My Brother's Keeper

A Pale Woods Mystery, Book One

Courtnee Turner Hoyle

Pale Woods Publishing

My Brother's Keeper
A Pale Woods Mystery
Book 1

Courtnee Turner Hoyle
Published June 2020, September 1, 2023

E-Book ISBN: 979-8-9876468-8-5

Library of Congress Control Number: 2020940137

You may contact the publisher:
Pale Woods Publishing
turnerco6@yahoo.com

To Tosha and Stereling,

You were the beginning of my story and the inspiration behind every chapter.

Chapter One

The sound was a shift. Then a bump.

My mother was the first to react. She gathered my two younger sisters in her arms and ran to the front door. She had a difficult time balancing them while frantically trying to turn the doorknob. I was several paces away when she finally opened the door and ran outside.

"Help!" my mother screamed.

She didn't stop running with my sisters until she was across the street and in the neighbor's driveway. My mother nearly dropped them on the asphalt and turned to look at the house. She put her hands to her mouth and paced, looking indecisive.

I bolted out the door behind her and ran into the street. My mother settled on an action and yelled, "Fire!" to get the neighbors' attention.

Two lights came on in the ranch-style brick to the right of our house. Worried faces appeared in the windows, but no one rushed to our aid.

My sisters were crying hysterically, but no matter how I tried to console them, they clung to my mother's legs. I couldn't blame them after what I'd put them through.

Finally, a man ran to my mother's side. I recognized his bald head and slim build. It was no surprise that he was the first person to respond to my mother's pleas for help. My mother was standing in his driveway.

"Mr. Fredrickson!" I shouted, but he focused on my mother. The concerned look on his face seemed strangely out of place, as he was dressed in Snoopy pajamas and a Number One Grandpa shirt.

People have their own ways of dealing with stressful situations. Apparently, when circumstances proved taxing, my mother's brain fell apart like tender meat.

Mr. Fredrickson grabbed her shoulders and shook her slightly. "Miranda! Are you and the children okay?"

My mother's eyes cleared a little. "Yes, but there's someone in the house!"

Mr. Fredrickson didn't ask about the phony cry about a fire. Apparently, he had watched the same crime prevention shows as my mother.

"Who?" Mr. Fredrickson asked. He thought it was a logical question, but sometimes I wondered how he and his wife became schoolteachers. The school system must not have given interviews that covered his lack of common sense and her hatred of children.

My mother was too scared to come back with a witty retort. Usually, she made sarcastic remarks about the obvious. Normally, she might have said, "I'm sorry, but I didn't ask for his driver's license before I ran screaming out my front door." Instead, my mother's fear filled her eyes. "I don't know, but no one *should* be in there."

Mr. Fredrickson handed my mother a large-screened phone with a case that read NAVY in bright yellow letters, then stepped into our yard. "Call the police!" he called over his shoulder in a whispered voice.

Mr. Fredrickson crouched down as he tiptoed across our lawn and went to the front door. He deftly maneuvered around my sisters' hula hoops and chalk boxes. He climbed the stairs one at a time in an over-exaggerated fashion in order to remain silent. Every step brought a knee closer to his chin as he held his hands out for balance. He stepped onto the porch and moved to the side of the door. "Hey! This is your last chance! Get out now, or the police will arrest you!"

I didn't know how scared I would have been if I had been on the receiving end of Mr. Fredrickson's threat, but I hoped the sound of his male voice would be enough to send the burglar out the back door. The intruder probably would have laughed on his way out with our television and my laptop if he had seen the bald man with chicken legs and Snoopy pajamas. I hoped the robber would dash out without investigating the owner of the voice.

More neighbors hesitantly came out to investigate. We lived in a suburban neighborhood, and it was almost ten o'clock on a Wednesday night, so most of them were in their bathrobes.

Our house was the only one in the neighborhood with vinyl siding. The house was even harder to miss since the vinyl was a canary yellow. My mother loved the sunlight, but I could never understand why our house had to be as bright as the sun. It may have made it an even better target for the robbers.

Why someone would try to vandalize our house, especially when we were awake?

The parade of toys around the swing set and the basketball hoop over the unattached garage should have alerted them to the presence of children, which showed our lack of valuables. I could see our outdated television through the open blinds, and the living room suit had seen better days.

Mr. Fredrickson kept darting his head in and out of the front door, but he made no move to go inside. After a few minutes, he proudly walked across the lawn and took his phone from my mother. "I don't know where he is, but I'll take care of him if he comes out. I still know a few techniques I picked up in the service," he bragged. He demonstrated a kick that caused him to grab his knee in agony.

A few moments later, Mrs. Fredrickson bustled into the driveway with blankets. She gave Mr. Fredrickson his coat.

"Anything we can do, dear?" Mrs. Fredrickson asked my mother. I don't think she really wanted to help my family, but her involvement in our situation would make her the bell of the ball in her ladies' circle the next day.

"No," my mother said. "I'm just going to wait for the police to get here."

Mr. and Mrs. Fredrickson looked at each other. They knew my mother couldn't call her husband.

I didn't hear any movement in the house, and soon police cruisers silently pulled into our driveway. Two officers in the first cruiser opened their doors and crept quietly around our house. They signaled something they both understood, and one officer went to the front door. The other officer walked slowly down the side of the house with his back to the sunshine siding.

Early in their marriage, my parents purchased a house that they felt would suit their lifetime needs. They signed thirty years of their lives away on a two-story traditional house with an attic and a lot of windows. Upstairs, there were three bedrooms, two bathrooms, a laundry room, and a long hallway. My mother's room was at the end of the hallway, and she had her own bathroom and walk-in closet. My sisters, Sydney and Ella, shared the room beside my mother's, and I had a room at the other end of the hall. The stairs emptied into the living room. A short hallway stood between the spacious living room and the kitchen, and a small bathroom was jammed off the hallway before you reached the kitchen. It looked like a door to a basement, but we barely had a crawl space under the house.

I watched the first officer go through our open front door and into our living room. It would probably take a few minutes for the officers to check the house.

A third officer emerged from the second cruiser and walked in our direction. He was much older than the other two officers, but he was taller and more muscular. He looked at my sisters kindly, but he had a face hardened from time and disappointment.

Miranda, did you phone in the disturbance?" he asked.

My mother nodded. There was no reason to be formal. We already knew the officer.

"Chief!" shouted the officer who had entered our front door. "The perp ain't here. He either ran out when he saw us, or he was already long gone."

The police chief bent his head a little so that he could look at my mother directly. It was easy to understand how his crystal-green eyes could pierce a criminal's lies. "Miranda?"

It was impossible to know if the police chief was trying to deconstruct my mother's calm or if he was simply waiting for her acknowledgment. The onlookers sensed the tension between them and inched back to their yards.

My mother stared back at him and held her head high. She seemed a little embarrassed, but she was determined to conduct herself with pride, especially since she knew she was safe.

"Where are your car keys?" the chief asked.

"They're in the kitchen, on the hook," my mother shakily responded. Her pride showed in her posture, but her voice betrayed her emotions.

"Novack!" the police chief shouted.

"Yes, chief," yelled the officer as he started down our porch steps.

"Go into the house and get the keys off the hook in the kitchen. It should be by the back door, over the trash can. And get some coats for the kids." The officer stopped mid-step, nodded, and ran into the house.

His attention returned to my mother. "Miranda, you need to get in your car and get these kids to the station. We'll talk more about this when you're there."

"But—" my mother began, but a dismissive wave from the police chief told her that her words would be wasted. My mother let go of her pride, and her posture, and followed the police chief to her car.

Chapter Two

It was hard for my mother to phone for help. She would rather have gone back into the house and faced a room full of burglars than call the police, but she had to think about her children.

Now her children were in a small blue room at the police station with two cups of hot cocoa. We lived in a small town, so this room probably functioned as the station's interrogation room and a meeting room.

The dispatcher, a kind lady with bottle-blond hair and a too-tight khaki uniform, had delivered the cocoa when my mother had gone into an adjoining room with the police chief. She smiled at my sisters and placed the cups on a long folding table in front of them. Steam rose from the white foam cups.

A random gurgle from the water fountain joined the buzz of the fluorescent lights. If I wanted a drink, I could go to the water fountain, but I would not give Double-Wide Dispatcher the pleasure of giving me a dirty look.

My sisters fell asleep with their heads together, and I silently looked around. There were award and donation plaques on the walls, and one plaque was from the DOA.

The Daughters of the American Revolution are still around? I thought. *Wouldn't they be more like the Great-Great-Granddaughters of the American Revolution?*

I could see my mother and the police chief through the large window that separated the rooms. A golden sign on the door told those who entered that Connor Murphy, Chief of Police occupied the space.

The police chief's office was covered with military service awards, American flags, and charity plaques. A large portrait of Andrew Jackson hung on the wall behind the chief's desk. I didn't have to be in the office to know that a small silver plaque at the bottom of the portrait declared the nickname of our country's seventh president: Old Hickory. On another occasion, the chief had explained to me that "Old Hickory" referred to Jackson's ability to remain firm and fearless in the face of opposition. Then the chief had smiled and stated, "Just like me."

I have above-average intelligence, and I still don't understand the comparison, but maybe I'm being too hard on him. I could have listed the reasons Andrew Jackson was not a great role model, but I doubted the police chief had investigated more about the past president than the story of the cane he used to beat a man who tried to assassinate him.

My mother and the police chief were in his office with the door closed, so I could only recognize the faint mumblings of words. Even though I couldn't hear the conversation, it did not surprise me when I saw my mother jump up from her chair and begin to shout and gesticulate wildly.

The police chief remained seated and spoke his words evenly, but a pink color crept up along his neckline and traveled to his face. He seemed determined to stay calm, but my mother flung an orange file at him and threw open the office door.

"You can't keep this up, Miranda!" His voice was firm and loud enough to project from his office. He held the file loosely in his hand.

The shouting had awakened my sisters, and they were staring at my mother with worried, sleep-soaked eyes. My mother gathered my sisters' coats, and she shot a piercing look at him.

"I have to keep going," my mother spoke through gritted teeth. "I don't run out on the people I love."

The police chief got up from his desk. He deliberately positioned himself three feet from my mother.

There would be no shouting. Only calculated words were spoken.

He raised one threatening finger and placed the other hand on his belt. The reaction was automatic. The long-time officer felt a threat, so he instinctively placed his hand within reach of his gun.

"Don't start this now, Miranda. You know I did the best I could."

"Save it, *Dad*," my mother spat. "I'm going home."

My sisters and I meekly followed our mother. The police chief continued giving his icy stare until he saw Sydney glance back at him. He met her eyes with a tired, sad smile.

Car rides after a fight could be uncomfortable and dangerous. I assumed it was because angry people made enraged drivers. Those individuals really needed to take a few minutes to cool down before they interacted with innocent relations.

My mother didn't squeal the tires of her late model Honda while driving out of the police station parking lot, but she was still clearly upset. She began mumbling to herself about being too old to be controlled as she fumbled through the radio stations. She settled on an alternative rock station and began singing along.

My mother shook her brown hair out of her ponytail. It spilled just over her shoulders in waves of shining chestnut. While most women complained about losing their looks as they got older, my mother became more beautiful every year. She looked her age, but her bright features, like her brilliant brown eyes and smooth olive complexion, did not betray her years.

My sisters were now wide awake, and they sat rigidly in the back seat, looking at my mother with worried eyes. I smiled when I noticed they were holding hands.

I turned around in the front seat as much as the seat belt would allow. "She'll be okay," I reassured them.

The youngest, Ella, glanced up and smiled wanly.

Ella was my favorite, but I would never say that to anyone. She had always believed in me, and she was the first one to forgive me after my worst mistake.

Ella squeezed Sydney's hand, and I thought about how quickly she seemed to change. One day she was a blue-eyed, blonde baby bouncing in my arms, and then she became a seven-year-old super-genius with the power to fill my heart or crush my soul with one look. Ella could be so smart that she was scary, but then she would dance with her dolls or make faces at our mother, and then you could see that she was still just a child.

My other sister, Sydney, looked and acted like an average nine-year-old. Her long brown hair tund brown eyes were the same shade as our mother's hair and eyes, but her complexion was a little darker. She tanned easily and was never burned by the sun. Sydney may not have been as smart as Ella, and sometimes she lacked common sense, but she tried to keep the family happy. It was Sydney who attempted to make my mother feel better.

"I think it's going to snow," she said brightly from the back seat.

My mother turned down the obnoxious lyrics and looked at Sydney in the rear-view mirror. "If it does, I'll build a snowman with you tomorrow," she said.

Sydney giggled, and my mother's smile went all the way to her eyes. Sydney started making snowmen by blowing her warm breath on the cold car window and drawing circles with her fingers.

I felt happiness spread from my chest to my face. Then I remembered I was the reason for most of our family's sadness, and my joy left me in a flash.

You deserve to be happy," Ella said from the back seat.

My mother smiled, and I looked at Ella in the side mirror. She stared back at me and winked. We had always shared a special bond, but I couldn't let myself get too close to her. I never wanted to hurt her, or anyone else, again.

Chapter Three

If fiery acid fell from the sky, our mother would put radioactive raincoats on us and take us to school. So after only a few hours of sleep, we piled into the car the next morning to walk the halls of education.

It had snowed as Sydney had predicted, but it wasn't enough for the school to close. It almost looked like a hard frost on the ground, the kind of freeze my dad had called a "hoarfrost."

"I only slept three whole hours!" Sydney whined. My mother opened the back door for Sydney, and she put her nose up as she climbed into the backseat. She wanted to ride in the passenger seat, but she was still too young, and I liked to be within reach of the car's thermostat.

"It's almost Christmas break," my mother explained. "Then you can sleep as long as you want."

I told my mother that it was clear on the road, but she checked both ways before she pulled out of the driveway. There had been a time when my mother had never doubted my word. I was determined to win back her trust.

"Am I getting the new Prissy Girl boots for Christmas?" Sydney asked. "It would be so much easier to go to school and face Lydia Sneed if I knew I was getting those boots."

My mother smiled slyly. "You won't know what you're getting until you open your presents on Christmas morning."

"I just need to know so that I can ask Grandpa to get them if you're not going to," Sydney said while looking through her Prissy Girl backpack.

My mother stopped smiling and pulled the car to the side of the road. She turned around in her seat and fixed her eyes on Sydney. I saw Ella tense up. I put my hand behind my seat so she could grab it.

"Don't ask that *man* for *anything*," my mother said slowly and forcefully. My mother was still upset over last night's argument, and she had gotten less sleep than Sydney. It was a bad combination on a morning ride to school.

Sydney usually knew when her whining had gone from playful to annoying, but she had hit a sore spot with my mother. My mother was still trying to assert her independence from her father, and it had been harder for her to establish autonomy since my father had left.

"Okay," Sydney squeaked. One hand froze in her backpack while the other trembled around its straps.

My mother continued to look at Sydney for a few more moments to let her know the severity of the situation before she turned around and resumed driving. We rode on in silence.

My family lived in a small town in Northeast Tennessee. Erwin was well known despite its size and population. We had hung a circus elephant, Murderous Mary, in 1916. Well, I didn't hang the elephant and certainly didn't condone the heinous act, but most people blame all of Erwin's inhabitants for the pachyderm's demise, and my grandmother wasn't even alive in 1916.

I liked living in a valley surrounded by heavy green mountains. Part of the Appalachian Trail ran through our county, and hikers were a common and welcome sight.

Our hometown was one of the two towns nestled inside Unicoi County. The town was small, but there were still several grocery stores and chain restaurants, along with, of course, plenty of churches and car washes.

I grew up with a rich Southern history and was raised by a motivated mother. Fortunately, I could absorb the culture without bias as I sought and understood information from the rest of the world.

My mother was a transplant from a city. She had grown up in harsh circumstances, especially after her mother had died. She was open-minded, but cautious, as she had taken care of herself since she was young. Her father would leave her for long periods of time while he ran down criminals in their urban streets. My mother learned how to cook, clean, and manage her time before she was ten. No one ever questioned my grandfather's parenting, because my mother was always at school on time and never caused trouble. She used to say she had secrets when we talked about her childhood, but she never told them to me.

My mother caused trouble one time, and it was so bad that it drove her father to move her out of the city and into the smallest town he could find. My mother had rebelled against her father about the move until she met my father. My mother never talked to my grandfather about moving again.

My father used to say one thing to my mother when she complained about not having the conveniences of a city: "A small town isn't so small when you have *big* love." Then they'd get into all that mushy stuff that made me throw up a little in my mouth.

My mother paused at the railroad tracks to wait for the last train cars to clear the roadway. "I'll be glad when they build the overpass," she said.

She drummed her fingers on the steering wheel. *They* had been talking about building a road over the railroad tracks for years. Ella would graduate from high school by the time the town officials finished the road. After all, the planning stage for a new public high school had taken almost thirty years.

My mother crossed two sets of tracks and quickly passed a long row of restaurants. Ella was known for her post-breakfast pancake attempts, but today Ella wasn't paying attention to her surroundings. She had her eyes closed and was rubbing her temples.

I loved the road that led to my school. I felt like I was literally ascending into higher learning as we climbed the asphalt that rose sharply into the curve of a mountain.

My eyes gravitated to the spot where my dad had grown up. The house where he had lived was no longer there. A single-wide beige trailer sat in its place. He had been raised close to the academy, but the school had only been an abandoned building when he was a kid.

Racer Daniels had built Pale Woods Academy on a property on a hill surrounded by trees. The building had been constructed during the Civil War as a lookout for Union soldiers who sought to use the Nolichucky River as a means of attack.

The town of Erwin could be seen from the front of the school. The Devil's Looking Glass and the Nolichucky River were visible from the right side of the building, and the woods seemed to creep up and surround the school.

Racer Daniels, the intelligent millionaire who originally bought the abandoned building, decided to name the school Pale Woods Academy. Pale Woods was the name the Native American Cherokee had given the woods.

shielded the students from rain and snow. Racer Daniels added the cafeteria and gym when he was still passionate about higher learning. Daniels had grown up with an irrational fear of tornadoes, so his buildings had domed roofs. The students walked to these buildings during a tornado drill because they were designed to withstand severe weather. It may have been an unnecessary feature because Unicoi County hadn't experienced the wrath of a tornado in decades, but I didn't mind getting out of class for the drills.

There were approximately 460 students who currently attended Pale Woods Academy. The students lived in Tennessee and North Carolina, and they admitted a new student only when a previous student left the academy. Sadly, there were times I had witnessed the speed of a student's exit when a wealthier student had applied for admission.

The kindergarten through eighth-grade classrooms were positioned on the first floor, and the high school students had classrooms and a library upstairs. Students who got caught outside their level were punished with detention or suspension, depending on the severity. Students who delivered messages to siblings or friends got detention, and kids who wandered around or played pranks were suspended. I had two detentions and one suspension in my first year, and the principal and I were on a first-name basis by the end of my first month at Pale Woods. Well, maybe I didn't call *her* by her first name, but she certainly knew mine.

The lower story of the school was larger than the upper story, and a playground was at the back of the school. The playground was small, so only two classes of children could play at one time. The play area ended abruptly at the edge of the surrounding woods.

My sisters and I were lucky to be students at the academy. Ella had earned some kind of scholarship when she was four, so we were all able to go to Pale Woods Academy for free. The school must have assumed we were all smart because we came from Ella's immediate family. I'm glad they didn't check more than our grades before we got our letters of acceptance. Sydney would have been turned away for her capriciousness, and they would have kicked me out of the school and into the river for my discipline record.

I was glad to be in a more challenging school because I had always been bored in public school classes. At Pale Woods, I had to pay more attention to the discussions in class, and I took my homework home to finish it. That cut down on my free time, so I wasn't in trouble as much.

Unfortunately, since the school waived my family's tuition to attend Pale Woods, it meant that almost all the other kids had more money than us. So Sydney, *Queen of Style*, had to find ways to compete with her arch nemesis, Lydia Sneed.

I will never understand the female species. I couldn't comprehend why Sydney claimed to be Lydia's best friend, but then complained at home that Lydia was snobbish and mouthy. My mother used to say to keep your friends close and your enemies closer. I was glad guys didn't think that way. If I didn't like something a guy said, I would punch him in the mouth, and then we could shake hands and be friends later if he fought well.

I glanced up at the school and saw the blinds move in one window in the center room upstairs. I had been in every room in the school except one. That one. I had abandoned my mission to see that room after I became a disappointment to my family. The less they had to deal with me and my crazy ideas, the better.

My sisters and I got out of the car, and my mother waved. Sydney didn't look at her or wave back. She was still pouting.

Ella was staring at the woods with a strange expression. Sydney stomped up the steps of the school before Ella was broken from her reverie.

"What did you see?" I asked.

Color crept into Ella's face, and I realized she was going to lie. She pretended to be concerned with a strap on her backpack.

"I have a headache. I was seeing spots," Ella whispered quickly.

"You don't have to lie to me. I'm your brother, and I'll help you with anything." I locked eyes with her and tried to convey my compassion for her, as well as my disappointment over her lie.

Ella smiled. "We better catch up to Princess Pout." Her angelic voice made me forget about our solemn moment.

A couple of kids turned and looked at us like we were talking to them. I put my hand on Ella's back and waved at them, but they rolled their eyes and didn't return my gesture.

Sydney saw Ella trying to match her pace, and she slowed her steps. Sydney had a soft spot for Ella, but she was jealous of Ella's intellectual accomplishments.

Sydney and I walked Ella to the first-grade section. We turned left inside the front door and walked past the kindergarten rooms.

"I'm big enough to walk to my class." Ella put a hand on her hip, and a piece of her blond hair fell into her eyes before she brushed it away.

"I know," Sydney agreed, "but it makes Mom feel better."

"Whatever," Ella said, and she walked into her classroom. I could hear some of the first-grade girls shout Ella's name as soon as she opened the door.

I was secretly glad that Sydney had explained it. The less I talked, the better I felt. I shouldn't even be allowed to be around such wonderful girls.

Sydney had ignored me since the incident, so the walk to her third-grade classroom was silent and uncomfortable. She was no different than everyone else. They all judged me and wrote me out of their lives, but it was no less than I deserved.

After my life-altering experience, I tried to talk to Sydney several times while we were alone. She completely ignored me and even sang over me. I thought she was acting childish and immature, but she was just a child, after all.

I watched Sydney go into her classroom and heard the third-grade drama begin. I could tell without even looking in the door that Lydia Sneed was showing off something new her parents had gotten her. *Didn't her parents want her to be surprised at Christmas?* Or maybe Princess Sneed already had tons of jaw-dropping presents under the tree.

I shook my head to clear it. I shouldn't be thinking so resentfully about an eight-year-old child, but part of me wanted Sydney to have everything Lydia Sneed could whine out of her parents.

I walked back down the hallway, up the stairs, and turned right. Ninth and tenth-grade rooms were on the left, and eleventh and twelfth-grade classes were on the right of the building. The library was at the back of the hall, separating the freshman and sophomores from the juniors and seniors.

I stared at the library without seeing it. I knew the room of secrets was directly behind me. All I had to do was turn left or right and walk up the narrow walkway on either side of the stairs to the room. I couldn't get in the room. It was locked, and I had already tried to open the lock. Several times.

I shuffled to the eleventh-grade section, painted with Greek—or Roman, if you prefer—gods and goddesses. I smiled at my favorite, Hermes, otherwise known as Mercury, the god of thieves. I knew he was also the messenger of the gods, but I didn't like to think of him serving anyone. I figured he only took the job because he wanted to mess with the gods. My first class was in the "Athena Room," and my English teacher was already calling roll.

I eased in without making a sound and sat down in the back row next to the door. I liked this spot because it was easy to get out of the class if I got upset or embarrassed.

My teacher, Mr. Knoll, droned on about our book reports and the research paper we'd start after Christmas break. There were no advanced classes at Pale Woods, so all the students got the benefit of accelerated lessons.

My siblings and I had always been a bit brighter than our peers, so we all did well at the academy. That also meant that I was almost as bored at a school for sharper minds than I was in my old public school. The work was hard, but the teachers had to pause lessons a lot to explain the material to not-so-smart rich kids.

Mr. Knoll was a nice man, but he wasn't very stimulating. I had already read Julius Caesar, and the entire class had seen the movie, so we didn't need the discussion of the story to carry on for a week. I had spent the previous week listening to my classmates stumble through the play aloud after Mr. Knoll had assigned the speaking parts.

The snow was blowing softly against the window, and my gaze fell upon the empty seat next to me. My eyes filled up with tears, and I left the room before anyone had the chance to see me cry.

Lunch used to be the best time of the day, but now that all my friends hated me, I couldn't wait to get back to class. I even tried to sit with the freaks, but they ate noisily and smelled like soured laundry. In the end, I just sat by myself and watched everyone.

You would think that a school for geniuses would have only one social group, but it turned out that smart kids came from all kinds of backgrounds. Most of the kids were from divorced families, but they lived in nice little suburban homes. Very few of the kids lived in mansions, and even fewer kids lived in mobile homes.

There was a "preppy" group, full of the kids on sports teams, along with their girlfriends and boyfriends. They had parties on the weekends and carried around hydro-flasks that told them when to drink.

The "redneck" crowd was small, but they were loud. They drove angry trucks on lift kits and yelled obscenities at people for fun.

The "nerds", "freaks", and "loners" rounded out our class. The nerds were like walking calculators, and most of them were stereotypical with their glasses and pocket protectors. Freaks were easy to spot because there was something extreme about them. They could have radiant hair, too many piercings, or maybe just a crazy style. Loners were the kids who didn't fit into any other category. These kids had no friends and no real social connections.

One of the loners sat across the cafeteria from me. He was a homeless kid with black, stringy hair and a white, greasy complexion. He probably would have been labeled a freak if he weren't homeless. I realized I didn't know his name or if he was in the same grade as me.

He lived in an old, green van on the Nolichucky River. I think the van had stopped running a decade ago, but there was space inside for the kid and his family. The van was close enough to the school for him to walk to his classes, but I didn't think anyone would have bothered bringing him to school if he had been farther away.

Some parents at the school heard about him, and they formed a fundraiser to help his parents afford an apartment. The concerned parents gave his parents a check in front of a news crew and left as soon as the news van pulled away.

The kid's parents seemed grateful, but I still saw them living in that same little van. My mother said they were probably drug addicts, and that they blew the money on their addiction, but I thought there might be more to the story.

The homeless kid picked up his tray and walked in my direction. I was sitting next to one of the garbage cans, and today's meatloaf was already making an unpleasant aroma from the previous lunch shifts.

He walked close to my toe on his way to the trash can, and he must have thought he stepped on me, because he muttered, "Sorry."

I looked up in surprise, muttering, "That's okay."

I wondered if it was only his lack of a residence that kept others away from him, or if he had done something to warrant the distaste of others. Did he relish solitude, or was he as lonely as me?

Chapter Four

I always thought I would drive myself to and from school by the time I was seventeen. I had taken the driving test the day I turned sixteen, but I failed the section on parallel parking. No one had encouraged me to retake the test, and I was too nervous to ask my mother if I could use her car, so I relied on other modes of transportation.

I spotted Ella's bright blonde hair in a crowd of kids waiting on the bus. She was talking to someone, but I didn't think anything about it until I noticed the stringy hair of the guy who had almost stepped on me at lunch. He glanced up at me as I approached them, and his demeanor changed. He was in such a hurry to get away from Ella that he tripped over the curb in front of the idling bus. He righted himself before he face-planted on the asphalt. I tapped the back of Ella's shoulder twice to let her know I was behind her.

Ella seemed bewildered. Usually, people wore a puzzled expression when *she* walked away from *them*, but the homeless boy truly perplexed my sister.

"What did he want?" I asked.

Ella flicked the zipper on her backpack. "I think he just wanted to talk."

Sydney had called our grandfather to pick her up after school. We noticed her climbing into his police cruiser and waved.

"I guess she is going to ask him for those boots," Ella said.

I hoped Sydney made it home before our mother, or it would leave me to explain my sister's absence. My mother would probably punish Sydney for calling her grandfather to pick her up, especially after the fight they had about him this morning.

The bus driver opened the doors to the bus, and students filled up the seats. I sat beside the window, and Ella moved next to me.

The world moved around Ella, but my sister hardly noticed. Her child-like features camouflaged an old soul and a numb spirit. I felt privileged to hear her thoughts, even though secrets hovered just above her words.

"What did you talk to the homeless boy about?" I tried again.

Color crept into Ella's features, but she spoke just above a whisper. "Why does it matter?"

"Because he's as old as me," I said. I was becoming agitated, but no one could hear my voice over the elevated chorus of exchanges from the other kids on the bus. "I just want to make sure he's not being weird with you."

Ella's spirited posture didn't relax. She reminded me a lot of our mother when she was upset. "He was just talking to me," she shot back. "And his name is Miles."

Ella and I both knew his living arrangements, and the irony of his name was not lost on me. I was going to pursue her talk with Miles further, but a voice shouted, "Hey, weirdo!"

A boy who looked a little older than Ella bounced up to our seat and pushed the back of it hard enough to jolt Ella. I had to remain motionless because the kid was ten years younger than me.

Ella didn't expect me to intervene. She jumped out of her seat and pushed her face inches from the bully.

"What is your problem, Kevin?" she yelled at him. Her hands were in fists at her sides.

Kevin didn't back down. "I don't like you," he said. His large body swayed back and forth as if to make himself seem bigger. "What did you tell the substitute today? Why did she bring us all off the playground and make us do worksheets the rest of the day?"

Ella's resolve dropped a little, but she stood her ground. "You want to blame people because you have to do schoolwork?" she started, but Kevin interrupted her.

"No, she was going to let us play the rest of the day. She was actually fun! But you come along and whisper something to her, and she runs us all inside and makes us work the rest of the day!"

All the bus kids gathered around Ella and Kevin. First-grade fights were rare.

Ella tilted her head and narrowed her eyes. "Do you know what I told the substitute?" she asked Kevin. "I told her about the Mugglies pajamas you wear to bed every night. I told her you cry for your Winky Blue, the blue blanket your grandma gave you. I told her that your mommy has to leave the light on every night until you fall asleep because you are scared of the dark!"

Kevin's face contorted as Ella roared out his secrets. None of the other kids wondered why Ella knew the information. They accepted it as a fact because Kevin deflated more with every word Ella spoke.

Kevin stammered some unintelligible sounds, and the kids moved back to their seats. No blood would be spilled.

The bus driver moved the bus into gear, and everyone sat down. The bus jerked cautiously down the hill.

I watched Ella settle into her usual posture. Her cheeks were flushed, but her hands were steady. Her special talent made it easy for her to lose bullies, but it didn't win her many friends.

I put my hand over hers and squeezed it. After a few minutes, she squeezed back.

We got off the bus and walked to the front steps. Our babysitter already had the door open for us. We had never needed a babysitter before last year's incident, but now we had Maria.

Maria was petite and had short, dark hair, dark eyes, and cream-colored skin. She reminded me of a singer in an eighties music video. My mother said Maria was 'spunky.' I guess she said that because Maria wouldn't let my mother complain about her job or the mess in her house. Maria would say, "At least your job pays so well that you can get weekly manicures," and, "At least you have a home that wasn't taken away by your husband." My mother always turned red after Maria's remarks, but she never held them against her.

Maria's husband had kept her from completing her high school degree, so when he left her, she didn't understand the paperwork in the divorce. Maria was left homeless, penniless, and without working skills. My mother heard about Maria from a close friend and hired her to babysit and do some light cooking and cleaning. Maria earned her GED quickly and started college courses at night.

Maria seemed to enjoy working for my family. She cooked, cleaned, and helped my sisters with their homework. I liked her, but her sarcasm could be harsh. It may have been a defense mechanism she had used to buffer her husband's abuse. Ella picked up on it, but Sydney thought she was just being rude.

Maria had dinner prepared and was lounging on the sofa. She placed a slip of paper in her Modern Psychology book and stretched.

"How was school today?" she asked.

"Fine," I said and started up the stairs to my room.

Ella reported she had won Christmas bingo, and then she explained Sydney's absence. *Good.* Maria could tell my mother that Sydney had gone to her grandfather's house instead of coming home.

My room was cold and quiet. There was a desk with a chair in the corner, and a reclining camp chair stood sentinel in front of the television.

I fell into the camp chair and closed my eyes. I heard somewhere that time heals all wounds, but I didn't think there would be enough time to heal what I did to my family.

Some of my tension was relieved when I heard Sydney come in the front door. At least Maria and I wouldn't have to tell my mother that Sydney was with her grandfather.

Sydney's feet pounded up the stairs. "Is he going to get you your boots?" I called without moving from my spot.

Sydney didn't respond as she hurried to her room. The metallic click of the lock bounced off the hallway walls as soon as she shut the door.

Let her have her secrets, I thought. I closed my eyes and tried to relax, but I still felt a constant nagging in my stillness.

I opened my eyes and stared into space. *What could I do to make them all love me again?* Ella told me she forgave me, but I missed my mom. We used to stay up late and talk while we drank hot chocolate at the kitchen table. It was our special time.

I jolted back to reality when the family phone rang. Our mother paid for a smartphone to stay in the house, like a portable landline.

Sydney would answer it. It was probably one of her friends.

I turned my gaze to the bunk beds in the center of the room, and tears tickled my eyes. The empty beds were just another sign that I was totally alone.

I didn't go to my room when I wanted to think about things. I went to my mother's bathroom. I didn't know why, but I always felt more comforted by the blue walls and warm vanilla smell than I was by my room.

My mother didn't like for her children to be in what she called her private rooms. We were not supposed to go past her bedroom door unless she was home. Her private areas were her bedroom, bathroom, and the two rooms immediately off her bathroom, her walk-in closet, and the laundry room.

The laundry room was the exception. I could walk through her bathroom and wash my clothes any time I wanted. Not that I ever would. She mainly cared about the things she hid in her walk-in closet. It didn't really matter, though, because I had already read her lonely poems and all the love letters from my father. My mother must have thought she had a treasure trove in her closet. It was all too lame to interest me anymore.

It was always quiet in my mother's bathroom, and Sydney and Ella were too scared to go into my mother's private rooms looking for me. I could have at least half an hour to myself before my mother got home. Then I would need to sneak back into my room before my mother came upstairs to change.

I sat on my mother's bathroom floor and stared at the wall. I felt like I had lost all my friends, including my best friend.

I was so lost in my thoughts that I almost didn't hear the sound. I concentrated on the stillness and listened.

A slide, then a bump.

I lifted my head and looked around the bathroom. The light was on, so I could see every space in the room. I was alone.

My mother always kept the doors open to the laundry room and her walk-in closet. Something must have fallen off the dryer.

I was against the wall, and I could feel the vibration of the water through the pipes, but the sound had been closer, within the walls of my mother's private rooms. My left shoulder ached when I stood up. I must have pulled it without noticing and woke up an old injury. It was an injury I didn't want to relive.

Curiosity overtook me, and I inched closer to the laundry room. Everything was in place. Nothing was on the laundry room floor except a hamper full of clothes.

Bump.

The sound had definitely come from the bathroom. I peeked around the laundry room door. Empty.

"Stop fooling around, sis," I said, feeling satisfied that I had caught one of my sisters trying to play a prank.

"Jerrod," a voice spoke softly.

I didn't know if it was Sydney or Ella, but I was sure one of them was trying to scare me. I could imagine them giggling behind the door. I would beat them at their own game.

I tiptoed to the bathroom door and pressed my ear against it. I didn't hear movement or stifled giggles, but I was *sure* at least one of my sisters was on the other side of the door.

I was going to fling open the door and growl, but I heard another bump. It was coming from the middle of the room. Behind me.

"Jerrod, it's okay," a voice breathed.

My bones chilled to their marrow. I waited for the voice to speak again, but I heard nothing more. I didn't really need to look at the owner of the voice to know who spoke. I had heard that voice so often that its melody lingered in my brain.

I dropped to the floor and screamed in anguish, driving myself crazy with grief and regret"Josh," I cried. "Please come back!"

Chapter Five

No one responded to my shouting. They probably expected irrational outbursts from me. I imagined Maria was trying to say something funny to keep my sisters from reacting to my screams.

I ran out of my mother's bathroom and into my room. I plopped onto my bottom bunk and closed my eyes. I needed to block it all out. I couldn't deal with the pain right now. The reality of it all would be too much.

All my energy slipped away. Pain and guilt turned into a deep, depressing stare, and I saw nothing and heard no one. I was in the blissful place of nothingness.

An hour later, there was a soft knock on my door. Ella pushed my door wider and stepped into my room.

"You scared me," she said. "Why were you yelling in Mom's bathroom?"

"I thought I heard Josh's voice," I admitted. My voice sounded a little raspy after my screaming fit.

Ella sat down on the end of my bed. She was still small enough to sit on the bottom bunk without having her head touch the top bunk.

"I would be the last person to tell you it was impossible," she said.

Ella had frightened her first babysitter by insisting that her imaginary friend was real. I knew she had an imagination, so she accepted almost everything with childlike certainty.

"He said everything will be okay," I related.

Ella's eyes filled up with tears, and she turned her head. I could hardly hear her when she spoke. "It will be okay when everyone accepts what happened."

"How can I?" I asked, jumping up from the bed. "I'm the reason for all the bad fortune in this family. If it weren't for my stupid tricks, I wouldn't be imagining his voice. I would *hear* it!"

Ella took a deep breath and looked from me to her hands. She always seemed to find the right words to say, even when I didn't want to hear them.

"You have a lot to sort out. I wish I could help you, but I can't." Ella didn't fidget often, but she wound one thumb over the other. "You have got to accept what happened."

I glared at Ella incredulously. Didn't she know I was trying to *sort things out*? Didn't she realize that every second of my life I was coping with what I had done?

"Why don't you just go play with your dolls?" I said bitterly.

I knew I had hurt Ella, but I didn't try to apologize. I sat on the bed and put my face in my hands.

I felt a small bounce when Ella lifted her weight off the bed, but I didn't hear her leave the room. I squeezed my eyes together so hard that I saw stars.

"We all miss him," Ella whispered, and she shut the door.

I skipped dinner, and no one bothered me. I crept downstairs when everyone was asleep and looked out the kitchen window. I could see dim Christmas lights on a couple of houses on the next street over, but I couldn't be happy about it. Christmas was my favorite time of the year, but all the magic had been taken from my life last winter.

I shuffled into the living room, and it did not surprise me to see my mother's artificial tree standing in the corner. She had been putting up that tree since before I could remember, but when I was younger, she had placed it in the upstairs window. A real tree had been in the living room corner, and Christmases had been brighter. The tree lights weren't on, but there were a few small presents visible in the streaks of moonlight.

I had my foot on the bottom step when I heard a faint rustling behind me. My mother was in the kitchen. She was wearing a pale pink, silk nightgown. I had seen her in that nightgown a million times, but tonight it looked shades lighter, and her face seemed just as faded. She kept her eyes down as she walked to the cabinet and got a coffee mug.

She paused. Then she nodded and took down another cup. I recognized the cup. It was a plastic mug I had made in the third grade when I was obsessed with cowboys. The writing around the cup read: "Best of the West." My mother put a pack of cocoa in each cup and ran warm water into both cups.

I felt a rush of excitement. I was finally going to have a heart-to-heart with my mother!

My mother walked to the table and sat my cup down at my spot at the table. I fought back tears as I crossed the kitchen to take my place in front of her. I pulled out the chair to take my seat, but she lowered her head, and sobs rattled her body.

"Hey, Mom, wait," I stammered. "Everything's okay. I'm sorry about whatever it is. Just don't cry."

My mother stiffened and took an unsteady sip of her cocoa.

"Sometimes it's still just so hard to believe," she whispered, staring hard at the floor.

"I know, Mom," I said. "It's all my fault."

I reached out to touch her, but she cleared her throat, grabbed our cocoa cups, and hurried to the sink. She poured out our mugs and stopped. She set the cups in the sink and grabbed the counter like it would hold her up.

She whispered something without turning around. It almost sounded like a prayer for strength. Then she took a deep breath and rushed out of the kitchen.

I hung my head and blinked back tears. I looked down at my stupid hands attached to my guilty body.

I wanted to run after my mother and comfort her, but there was nothing else I could do.

Chapter Six

It was the last day of school before the holiday break, and I decided I wasn't going to go. I thought my mother and sisters would harass me about it. Until a year ago, my mother would have dragged me out of bed and carried me kicking and screaming to school, but no one even knocked on my door to ask if I was okay.

They clanged dishes and mumbled groggy pleasantries as they readied themselves, and I listened to the metallic clicking of the engine as the car pulled out of the driveway. I was finally alone.

I wasn't aware of how much I needed some time by myself until I walked down the stairs and stared at the empty house. Relief washed over me when I realized that I would have the next seven hours alone.

I put my hand on my left shoulder and rotated my arm. The soreness had become a familiar inconvenience.

The dim light in the room was a reflection of a sky heavy with snow. The pregnant clouds looked ready to deliver frosty precipitation at any moment. School would probably be dismissed early because of the weather.

I tried to get into the Christmas spirit, but I could only feel a sharp ache in the middle of my stomach. The holidays would never be the same in our house.

I didn't deserve to enjoy Christmas, but my family needed the feeling that shines like a halo around the people who can experience the joy of togetherness. I had ruined it for everyone. Christmas was once my family's favorite time of year, but now it seemed like a piece of barren ground where flowers were planted but never grew.

I spent most of the morning hanging out in my room, even though I had the whole house to myself. My mother never called to check on me, but I stuffed my feelings about it into the same abyss I used for everything that hurt me. Usually, when I was sick, she would call during lunch to tell me to feel better and sleep on my side. My mother was always worried that one of my siblings or I would die from asphyxiation because we had vomited while asleep on our backs.

My mother may have known that I wasn't sick and wanted to give me some space. I had to respect her observation.

She had seemed so upset when she had fixed our cocoa. It was almost like she was trying to forgive me, but she couldn't get past the pain she felt. I couldn't blame her.

A wave of unexpected sadness seized my body, and I ran to my mother's bathroom. I hadn't been there since I'd heard the voice, and I only thought of it fleetingly as I struggled to hold back my tears.

I pushed away the thought of my father shaking his head over me as one traitorous tear escaped and ran as fast as rain down my cheek. He may have thought I should toughen up, but there was only so much grief one person could manage alone.

At some point, I must have fallen asleep, because I could smell food. I hadn't heard my family come back home, but I seemed to have slept the day away.

I slowly opened my eyes in the darkness, and I almost freaked out, but then I remembered I hadn't turned on the light in the bathroom. I stood slowly and limped down the hall on tingling feet. I had expected the house to be dimmer, lit by artificial light, but it seemed more like early afternoon, with the natural sun coming through the windows. There was a scent in the air, too, like very strong vanilla.

Wait.

Why did I hear a man's voice coming from the kitchen?

I ran down the steps and stopped. Everything was different.

The tree was up, but from the smell, I could tell that it was a live tree and not my mother's ancient artificial one. Blue and white lights danced on its branches, and the ornaments seemed to move with their rapid blinking.

Homemade ornaments adorned the branches. The reindeer I had made out of pipe cleaner and Mom's candy cane she had constructed from beads twirled as if propelled by an invisible nudge of the tree. Sydney's angel was on the tree. It must have been one of her first creations because the angel pattern that covered the toilet paper roll was decorated with three or four dark circles of crayon. It was evident that a toddler had been responsible for the masterpiece.

There were so many presents under the tree that it looked like a wave had carried the gifts forward from the wall. The daylight that streamed through the windows seemed to suggest that the time was much later than morning, but the Christmas packages sat unbothered.

My family was gathered around the tree. My mother, Sydney, and...me?

We were different. Not different, but younger. Sydney was closest to the tree. She was barely a toddler, and she was trying to get an ornament down by pulling on it. My mother guided Sydney's hand away and turned her to sit in her lap. She began braiding her hair, and Sydney sat silently, looking into the kitchen.

I—or Little Me—was sitting next to my mother, my back against the couch. I had a large blanket wrapped around me, and I looked sick. My face was sweaty and pale, and every few minutes I would cough and groan.

"Why do I have to be sick on Christmas?" Little Me complained.

"Because you just had to build the *biggest* snowman on the street," my mother said with a smile. "On the *coldest* day of the year."

Little Me was defiantly sulking about my sickness. I stuck my tongue out at my mother.

Was I dreaming? Everything seemed so real! I had heard that a person could think everything he or she saw or heard in a dream existed. I put my hand against the wall. I felt the cold firmness of the sheetrock.

I pinched myself. Yep, it hurt.

Could everything you touched feel real, too? While I was trying to understand what was happening, I heard the man's voice again.

"Okay, we're ready!"

My mother looked up from braiding Sydney's hair and said, "Okay, babe!"

I heard a few heavy steps, and then I saw him. My father. And that wasn't all.

"Merry Christmas to you! Merry Christmas to you!" Josh sang as he carried a cake from the kitchen. My father stood by my mother and put his hand on her shoulder as she rose.

"Remember, it's not Christmas yet," my father said, mock scolding. "We decided to put your mother first this year. Can you imagine how hard it must be to share your birthday with Jesus?"

My mother blushed and put her face in my father's chest. Little Sydney jumped up and down, holding her hands up to our mother.

I remembered that day! My father had suggested that we celebrate my mother's birthday during the first part of the day and Christmas during the last half of the day. It was all in an effort to make my mother feel special.

It had been a hard year for my parents. I didn't want to remember the reason my memories of that time had been cloaked with sadness. During that year, our parents had often told us to play quietly, and I wondered how Sydney learned to speak so quickly when so little was spoken to her. I guessed that was why she didn't find it strange when people told her to be quiet. She was used to it.

Josh dropped his head, but he was still smiling. "We made you the eggnog cake."

The eggnog cake had been a birthday tradition for our mother since she and our father had gotten married. My mother's mother had died when my mother was young, and her father was always on duty, so she never really had parties and cakes on her birthday. When our father's mother, our nana, heard that her son's new wife had never had a birthday cake, she was shocked.

"My birthday is on Christmas," our mother had explained to our nana. "My dad always gave me a card with money for Christmas and my birthday."

"Sharing a birthday with our Savior is only a better reason for celebration," our devoutly Christian nana explained. "I'll make sure you get a birthday cake every year."

Our nana made my mother her first birthday cake, an eggnog cake. Most people hadn't heard of an eggnog cake, but it was a wonderfully moist French vanilla cake with rum, eggs, cinnamon, nutmeg, and vanilla extract. Our nana had a special way of making the cake, but her recipe was lost in the fire that ended her life. My father worked the recipe from his memories with his mother in her kitchen. He had carried on the tradition by baking the cake with one of my siblings or me on Christmas morning. It had been my turn to help my father with the cake, but I had gotten sick, so my brother mixed the ingredients and licked the frosting spoon. It had been a relief that Josh had taken over as junior kitchen assistant that year because my father and I had not been on the best of terms.

"You remembered!" our mother said, just like she did every year.

Josh's smile stretched to his eyes. "We will never forget your birthday!"

My father took a lighter from his pocket and lit each candle. Even though my mother must have been in her late twenties, there were only eleven candles on the cake. It dawned on me that Josh must be eleven because he always put the same number of candles on our mother's cake as his age.

I watched my father light the candles. He almost had to bend over to reach the cake Josh held. His blue eyes danced in the candlelight, and a small smile played across his mouth.

I remembered thinking he was as big as a giant, and he must have seemed that big to Little Me, but he didn't seem that tall to me now. My father was just over six feet tall. He had a lean, muscular frame, but you could tell the muscles were from manual labor and not from weight training. He was always hot, so he wore short-sleeved shirts all year. It showed off his frame and made a lot of women do a double take. My mother said that I had my father's shoulders, and I never had to work for my muscle tone, but it didn't seem as though my body could support the type of muscle my father carried.

"We didn't put the right number of candles on the cake, because we didn't want the house to burn down," my father joked as he lit the last candle. Everyone laughed with good nature, and my mother blew out the candles.

"Wait, Mom," Little Me said from the corner. "You didn't make a wish."

"Yes, I did."

"What was it?" Josh asked.

Our mom laughed and held her finger up. "I can't tell you, or it won't come true."

My father grabbed my mother and pulled her close to him. She pretended to be shocked and concerned.

"Ve have vays of making you talk," he said, mimicking a villain. He bounced my mother onto the couch and tickled her.

I looked around at my family. Sydney was trying to help my mother push my father away. Josh was laughing and still holding the cake, and I was watching from the couch with a dopey smile on my face. Ella was looking at me.

Ella

Ella was not only present in my Christmas past, but she was the only one who was the right age. And she was looking right at me. The older me.

"Okay, stop!" my mother said.

"Well, let's hear it," my dad said, helping my mother to her feet.

"I only wished," my mother began, fixing her gaze on my father, "that we could always be this happy. That we could be the same as we are right now."

My father's smile faltered, but he picked it back up quickly. "Of course we will." He started tickling my mother again.

My mother stopped my father's merriment and looked at him soberly. "Pinky swear?" She extended her pinky.

"Yes." He quickly locked his pinky with his wife's pinky finger.

My eyes were watery, and my body felt cold. Maybe my mother shouldn't have told us her wish. Maybe it was bad luck because that was our last Christmas as a family. My father walked out the back door for the last time in the spring, and nothing was ever the same.

"Is it time for Christmas to start?" Josh asked.

Our father gave him a disapproving look, but our mother ruffled his hair playfully. "Of course it is! And I have a Christmas present for all of you!"

"Is it a trampoline?" Little Me asked.

"Is it a puppy?" said Josh, jumping a little off his heels. The cake threatened to slide off the plate.

My father was puzzled. He looked down into my mother's face.

Ella, *my* Ella, was still staring at me. She nodded her head like I should have gained some knowledge from the scene. She didn't look at our father. She didn't turn around at all. It was as if she was only there to make a point to me. Maybe it was my subconscious trying to bring a physical presence to all my family members, but I couldn't believe Ella could be so indifferent to a scene that held her father and brother in a precious moment in time.

"I'm going to have a baby!" my mother shouted. She pulled her shirt a little tighter around her belly. I couldn't see a bulge, but everyone nodded as if my mother was noticeably pregnant.

We all cheered. My father picked my mother up and twirled her around the living room.

"Put me down, Johnny," my mother scolded. "I'm in the sick stage."

My father placed my mother on her feet and beamed at his family. His perfect grin was contagious. We were all smiling, lost in a rare moment of sublime happiness.

"This is my best Christmas," he said. "Let's thank the One who made it all possible."

We all lowered our heads to pray. I watched each member of my family as they nodded at the appropriate places in my father's prayer, and I could almost remember the excitement I had felt.

Little Me peeked during the prayer and stared into an identical face. Little Me and Josh winked at each other and bowed their heads again. We all loved Christmas, and we were happy to celebrate our mother's birthday and the announcement about the newest member of our family.

My father finished the prayer and knelt down. He put his ear to my mother's belly and acted as if he were listening. "She says she can't wait to meet us."

My mother laughed. "How do you know it's a girl?"

"Father's intuition," my father said, and he got to his feet.

He patted my mother's almost flat stomach. "I can't wait to meet you, Ella."

But my father never met the baby he pretended to hear. He was gone three months before she was born.

Chapter Seven

A thud woke me from my unintentional slumber. The sound of my little sisters' voices drifted to my ears.

I opened my eyes in the darkness, and I peeled my face off the linoleum in my mother's bathroom. My left shoulder roared its disapproval over my position on the floor.

It *was* a dream. My family had been unbroken for that last holiday. I hadn't thought about the completeness of my family that Christmas, but I realized that was as whole as we had ever been.

I sat up and rubbed my eyes. I could smell meat and ketchup. Maria must be making Monday night meatloaf on Friday pizza night. My mother probably forgot to go to the store, because traditions were rarely broken in our house.

I shuffled downstairs when I heard the dishes rattling, and I sat down as Sydney was placing the last plate on the table. Ella rattled the silverware onto the placemats.

Sydney hopped up and down when my mother brought in the food. Meatloaf with mashed potatoes and broccoli steamed in a large casserole dish.

Maria had been sent home. It was odd to see my mother home so early, but stranger things had happened. Like reliving an almost tangible memory.

"Can I go first tonight?" Sydney asked.

My mother had read in some family magazine about a study where kids who got to share their day at the dinner table were less likely to do drugs. She insisted that we recount our day at the table every evening, even if we were eating at a restaurant. It was a familiar family tradition, like keeping a promise when we pinky swore.

"Yes," my mother said as she sat down. She filled my sisters' plates with food and put the platter of meatloaf in front of me. I guess that was my cue to help myself.

My mother ate while Sydney, Ella, and I bowed our heads in silent prayer. She was respectfully silent, but she didn't participate in our religious custom. Sydney held Ella's hand, Ella joined her hand with mine, and I reached toward the place where my hand and my mother's used to join and clasped empty air. After a moment, we looked up.

My mother aired out her paper napkin and smoothed it onto her lap. "What happened in your world today, Sydney?" She looked up with a small smile.

"Well," Sydney began jubilantly. "I was the pod monitor today! And that doesn't mean section monitor! I was in charge of the *whole* pod!" she finished in a rush.

"That's great, honey!" my mother said.

Every month, the elementary school teachers picked their own room monitor. Most of the time, the room monitors stayed the same unless a room monitor was promoted to section monitor or pod monitor.

A section monitor supervised their grade, and a pod monitor was in charge of four grades. The pod monitor stood in the hall and watched the students in their pod during the mornings and afternoons and made sure the section monitors were doing their jobs. I called them glorified hall monitors because they never really enjoyed any perks with their job, except writing up their enemies.

The only time Sydney was in detention was when Lydia Sneed wrote her up for pushing a kid in the hall. Sydney was pretty upset over it. She claimed it was an accident, and she cried for a week after she served the detention. Sydney never forgave Princess Sneed for that one, and she had vowed revenge.

I talked to the kid Sydney supposedly pushed. It was a nerdy third-grade boy named Peter Perkins, better known as P.P. I don't have to tell you how many times he's been stuffed in a locker.

P.P. said that he had accidentally brushed up against Lydia when a bully pushed him into the wall. Princess Sneed began yelling, and Sydney defended him. Lydia screamed that Sydney was so stupid that she probably bumped into him and caused the whole mess. Sydney had simply grabbed P.P. by the arm and stormed off. Lydia wrote Sydney's name down, and Sydney was required to serve a punishment.

I was angry with P.P. for not informing the principal about the situation to help my sister, but I was livid over Lydia's deception. I promised that I would have my own revenge, and I didn't let another day go by before I had it. I placed some brownish goop on the seat Lydia occupied at lunch, and I was happy to hear about the dark brown stain on her bottom when she got up to clear her tray. Lydia still looked in a seat before she sat down, and a lot of her *friends* still called her "Poopy Pants" behind her back. *I love chocolate pudding!*

An early elementary school pod monitor also enjoyed the privilege of locking and unlocking the flag cabinet for the ROTC students. Six ROTC students were chosen to raise the American and Tennessee flags in the morning and lower them in the afternoon.

The ROTC students had their hands full when they reverently carried the flags, so the lower elementary pod monitor would lock and unlock the flag cabinet for them.

The early elementary pod monitors were given a set of keys. The pod monitor only needed the key to the flag cabinet, but the janitor got tired of running the flag cabinet key around the key chain twice a day, so he just let the pod monitor hold all the keys on the second set of keys the school had in case the first set was lost. The key ring held a key to every door in the school, even the room I wanted to enter so badly.

I had tried once last year to get the janitor's keys. I made the mistake of asking Lydia Sneed to let me borrow them when she was pod monitor, but she was smarter than I thought, and she told the principal. Principal Bailey gave me a long talk about integrity, but I was glad she only gave me detention.

Principal Bailey called my mother, and she made it sound like I was planning on stealing school property. That was kind of true, except I didn't think the thing I wanted really belonged to the school.

Mom gave me a lecture that made me feel ashamed, and she didn't look at me with a smile for almost a week. Mom's punishment was worse than all the detentions I'd ever served, so I never tried to liberate the keys again.

Sydney was bursting with pride. She told our mother and Ella about the keys she held and the way that people looked at her when she wore the pod monitor badge. Sydney thought they stared at her with admiration, but the kids she thought were looking at her with respect probably just wanted to make sure that she didn't write them up for detention.

"I got it because I'm so trusting," Sydney beamed.

"You mean trust*worthy*," Ella corrected.

"That's not what matters," Sydney began with her nose in the air. "What matters is that I'm in charge and you're not."

"I do not care about your silly title," Ella snapped. "You are not in charge of me."

"That's where you're wrong! Being in charge of the *whole* pod means I can write up people in *first*, second, and third grade."

"I would rather be written up than be a prissy goody-goody!" Ella shouted. "Besides, school dismissed early, so you were not even in charge for a *whole* day!"

I started laughing, and I tried to cover it with a cough.

"Okay, girls," our mother intervened. "That's enough!"

"She started it," Sydney said. "I was just telling you about my *trustworthy* day."

My mother rolled her eyes. Ella and I smiled.

"Well, you cannot be hall monitor over Christmas break, Goody-Goody," Ella said. "So I am glad you were the hall monitor of the *half* day."

"*Pod* monitor!" yelled Sydney.

"Okay," my mother said. She seemed determined to salvage the family meal. "What happened to you today, Ella?"

"I saw Dad." She spoke it casually, without looking up from her plate.

I stopped smiling. Sydney had her mouth open in surprise, and my mother looked like Ella had just slapped her.

"Don't start lying again, Ella," my mother whispered. "I can't take it."

"Where did you see him?" Sydney asked. "Was he near the house?"

"But I did see him!" Ella exclaimed to our mother, rising from her chair. "He was happy, and we were celebrating your birthday!"

I thought of Ella in my dream. How she looked right at me. The *real* me.

"We were all there. You, me, Daddy, Sydney, Josh, and Jerrod!"

"Stop it!" my mother screamed. "I can't take it! Not today or ever!"

My mother's chair clambered to the floor as she shot up and raced upstairs. I wondered if she was going to her bathroom to cry.

"Nice," Sydney said. She got up and started scraping the rest of her meatloaf into the trash. "You never even saw Dad in your whole life."

"He was tall and blond, with blue eyes like mine," Ella said indignantly. "He was like me."

That seemed to confuse Sydney, but then she shook her head. "You could have gotten that from the pictures."

Sydney stomped out of the kitchen and went upstairs. Ella slumped in her chair and stared glumly at her plate.

"But I did see them," Ella whispered.

"Me, too."

Ella looked up as if she had just noticed me. All of the frustration and sadness left her face.

"I'm sorry," Ella sighed. "I shouldn't have peeked at your memory, but you sent it right to me."

She seemed a little more confident, pushing herself up in her chair. "So you understand what I wanted you to see?"

"Sure. Josh and I used to dream the same dreams sometimes," I explained. "I didn't know I could do that with you, too. Did you fall asleep in school?"

Ella dropped her posture and stared out the window, sighing in resignation. "Yeah, I fell asleep," she said. "Just like everyone around me."

She must not have understood my response. Ella's face was unreadable, and I couldn't find the right words to say. She stood up quietly and left me to stare at my family's unfinished meal.

Chapter Eight

I dreamed of Josh.

I was sleeping comfortably on my bottom bunk when I heard a noise. I assumed it was one of my sisters going to the bathroom, so I didn't feel the need to investigate. Then I heard it again. It was like someone was pacing outside my room, and they were bumping into the wall occasionally in the dark.

"Fine. I'm up," I mumbled.

I peeked out my door, but I couldn't see anything. My eyes adjusted to the darkness, but I could still see very little.

"Why don't you want to remember me?" said a voice.

I almost screamed.

Josh was right behind me. I turned around and looked at my twin for the first time in almost a year. He and I were mirror images, except for the horseshoe-shaped scar across the bridge of my nose. He had on the same blue jeans, button-up flannel shirt, black combat boots, and brown leather jacket he had worn on the last night I saw him. A drop of blood near his lower lip sparked a memory that was quickly extinguished.

I just stared at him. I couldn't think of anything to say.

"What are you doing?" Josh asked.

I often wondered the same thing. *Why did I stay around when I was so obviously hated?*

"I can't run away, because Ella needs me," I told my brother's ghost.

My twin threw up his hands. "I really don't know how to respond to that!"

What did he mean? It seemed like he was communicating pretty well for a dead guy.

"And we both know Ella is perfectly capable of taking care of herself," Josh said. The frustration he felt showed clearly on his face.

I shrugged and looked at the floor. I couldn't think of any other defense.

Josh ran a hand through his closely clipped hair. "Okay, we'll try it this way. Did you ever find out what was in that room?"

"N-no," I stammered, "b-but I didn't want to hurt anyone else after last time."

Josh just stared at me. He moved his lips as if he were about to say something, and his eyes watered. He sighed and looked at the ceiling.

Then I cried. I used to think that a crying boy was a sissy. I would laugh and throw rocks at the boys in our neighborhood who would collapse in tears when they fell off their bikes or blubber for their mothers when they didn't get their way. Over the past year, though, I had learned that a sadness could be so great that it was even forgivable for grown men to cry.

I couldn't seem to do anything else but weep. I avoided looking at Josh as large tears rolled down my cheeks and onto the floor.

After a few minutes, my brother touched my arm. I hadn't felt the warmth of his touch in so long that it startled me. I wanted to hug Josh or trap him in some other way to make him stay. I wanted to shout to my mother, "Wake up! You can love me again. I brought Josh back!" But nothing is easy, and dead people stay dead. I yearned to stay in my dream and talk to my brother, even if it meant that the world would go on without me in it. But every dream has to end, no matter how hard you try not to wake up.

Josh smiled at me sadly. "I guess it's best to go through with the plan. I thought you would have wised up before now. I only hope that it will make sense to you when you get there." Josh's words would have seemed condescending to the outside observer, but I needed a course of action, and Josh's voice was a comfort.

He reached out to touch me again, but my vision blurred, and I felt the sensation of falling. My brother slipped away, and I tried to hold onto the dream, but the forces of consciousness enveloped me.

I jerked awake. I still felt the residue of my falling sensation, but it made my bed seem softer and more comforting. My skin felt tingly and warm, like my body had just gotten its circulation back.

I opened my eyes and looked at the bottom of the mattress on the top bunk and an intense sadness devoured me. I was so angry with myself! I saw my brother for the first time since his death, and all I did was cry like a stupid baby! I didn't beg for him to forgive me. I didn't even ask why he was here!

Josh had told me I needed to go through with the plan. I knew what he meant, but I had no intention of trying *the plan* again. Too many people had been hurt by my rebelliousness. The plan had ended disastrously, and I was simply going to wait until enough time had passed so that everyone would forgive me.

But how could I expect anyone's forgiveness? I didn't even think *I* could forgive me. What sane person could cause his brother's death and forgive himself?

Chapter Nine

When you grow up with the same people for seventeen years, you learn a lot about them. You don't just learn the way they like their coffee or tea, but you discover a side of them that the rest of the world never sees.

My mother loved surprises, so Christmas was the best day of the year for her. *She* didn't want anything unexpected. In fact, she hated the idea of not having complete control of every situation, but she enjoyed surprising other people.

When I was a young child, my mother's surprises always made me feel important, and I wondered how she shocked me, but when I became a teenager, I started to pick up on familiar patterns. Every year, my mother would add some flare to her gift-giving by adding a little deception to her presents. Some of my mom's favorites were the "box in a box" joke or the "I forgot about this one" trick. I learned to roll my eyes and play along when I needed my Scout knife to cut zip ties or duct tape.

My mother led us on Christmas scavenger hunts for large presents. There were gifts inside the Christmas tree, and we even watched videos that showed us the present, but we had to find it in the house with no other clues. I could always count on having to *work* for at least one of my presents every Christmas.

Sometimes my mother got really carried away, and her Christmas tricks weren't funny. One Christmas, Sydney started bawling because she couldn't get all the duct tape off her doll house. Another Christmas, Josh got really upset because his new video game was glued shut, and he cut himself with a knife trying to open it.

The tricks were just ways to prolong my mother's happiness. I think she meant well with her gags because my mother's favorite part of Christmas was seeing our reaction to the presents she got for us. There were some Christmases, though, when my mother lost her holiday spirit because someone complained about the way they received their present or she had to swallow her pride so our Christmas wishes would come true.

The Christmas I remember the most was the one before I turned fourteen. I wanted a computer so badly that I begged every member of my family to pool their holiday money together and put it toward a laptop for me.

Every time I went to the store with my mother, I would point at the laptops and say, "One of those would really help me with my schoolwork."

Josh did the research for his projects on my mother's outdated PC, so I thought that my mother would be more likely to get me a laptop if I insinuated that it would be used for homework.

I never had a reason to suspect that my Christmas hints had gone unnoticed. When I penned my list for my mother, it had one item on it. My mother smiled, so I thought she had found a way to get the laptop for me.

A week seemed to last forever when I was young, but memories now blurred together when I tried to recall the days of my early adolescence. It seemed like I waited forever for Christmas to arrive, but I couldn't remember a lot of the days between Thanksgiving and Christmas.

I was wrapped up in my juvenile worries and Christmas dreams, and I never thought about the emotional and financial strain my mother must have experienced after my father left. I didn't realize that my mother tried to meet financial demands without sacrificing the wants and needs of her children. Looking back, I shouldn't have complained about the lack of space in my mother's older model Honda when she traded her new, roomier mid-sized car. I certainly shouldn't have whined when I had to trade video games at a bargain store when my parents used to let me buy a new one every month.

My mother wasn't in the habit of expressing her concerns to her children. She only asked that we work hard in school, so I thought that my near-perfect grades would get me anything I wanted.

On Christmas Eve, my mother sat down at the kitchen table for one of our talks, tears in her eyes. She looked out the window after she handed me my cup of cocoa. She seemed to be gathering her courage to tell me something.

The cocoa cup was hot in my hands, but the liquid was tepid. I started with a careful sip that turned into a long drink.

"Is everything okay, Mom?" I asked, licking the chocolate off my lips.

My mother took a deep breath. "I wanted to get you a computer, but I have to pay the taxes on the house. I tried everything, Jerrod, but I can't make your Christmas this year." She said it in a rush, like she was purging the words from her mouth.

I was shocked that my mother was talking to me about a Christmas present. She had always been concerned about the mystery of Christmas gifts, so revealing what she had or hadn't gotten me breached her usual protocol.

All I could think to say was, "It's okay." It was an automatic response, but my mother smiled and hugged me across the table. She kept her almost happy smile as she cleared our cups from the table and prepared to lie down.

I went to bed wondering if she was deceiving me or if her tears were real. *Could she be hiding my laptop? Would my mother lead me on a scavenger hunt, or would she give me a string that would guide me to my most desired gift?*

I had examined all the presents with my name on them, and none of them looked like a laptop. In fact, most of the presents were wrapped in boxes that easily rebounded from the soft material that was unmistakably clothing.

I stayed up most of the night thinking of ways I could get my laptop and what I would do to my mother if she tricked me. As soon as I decided that it was too late to go to sleep, I dozed into a peaceful dream.

Dawn came creeping through my window on Christmas day, and I heard Sydney run into my room. I had to hold back a chuckle. The buttons on her candy cane pajamas were slightly off.

"Mom's up!" she said. "Race you to the tree."

Josh swung the upper half of his body from his top bunk and grinned. He had a rare mischievousness in his eyes. I decided to take advantage of it.

"Let's get her!" I yelled and shot out of bed.

Josh flipped off his bunk and ran after me. We each grabbed one of Sydney's arms and started dragging her to her bed.

"Let's tie her to her bed and open her presents!" I yelled over Sydney's protests.

Sydney tugged the arm I held until she realized she couldn't free herself. She turned to Josh, her lip in a pout, but he held her firmly. The hallway echoed with Sydney's protests.

"Boys! That's enough!" My mother's stern voice resonated through the hall. My mother's features reflected her broken spirit as she held a wriggling Ella in her arms.

Josh and I simultaneously let go of Sydney's arms. "What's wrong, Mom?" Josh asked.

"Nothing," she said and forced herself to smile. "Let's go open presents!"

I was still so overcome with Christmas joy that I ran downstairs without another thought about my mother's depressed expression. I was the second one to the tree—Josh had always been a step faster than me—and I grabbed a present.

I knew the present was mine because I had memorized the position and the wrapping paper of each of my presents. I ripped open the paper.

Socks. Oh.

I found out early in life that parents used days like Christmas and your birthday to give you things like socks and underwear, which they should be giving you anyway. It seemed like you were getting more, but really they were cheating you.

I reached across my brother to get a present wrapped in red and gold paper. My brother had already torn through two presents and was holding up a shirt so that our mom could snap a picture.

"Out of the way, Jerrod!" she scolded, but she must have gotten the picture. She didn't ask Josh to pose again.

I rebounded back into my sitting position and pretended to check the tag. I tore the paper and ripped open the box.

Jeans. Wonderful.

Sydney brought me a present wrapped in green, metallic paper. She was smiling excitedly at Josh, who had a present with identical paper.

"I want you to open them at the same time," Sydney said and ran over to where Ella was quietly sitting. "Mom, get a picture of their faces."

Josh and I chanced a glance at each other and started opening at the same time. I lifted my present up so that Sydney could beam her delight at me.

A lot of people thought that twins should dress the same because they looked the same. I supposed these people thought it was cute to pinch the cheeks of the little babes who were dressed in identical sailor suits. The suits were so ridiculous looking that you couldn't tell if said babes were crying because of the itchy material or because they caught a glimpse of themselves in a mirror. These individuals would probably also scream in delight if they saw twin darlings playing with the same toys, working in matching notebooks, and tucking themselves into identical bed sheets at night. I would have died of embarrassment before I went into kindergarten if my parents had thought that way.

My mother and father believed that our matching physical features were the only things about my brother and me that should be identical. They may have bought us the same types of shoes, but they were always different colors. Josh and I had to share a room, but my brother had Marvel bed sheets, and I had a comforter that reflected my Star Wars obsession.

Our room was littered with proof of our differences. Josh loved science, and half-finished experiments grew in our room. He had an herb garden placed in our window, a jar of sugar water forming crystals on a string, and eggs developing under the warmth of an incubator. He also loved cars. I thought cars were scientific to him because he could take apart the components of a motor and fix them.

To my mother's horror, Josh wanted to be an auto mechanic. He had car magazines, posters, and silly model cars that he put together with our dad. I used to love to hide them. He'd get so freaked out, and I would get grounded for a week, but I loved to watch him run all over the house shouting and crying as he threw pillows and toys out of the way in search of his beloved models.

I was a gamer. I had a padded camp chair that cradled me as I played the latest trend in video games. Gaming was the main reason I wanted a laptop. I wanted to play online games with my friends and with people around the world who might be better at gaming than me.

At that age, I didn't put a lot of thought into my life from one day to the next. I enjoyed the freedom that intelligence allowed me. I didn't have to study to easily ace my challenging exams, so I did a lot of lounging and practical joking. I had a couple of ideas for video games, so I thought I might design video games later on in life. In my teenage mind, I thought I could release one video game that would sustain all my adult needs. I had researched several colleges that could help me develop the skills I needed to create next-generation video games, but the colleges were all miles away from home, so I didn't share my college plans with my family.

It was a running joke that Josh was on his way to great discoveries. The lack of growth on my side of the room proved that I was destined to live in my mother's basement.

Our parents embraced our differences and catered to our separate personalities. My father fueled my brother's automotive dreams, and my mother fostered my love of video games and Star Wars.

Sydney didn't seem to think the same way as our parents. Josh held up a green sweater with a smiling Santa on it. I pulled aside the red and green tissue paper in my box to reveal an identical sweater. We gave idiotic smiles when our mother took a picture, and we put on the sweaters to make Sydney feel like her presents were appreciated.

"She better not do that every year," my brother mumbled while Sydney was busy opening one of her presents.

I opened my other gifts: a movie, underwear, and more socks. I acted excited about every present, but I may have performed too much. The sad look returned to my mother's face.

My brother picked up a large box. He shook it slightly, and our mother's face paled. "Josh, be careful."

Josh tore open a box that held a chemistry set. His eyes danced with happiness.

"Don't always believe your gift is what's on the package," our mother teased.

Josh was too excited to debate with our mother. Even little Sydney knew that no one had ever gotten a chemistry set, and our mother couldn't be reusing the box, but we all played along.

Josh opened the packaging, and he found a gray shirt wrapped in tissue paper. He held up the shirt while he tried to act disappointed and grateful simultaneously.

"Maybe you should take the tissue paper out so I can reuse the box next year," our mother suggested.

Josh bent his head toward the box and cracked a smile as he lifted the tissue paper off of the chemistry set that was "hidden" in the box. "Mom, you're the best!" Josh said, and he almost knocked our mother to the floor when he ran to hug her.

Twenty minutes later, everything under the tree had been un-wrapped, and my family was in a present coma. Ella was drifting to sleep in her playpen while Sydney and Josh played chess, drowsi-ness cloaking their faces. My mother was watching them as her eyelids crawled down her eyes, then shot up to her eyebrows, only to creep back down again. I was too frustrated and disappointed to be tired. I had not gotten my laptop!

Everyone had received the presents they had wanted most. Ella had even squealed in delight when Sydney helped her open a motorized toddler car. All the gifts had been unwrapped, and there wasn't a surprise package or even a present scavenger hunt.

A knock at the front door caused us all to jolt to alertness and look at each other. "Is anyone expecting company?" my mother whispered. Three heads shook at once.

Our mother crept to the living room window and peeked behind the curtain at the edge of the window. She stood squinting into the morning for almost a full minute.

"There's no one there," she said.

Josh raced to the door and slung it open. He started to run out onto the porch, but he tripped over a box that had been pushed against the door. Josh recovered quickly from his fall and grabbed the package.

The box was wrapped in plain brown paper, and it had a flat, rectangular shape. I thought it had been delivered by the postal service, but there wasn't an address on the box. Someone had personally delivered the package.

Josh shook the parcel. "Well, it's not ticking or smoking, so I'm gonna open it."

"No, give it to me," our mother said. "I need to open it in case something's up with it."

Our mother carefully peeled the tape on the side of the box and opened it enough to try to see what might be inside. Sydney, Josh, and I stood as close to her as we dared.

I didn't know if I imagined it, but I thought my mother's eyes grew wide when she recognized the item in the wrapping. She handed me the box and said, "I think this is for you."

I took the box and felt the weight of the package. It was between five and ten pounds. I guessed my mother thought it was safe because of her reaction, so I tore off the rest of the brown paper. It took me a moment to realize what I had unwrapped.

I had researched a lot of laptops. I had scanned pages of advertisements with electronics, but I had never really pointed out a certain brand when I would drop hints to my family about my biggest Christmas wish. In my mind, the perfect laptop was one with the most memory and a powerful processor. The laptop I held was a machine that fulfilled all my desires. I could open the box and use a satellite connection to search for information or send messages to my friends. I could also gather together as many of my stories and video game ideas as I wanted without fear that the amount of storage would slow down the machine.

I looked at my mother with a silly grin on my face. My excitement crept away when I noticed that Sydney was the only one staring at me as I explored my gift. My mother was on the couch, holding her head in her hands as Josh tried to comfort her.

"What's wrong?" I asked my mother.

My mother looked up from her hands, and there were tears in her eyes. "Nothing, honey," she said. "Sometimes Christmas wishes find a way to come true."

I was momentarily curious about her statement until my computer beeped. *My first message!* It was only a welcome message, but it was still fun to read it on my new Christmas present.

I absentmindedly closed the front door and cleared a place on the living room floor. I was so wrapped up in my gift that I didn't analyze my mother's reaction to my granted Christmas wish.

My mother stayed busy preparing dinner, cleaning, and taking care of Ella, so I really didn't notice a difference in her attitude until there was another knock at the door.

"Maybe that's someone dropping off my Lamborghini!" Josh said as he ran to the door.

My mother stopped him in mid-stride. She bent her head down, almost like a beaten dog, and she walked to the door. "I should be the one to answer the door."

We all stood around the door as my mother checked the peephole and opened it. The doorway opened to reveal a tall, muscular man with broad shoulders and a hardened face. His piercing green eyes were alert under thick, white eyebrows. The stranger had full, white hair and a moderate, well-groomed mustache. He was dressed in shiny black boots and a navy blue policeman's uniform.

My first thought was that the police had found my father, dead or in jail, and our family's biggest mystery had been solved. Then I studied our visitor's eyes, and there was something familiar about them.

"I guess it's time you guys met your grandfather," my mother said.

Chapter Ten

All the children concentrated very hard on their plates that evening. My turkey and mashed potatoes were a much better sight than looking at a strange man in my father's place. No one had sat at the head of the table since my father had left.

My mother had gone to a lot of trouble to make the room festive. There were small Santa hats on the edge of each picture on the wall. She had also put out the red and green checkered Christmas tablecloth and her best china. The china was a cream color, with holly around the rims of the plates and bowls and mistletoe engraved into the handles of the utensils.

She had placed her father's plate between Josh and me. Sydney and my mother sat on the other side of the table and Ella's highchair was between our mother's chair and our absent father's place. When we walked into the dining room, the large man lifted his plate and put it at the head of the table. He sat down and winked at Ella. It was almost like he had no respect for my father.

My mother was very uncomfortable. She kept fidgeting and barely touched her food. She was quick to assist Ella with every bite of her dinner, and she tried to make some strained conversation about the neighbor's Christmas lights. The giant man seemed uninterested.

We were supposed to think of this stranger as our grandfather, but I couldn't remember seeing him. My father had mentioned our grandfather when he and my mother argued, so I always suspected my mother and her father had become estranged after she married my father.

"You can thank him for your laptop," Josh whispered while Ella cried over peas. He jerked a thumb in the direction of our strange guest.

My brain fully processed my mother's sadness over her inability to buy my Christmas present, her broken spirit on Christmas morning, and the sudden appearance of her father. My mother had paid for my laptop, but she had not paid for it with money. She had paid for it with her pride.

"Miranda, do you let the boys finger their food all the time?" the stranger asked.

Our mother sucked in her breath, and Josh stopped lifting a piece of turkey to his mouth. He put it back on his plate and picked up his fork.

"Thank you, Josh," our mother said and turned to her father. "I don't get mad over the little things. Besides, it's not as if he were sucking mashed potatoes off his fingers."

"No, but I can hear them all eating like they have a trough in front of them instead of their plates," he commented.

"Please eat more quietly, children," our mother said curtly. "Your grandfather is used to having everything orderly." She glared at her father until Ella demanded her attention.

After a few minutes of silence, my mother sighed. Her posture deflated, and she put her fingers to her temple. She seemed determined to save Christmas dinner. "How has your holiday been so far?"

"I had a suicide and a murder this morning and a car accident to clean up before I left the station," my mother's father began, but Sydney cut him off with a gasp.

My sister's eyes had gotten larger with each event my mother's father recounted, but she couldn't handle the details she knew were coming about the accident. Our mother looked pointedly from us to her father.

He cleared his throat and straightened in his chair. "I guess it's been a while since I've been around children." He looked at Sydney. "Are you okay?"

Sydney nodded and stared at her plate.

The familiar stranger looked at my mother and winked again at Ella like they had a special secret. I couldn't be mad at Ella for cooing back at him. She was just a baby.

Josh and I exchanged a glance. Through our twin telepathy, or just a regular analysis of the situation, we concluded: *We don't like him. He will never be our grandfather.*

At that moment, the powers of God, fate, or chaos did not agree, because Sydney began to choke. We all turned our attention to her in alarm.

She had been holding back tears from thinking about the poor people who had been involved in the accidents. Sydney explained later that she had been about to swallow a bite of turkey when a sob had come up from her throat. The turkey had gotten lodged, and she panicked. My sister knew to put both her hands to her neck to give the sign that she was choking.

My eyes went from Sydney to our mother. My mother knocked her plate to the floor as she jumped out of her chair and grabbed Sydney. She thumped Sydney hard on the back with the palm of her hand. I knew that you were not supposed to hit a choking person on the back, but I felt frozen. I could only watch. My brother seemed unable to move, too. He still had his fork in his hand.

"Stop it!" our mother yelled at Sydney, but of course, Sydney couldn't help that she was choking. My mother shook her roughly and pounded her back again.

My mother's father pushed back his chair, walked calmly over to our mother and Sydney, and firmly removed my mother's hands from Sydney's body. He then placed himself behind Sydney, put a fist into her stomach, and pushed upward with his hand. He must have done his own version of the Heimlich maneuver because he had to hold my mother back with his other hand. Regardless of the lack of procedure, my sister spit the chunk of turkey across the table and onto Josh's plate.

Sydney gasped mouthfuls of air, and my mother hugged her and cried. My mother's father sat down and began eating again. Sydney looked at him as if he had a wondrous white light around him. She untangled herself from our mother's arms and walked over to his chair.

"You saved me," she said in awe. I could see the beginnings of some serious hero worship.

My mother's father opened his mouth to say something, then closed it and lowered his fork. Sydney took the opportunity to climb into his lap. At first, the large man sat with his arms out and his hands open. Then he hugged my sister for a long, silent moment.

Sydney could brighten anyone's day, and my mother's street-hardened father was no exception. Maybe it had been too long since he had been loved, or perhaps he was remembering my mother at Sydney's age, but I heard tears and regret in his words when he said, "I love you, Little Lady, and I'm gonna start showing it."

He looked up at my mother expectantly. My mother simply stared back without a comment or commitment.

Sydney buried her head in his chest. "Thank you, Grandpa."

He smiled and stroked her hair. My mother continued to stand beside Sydney's chair, and Josh and I were still frozen. Finally, Josh shook his head, and we exchanged another look: *I guess we're going to have to call him Grandpa, too.*

Chapter Eleven

We tried to familiarize ourselves with our grandfather. He attempted to bond with all of us and wanted to reconnect with my mother, but Sydney was the only one who formed a true attachment to him.

Josh and I liked our new family member, but it was hard for us to feel a true connection to someone who had not known us in our youth. It seemed like so much was expected of us right away, and you can't build a house without a foundation.

Ella liked our grandfather about the same as everyone else, but as she grew, she put more distance between herself and him. She cared for her grandfather, but it was almost physically painful for her when he visited. I could never understand it, and there was always something else on my teenage mind, so I filed it away with all the other odd things about my family.

Years of seasons and holidays moved past us with no sign of my father. It was strange to celebrate holidays with a missing family member. It almost seemed like our family felt guilty for being happy. We were slow to smile, and a rainbow of emotions whizzed through our house in a matter of moments.

My mother's birthday fell on Christmas, but after my dad left, no one knew how to celebrate it. We would all wish her a happy birthday, but we never separated her birthday and Christmas presents. My mother's friends would call her, but they would recognize her birthday as an afterthought. "I hope you have a great Christmas!" her closest friends would say. "Bye. Oh! Happy birthday, Miranda." My mother would smile sadly, but her voice wouldn't betray the disappointment she felt.

My father always made a big deal out of my mother's birthday. We devoted the morning of Christmas to the spirit of the holiday, but in the early afternoon, we celebrated my mother's birthday. My father used to say that Christmas became December twenty-fifth after noon. We made her a cake and cookies, we sang and danced together, and we gave her presents. We always constructed the presents. My father insisted handmade presents helped separate Christmas from December twenty-fifth.

The Christmas my brother and I were almost sixteen, Josh, Sydney, and I tried to continue my father's tradition. The day ended with my mother locked in her bedroom, the sound of her tremendous sobs echoing down the hall.

That was the day I decided to find my father. I didn't know how to begin my search, but I was prepared to travel the world to locate him. I didn't expect my grandfather to be the key to unlocking his whereabouts only days later.

One night, shortly after my sixteenth Christmas, I awoke to hushed screaming. It's the special type of yelling where your face is red and you gesticulate wildly, but you speak in a voice just below regular talking. It would have been better to talk in a regular voice because my mother's strained voice probably wouldn't have awakened me.

Her angry words carried up the stairs, even though she was trying not to wake her children. My grandfather's deep, calm voice barely made it to my ears.

I could tell Josh was awake. I could feel his curiosity and fear.

My mother seldom yelled. She was firm, but she would always find an example or song to smooth ruffled emotions.

My mother was very upset about something. Our room was right above the stairs, so we listened as the echo of my mother's words carried into our room.

Josh and I silently got out of our beds and crept to the top of the stairs. From our new position, we could hear both sides of the conversation clearly. Our grandfather's voice drifted to us, and he was not sparing his sleeping grandchildren the hostility of his remarks.

"I am so tired of your excuses, Miranda," he said. "You were so in love with him you didn't even see what was going on."

"Nothing was going on," my mother countered. "He had a problem, and he'll be back when he's fixed it."

"You act like he's on vacation!" our grandfather shouted. Then he paused, and I could feel a strong emotion gathering. "Good God, girl! What's wrong with you?" he asked seriously.

I knew enough about my grandfather to understand that he was staring at my mother in disbelief. I knew my mother well enough to picture her crying silently. Her tears were falling on her own shoulders.

"I don't want the file." Her words pleaded with her father to let her maintain her ignorance. "He loved me so much. I know he did. He had his reasons for leaving." The increased volume of her words showed that my mother had looked from the floor to my grandfather's face.

"I know you didn't like him," my mother continued. My grandfather made a noise, but my mother kept talking. "When you took me away from the city, I was ready to rebel. I know you think that's why I married Johnny, but he *saved* me. You don't know everything about him. He *defended* you. He wanted me to forgive you." My mother took a moment to get control of her sobbing. "Johnny and I were together for almost fifteen years. Just like you and Mom."

A slap made us jump. We looked at each other.

He slapped the file on the table, Josh sent. He hadn't hit our mother.

"Get a clue, Miranda!" our grandfather shouted. "He could have faced God Almighty in my defense, but the fact remains that he abandoned his family. That means any free pass for his craziness flew out the window when he walked out that door. As for the file, I think you're stupid for not keeping it! You do this all the time. You were in denial over your mother's sickness until she had been buried almost a year, and you didn't accept that we were staying in the country until Mr. Wonderful brought you home from that silly hayride!"

Josh and I could only stare at each other. We couldn't help our mother without possibly making the situation worse, but neither one of us could bear to hear her muffled cries.

Josh seemed inspired by something and quickly got up and walked down the hall. I paid more attention to the conversation downstairs than I did to my brother's intentions.

My grandfather's heavy boots walked across the kitchen. "You're gonna have to grow up one day and stop living this way!" my grandfather finished. He was out of breath from his rush of emotion.

His heavy footfalls boomed across the floor. I heard the file slide across the table.

I could feel my mother crying. I wanted to kick my grandfather right out the door for causing her pain, but there was a large part of me that wanted to know what was in the file. Maybe if I let him wear her down, he would read it out loud in his frustration.

"Please take it," my mother said weakly. "I gave a copy to the school, but I don't want to know what's inside. If he's in jail or he has another family—" my mother said, but her sobs choked her.

"Miranda, you know *exactly* what's in this file."

Josh had returned with a sleepy Sydney. She rubbed her eyes with tiny fists, and one side of her face was marked with the folds of her pillowcase.

Josh ran Sydney down the steps and placed her on the bottom step. She looked back at him and stumbled down the last step and into the living room. My mother must have noticed Sydney, because she said, "Honey, what are you doing out of bed?"

"I don't know," Sydney said, but her grandfather scooped her up before she could say anything else.

Josh and I had not had enough time to run into our bedroom. We were at the top of the steps, staring down at our grandfather's intimidating form. He held Sydney in one arm and was trying to soothe her.

"It's okay, Little Lady. There'll be no more fussin'. You can go back to sleep," he said.

Our grandfather turned to give Sydney to our mother, but his acute senses picked up on the presence of other people. My brother and I were completely exposed! He locked eyes with us briefly. Josh and I had the same flashing red thought: *We're caught!* But our grandfather nodded knowingly and focused his attention back on Sydney. He quickly moved away from the bottom of the stairs.

We took the opportunity to bolt into our room and dive beneath the covers. We waited a few minutes before we spoke. I could still hear muffled patches of conversation.

Josh was the first to speak. His words startled me after my adrenaline had spiked.

"Why didn't he bust us?" Josh said.

"What good would it have done?" I shrugged in the dark. "Mom would have freaked out, and she's already upset. He probably wants us to know anyway."

"Oh, about Dad, you mean?" Josh said.

I tried to hear some more of the conversation. My mother and grandfather were talking more quietly. My mother had calmed down, and she was soothing Sydney.

"I'm gonna go listen some more," I said, throwing back the covers.

Josh shot up from beneath his comforter. "Stop! Grandpa didn't say anything the first time, but if he sees you sneaking again, he might tell Mom!"

"Then stay in bed, and I'll be the only one who'll get caught," I whispered on my way to the stairs.

I felt a little braver, so I sat down on the third step from the top. I could hear every word exchanged between Sydney, my mother, and my grandfather.

"I love you, Grandpa," Sydney was saying. There was a rustle of heavy fabric as my grandfather put on his coat.

"'Bye, Little Lady," he returned softly.

"Please, Dad," my brother pleaded. I knew she wanted him to take the folder, but she didn't want to say anything more in front of Sydney.

"Don't build him up to be something he's not," my grandfather warned. "Remember him how he really was. I bet your boys remember him."

What was that all about? I remembered my father, but he was a loyal, loving, hard-working man. There had been a couple of incidents, but I had put them out of my mind. I was really worried about him.

My grandfather's footsteps grew louder as he neared the front door. I didn't even bother to move. I was tired and sad.

My mother didn't walk her father to the door. He glanced up the stairs briefly and held up the orange folder in his hand. *Was he trying to tell me to come get it?*

My grandfather opened the door but paused before he stepped into the night. "You know where you can find this file whenever you need it."

My mother didn't answer. I didn't think he was talking to her anyway.

I got up and quietly tiptoed into my room. Josh was awake, but he said nothing.

"I'm gonna ask Grandpa to give me that file," I told my brother, but I secretly wondered how I could ask my grandpa for the file without my mother finding out.

Josh surprised me when he said, "Why don't you just leave it alone?"

I was about to climb back into bed, but I shot back up. "What do you mean? Don't you want to get Dad back!" Josh had always been closer to our father than me.

"Why?" my brother responded. "*He* left *us*. If he doesn't want to be around, I don't want him here."

I climbed quietly back into bed. I had no response.

Chapter Twelve

Since I had caused my brother's death, I experienced periods of insomnia. I'd hear soft sleeping sounds from my mother and sisters, but I was confined to my bed, looking at the bottom of the top bunk where my twin used to sleep. I would lie awake for hours, wishing for the blissful escape of sleep.

During my periods of unwanted wakefulness, I would reflect on times in my life that were happier, or simpler, but I couldn't keep my mind from drifting to more difficult years. I often thought about my family before my father left.

The house had been dark the year before my eleventh Christmas. Not physically dark—Josh wouldn't even let me watch a movie with the lights out—but emotionally dark. I remember thinking it was strange that our mother kept us quiet, especially since we used to be encouraged to act as happy and childlike as possible.

We still had great times together. In fact, I could remember the good times better because of the cheerlessness that echoed through our house most of the time.

There was a lot of light before the dark year. Our mother and father acted like the perfect family before Sydney became a toddler.

We danced around the house, we went to sporting events and out on picnics, and my parents always made sure that we were happy.

My father was so excited when my mother told him she was pregnant with Sydney that he went out and bought a minivan. He pulled into the driveway and smiled proudly, waiting for praise.

"Can we afford this?" our mother asked, patting her growing belly.

"Miranda, we've always found a way," my father said. "Besides, would you want to sit in between two boys fighting over chips or an action figure?"

Our mother laughed. "Just make sure it has seat warmers."

Our parents took us everywhere with them. They used to tell family and friends that if children were excluded, then it was a place they didn't need to go. Our parents even took us to parenting classes with them so that we could learn how to take care of the new baby.

Our family celebrated Sydney's arrival in the summer. Our mother had hardly given herself enough time to heal before she announced that she was pregnant again. It was one of the last hot days of summer, and our family went out for ice cream. My father snuck tiny bites to baby Sydney when he thought his wife wasn't looking.

Several weeks later, Josh and I were playing video games when we heard a horn blow in the driveway. Sydney was stretched out on a blanket, trying to keep her head up, and our mother was reading on the couch.

"Josh, look out the window," my mother said. "Tell me who it is."

Josh walked across the room and hopped over Sydney. He jerked the blinds to the side. "Looks like a big pink van."

"What?" our mother asked, coming into the living room. She carefully pulled the blinds over. "Tell me he didn't."

Our mother strode to the front door, picking up Sydney, who was trying to push and grunt her way to her mother's feet. Josh and I followed our mother and walked outside.

It was almost Halloween, and cold weather was supposed to come in overnight, but the day was sunny, and the warmth of the sun was almost tangible. Everyone had at least one pumpkin outside their home. Our father had helped Josh and me make one a few days before, and it watched us from our porch with its gap-toothed grin. A lawn mower hummed, and someone's end-of-season barbecue drifted in the gentle breeze.

I knew it was my dad before I looked into the van. I could hear the heavy metal music pounding out of the windows.

"Only you would be proud to sit in an electric pink van and jam out to Rob Zombie," our mother said. "Have you no shame?"

"What do you mean?" our father asked innocently. "This van is the bomb!"

"Bomb is right," our mother countered. "It looks like a bottle of pink stomach medicine exploded over it."

"Oh, just get in. Let's take it for a ride."

"Please tell me you didn't trade our minivan for that thing," our mother groaned. "The neighbors will get us for violating the Neighborhood Agreement. It's an eyesore!"

"Get Sydney's car seat, and we'll go get a pizza," my father offered with a wink.

Food is a magic word to any pregnant woman, so my mother agreed to take a ride. Ten minutes later, my family was ready for their maiden voyage in the pink van.

"Turn down the radio," our mother shouted over the music. "You're going to burst the baby's eardrums."

I'd noticed that in any family with more than one child, the parents often referred to the youngest as the baby. Unless they added another child to the family tree, the youngest child would be called the baby until he or she was well past infant years. At seven, Ella was still sometimes called the baby.

"She likes it," my father yelled back. "Sydney has great taste." He turned around and winked at Sydney. Sydney kicked her legs in her seat and cooed at him.

"Well, she can like it at a lower volume," my mother said, turning the chipped volume dial.

I didn't think I had seen my mother more embarrassed than she was on the five-minute ride to the pizza parlor. My father waved at all our neighbors, who would look up to wave at the approaching vehicle. They looked surprised, and their mouths hung open slightly as they realized who was driving. Our mother covered her eyes and shook her head in shame when a neighborhood girl called to her parents, "Why can't we get a Barbie van, too?" After that, our mother told her husband to roll up the windows because there was too much air on Sydney.

My father thought the van was wonderful. "I figured we needed more room, and I found this baby for a steal." He patted the dashboard. "Can you believe the original owner only put forty thousand miles on her?" Our mother just stared back at him, shaking her head with her mouth open.

"We look like an advertisement for breast cancer awareness," my mother commented.

"The rolling Ta-Ta machine," I shouted, and laughter exploded in the van. Josh held his stomach and could hardly catch his breath.

The name stuck. Every time we left the house, our mother would say, "Go start the Ta-Ta machine," or "Put Sydney in the Ta-Ta van." The bright pink van marked our home and was part of the rest of our adventures as a united family.

Chapter Thirteen

Josh and I didn't always attend Pale Woods Academy. We had once been cogs in the wheel of public education.

Public school kids were mean. The children at our school were no different. Our mother made sure that Josh and I were stylishly dressed, but kids still targeted us because we were smart. It didn't help that Josh was a complete show-off.

I was content making good grades and keeping my head low when the teacher asked a question, but Josh had to be the first to raise his hand. Then he would look around the room at the other students while reaching straight into the air. He'd lock eyes with me: *You know the answer. Why don't you raise your hand?*

I'll tell you why I didn't raise my hand. I liked the smell of my shampoo. Josh must have liked the smell of public toilet water because the toilet was where bullies would put his head almost every day before lunch.

Kids still made fun of me because I'd take up for my brother, or I'd get chosen for an academic honor, but they left me alone most of the time. The difference between Josh and me was that I wouldn't let kids push me around. I'd shout back at them and call them names. I even shoved a kid into a locker and closed him in it in second grade for calling me a nerd.

I got into my biggest fight in the fourth grade. I was punished severely for it, but I never regretted standing up for my brother.

This fifth-grade kid, Tony Spumoni, liked to pick on all the kids. Well, all the kids who were smaller than him. He would just reach out and randomly grab a kid by the coat or collar and pull him close, like they were best pals. Then he would look to see if a teacher could see him. If the kid was lucky, a teacher would catch Spumoni's eye, and he would let him go.

The teachers knew Tony was bullying the younger kids, but they couldn't do anything to him unless they saw him hurting someone. The worst part was that he plagued the school much longer than most bullies. He had repeated at least two grades. He was the oldest fifth grader I had ever known.

Every bully had goons. Goons were the guys who followed the bully around, laughed at his jokes, and sometimes endured a small amount of physical abuse when the bully had no one else to intimidate. Spumoni's goons were Edward "Frek" Rice and Kelly Johnson.

Frek had red hair, glasses, and freckles. All the kids called him Frek because he had so many freckles that you couldn't tell if his skin was brown or white. His laugh sounded like a donkey with a cold. We all thought Frek had failed fifth grade the previous year just so that he could terrorize kids with Spumoni a little longer.

Kelly Johnson had brown hair, brown eyes, and no noticeable deformities. He would have passed outside Spumoni's radar except for his name.

Kelly Johnson's parents must have hated him. They gave a perfectly normal boy a girl's name.

Since he had a girl's name, he tried extra hard to assert his masculinity. He had been mean and aggressive since he started school. He was the bully of his grade until Spumoni failed last year. A lot of kids couldn't wait until the two bullies collided, because they thought Kelly Johnson would get his butt kicked by Spumoni on the first day of school. Instead, he teamed up with Spumoni over the summer, and he came to school ready to do Spumoni's bidding. Spumoni referred to Kelly as Johnson. Spumoni probably didn't want to embarrass him by using his real name, or he may have told Spumoni that his name was Johnson.

The only reason Johnson and Frek didn't get thrashed was because they lived on the same street as Tony, and they pretended to worship him. Tony was probably just smart enough to know that he needed goons as scapegoats or to help spread around gossip about the kids he'd beat up.

One day in the winter of our fourth-grade year, Josh and I were walking out to go home when Josh spotted Spumoni. Spumoni was watching kids go out, looking for one to send home with fear. Josh grabbed my arm and whispered, "Let's go out the other way."

"No way, Josh. The door's right there," I told him, pointing to the exit five feet away.

"You don't understand," Josh said, his voice breaking. "Tony doesn't like me. I corrected him in the hallway."

Most kids only had to worry about what they said in front of teachers and their parents, but everyone was *corrected* when my brother was around. Most kids just avoided him because they thought he was a know-it-all.

"So what?" I said dismissively. "He doesn't rule the hall, and I'm going home. Mom has a doctor's appointment today. If we go out the other door, we'll have to walk around the school, so she'd probably be late."

I pushed Josh forward. Josh may have gone by Spumoni unnoticed if he hadn't been watching him so closely. We were almost out the door when I felt Josh grab my arm. I almost fell backward, but Josh's grip loosened.

I turned around, ready to yell at Josh, but I saw Spumoni pinning his arms against a locker. Josh's feet were kicking, trying to find the floor. "Look guys," Spumoni said. "It's the smart boy."

Josh was looking from Spumoni to me with fear in his eyes. *Go get someone.*

I was not the type to run to a teacher when there was a fight, and my pregnant mother couldn't improve the situation, so I stood and watched. My brother would have to face Tony at some point.

A crowd gathered around my brother and Spumoni. Frek and Johnson stood like sentinels on either side of Spumoni and Josh so that they could look for teachers and still watch the scene.

"You think I'm dumb, don't cha?" Spumoni asked my brother.

"No," Josh squeaked. "I just pointed out that you shouldn't end a sentence with a preposition."

I lowered my head and shook it. I probably would have roughed my brother up, too. *Did he want to live through elementary school?*

"Well, you were real funny, smart boy," said Spumoni. "I was laughin' so hard. I'm gonna be laughin' even harder when I knock the preposition out of you."

"Good one, Tone," Frek brayed. Spumoni looked proud of himself.

Josh struggled, and Spumoni pushed him harder against the lockers. He put one hand on Josh's chest and placed one of his massive hands over my brother's throat.

That was enough for me. I could never beat Spumoni in a fair fight, especially since Frek and Johnson would back him up, so I yelled, "Hey, Tony!"

When Spumoni turned around, I hit him as hard as I could in the face with my math book. Spumoni's hands let go of my brother, and Josh slid to the floor. Spumoni was yelling and holding his face, but

Josh wasn't taking the opportunity to run. He just sat on the floor, like he was waiting for the next round of abuse.

I didn't wait for Spumoni to recover. I had surprised him for a few seconds, so I used those seconds wisely. I hit Frek in the stomach with my math book, and when he doubled over, I brought my knee up to his face.

Johnson was ready for me. He hit me in the nose so hard that I saw stars. *Why had it hurt so much?* Johnson had not used his fist to hit me, but my adrenaline was too pumped to register the combination lock in his hand.

I swung blindly at Johnson, but my fists never connected. Blood was getting in my eyes and running down my face.

"What in the world is going on here?" a woman's voice shouted. I was still trying to swing at Johnson when Mrs. Fredrickson grabbed me around the collar and pulled me a foot across the floor. "What did you do to these boys?" she asked me.

I don't know why I couldn't tell her. I should have told her about Spumoni threatening Josh, but all I could do was try to squirm out of her grasp.

Josh didn't speak up. He just sat looking at me from his place on the floor.

Mrs. Fredrickson turned to Josh. "Is your mother here?" she yelled a little too loudly.

Josh snapped out of his daze. "Yes, ma'am," he said.

"Then go outside and get her. Tell her to come into the office."

Josh got up, but he had to squeeze by Spumoni to get out the door. Mrs. Fredrickson's attention was on me, so she didn't see the menacing smile that walked across Spumoni's face when he looked at Josh.

"You're coming with me," Mrs. Fredrickson hissed at me with venom and distrust.

She turned her attention to Spumoni and his goons. "You and you," she said, pointing to Spumoni and Frek, "will walk in front of us to the office. The nurse will take care of you there. The rest of you can go home. Show's over!"

Johnson walked off as if he had never been involved. He looked back over his shoulder at me and smiled. I didn't know what Mrs. Fredrickson saw when she stopped the fight, but she hadn't seen Johnson and the combination lock.

The walk to the office took about thirty seconds, and I wasn't scared at all. I knew I had done the right thing.

Mrs. Fredrickson opened the door to the office. The receptionist didn't look up until Frek and Spumoni were in the office, so she saw my bloody face first. Her expression changed from inviting to shocked to concerned. Mrs. Fredrickson unceremoniously went past the receptionist and opened the door to the principal's office.

"Robert," Mrs. Fredrickson said shrilly. "I found one of the Miller boys fighting in the hall. Look what he did to these two before I could stop him." She motioned to Spumoni and Frek.

Mr. Robert Gouge had been the principal at Elm Street Elementary School for ten years. He was funny and kind, but he was firm with troublemakers. He always addressed students with a salutation, adding mister or miss in front of their last names, and when I asked him about it, he said it was to show respect.

Mr. Gouge had been sitting in front of the desk, going over a stack of lesson plans. He calmly folded his hands in front of his face and rested his nose against his thumbs. He picked up his phone and looked at the door of his office. I heard the mumbled buzz of the office phone. The garbled voice of the receptionist, Mrs. Jackson, said, "Yes, sir?"

I was seated two or three feet away from Mr. Gouge, but he was great at whispering. The adrenaline also still had my blood pumping, so my senses should have been more acute, but all I heard him say into the receiver was, "Spumoni's mother" and "Rice's grandmother."

Mr. Gouge hung up the receiver without a goodbye. He leaned back and rested his arms and hands on the armrests of his chair. He did not smile, and his expression seemed alien. I was used to seeing him laughing playfully as he joked with students in the hall.

Mr. Gouge became a principal after twenty-five years of teaching. Many of his students came by to visit or ask for advice, even after they graduated high school. He seemed enormous to me in the fourth grade. He was not as tall as my dad, but he was probably six feet tall, so he was much larger than all the elementary students, and none of the teachers matched his height. He dressed in a white button-up shirt and khaki pants every day, unless the school celebrated Christmas or national holidays.

Mr. Gouge's tattoo intrigued me the most. I had spied it during a tug-of-war match in the spring of my second-grade year.

I had to sit out of the game because I had recently been sick, but I felt fine, so I sat behind the girls' line. My teacher put boys against girls because there were more girls than boys in the class, and she asserted girls were not physically limited. I sat close enough to see up any of the girls' dresses if they should bend to get a better grip or fall if they lost. Mr. Gouge must have seen my vantage point, and he made an elaborate excuse that the lines were unfairly matched, holding the end behind all the girls. I had a perfect view of him from the waist down. The girl's side began to lose, and as Mr. Gouge dug his heels into the ground, I glimpsed a design on his right ankle. I reproduced the image later that afternoon, and Josh looked it up on the computer.

"It's the symbol for pi," he confirmed.

"I've never seen Mr. Gouge eat a piece of pie," I told him.

"No," Josh laughed. "I've seen the symbol before. It's Greek. It was used to build pyramids, but now mathematicians use it to find the circumference of a circle."

"The Greeks built pyramids," I teased.

"No," Josh said, missing my joke. "Egyptians were the first ones known to use it when they built the Giza pyramids."

I wanted to know why Mr. Gouge had a symbol for math on his leg. He had taught third grade, and none of his past students had mentioned him putting extra emphasis on math, so I asked him about his tattoo the next day after school.

Mr. Gouge watched the students leave almost every day. He would call out the names of the students he knew and high-five anyone who made eye contact with him as they left. He was standing just outside the door of the school, talking into a walkie-talkie. Josh ran to our van while I stood looking at Mr. Gouge. When he noticed me, he jumped.

"Oh, hey, Mr. Miller, your mom's over there," he said, pointing to my mother's car.

"I know."

Mr. Gouge looked puzzled. "Is there something I can do for you?" He turned his whole body to face me, but he didn't bend down to be level with my height.

"I want to know why you got your tattoo," I said. I talked through his look of shock. "You don't eat pie, you're not Egyptian, and I didn't think you liked math *that* much."

Mr. Gouge's friendly face hardened. "Tattoos are a form of expression, and they sometimes mean a lot to the person. Sometimes," he continued, squinting his eyes, "they can be very personal."

"Well, if it was *that* personal, why did you get it where *I* could see it?"

Mr. Gouge chuckled, and his easy-going manner returned. "I guess you're right, Mr. Miller. I should have thought about that."

He took a deep breath, glanced at the departing buses, and bent down to meet my eyes. "I guess the best I can explain it is that pi is a number that never ends and doesn't repeat in a pattern." He looked at the concrete sidewalk. "I think I got it to show me that life goes on and to remind myself not to repeat my mistakes."

Mr. Gouge looked at me expectantly. He probably anticipated more questions or comments on his explanation. I was satisfied with his answer, so I had nothing more to say.

"Okay, thanks," I said, and I ran off to join my family.

I wondered briefly that night about what Mr. Gouge didn't want to repeat. I hadn't thought about his tattoo again until now.

Mr. Gouge sucked his lips back onto his cigarette-stained teeth. I heard the chair creak as he rocked it slightly. "Boys, who started the fight?"

There were a lot of tattlers in the world, but once a guy reached a certain age, he quit telling on people. In fights, it seemed, there was an unspoken code that was followed. Spumoni, Frek, and I looked at the floor. No one was talking.

"Last chance," Mr. Gouge said. He didn't want to drag it out all afternoon.

I could have gotten Spumoni kicked out of school and Frek and Johnson suspended, but I held my gaze firmly on the carpet. I wasn't going to snitch.

"That gives me no choice but to distribute the punishment evenly among you three," he said.

Mrs. Fredrickson looked scandalized. She pointed her stubby finger at me. "But don't you see what he's done to those boys?"

Mr. Gouge looked up from his hands and said, "Mrs. Fredrickson, I think that you're well aware of Tony's reputation, and I'm sure that he and Edward are not blameless." Mr. Gouge looked from Spumoni to Frek. Apparently, Mr. Gouge did not respect Tony and Frek. "Boys," he said, and we all looked up. "Edward, Tony, are you a victim in any way?"

"No," Spumoni and Frek mumbled together.

"See, Mrs. Fredrickson, I'm not being unfair." Mr. Gouge smiled and looked at me. "In fact, Jerrod was probably defending himself."

Josh picked that moment to knock on the door. "Come in," Mr. Gouge said.

Josh slowly eased the door open a crack. Mr. Gouge motioned for him to come in. Four faces turned to look at Josh. I didn't know what kind of expression Spumoni had on his face when Josh walked in, but he turned around quickly when he saw my mother behind Josh.

I got up from my chair and let my mother sit down. She settled and looked up into my face to thank me, but she stopped short when she saw the blood.

"Jerrod, are you okay?" she shouted, rising to her feet.

"I'm fine, Mom."

"No, you're not! There's so much blood!" my mother yelled. My mother didn't carry a purse, so she grabbed handfuls of tissue off of Mr. Gouge's desk. Much to my horror, she licked the tissue and cleaned the blood off my face.

"Why are you standing around looking at us?" my mother scolded Mr. Gouge and Mrs. Fredrickson. "Get my son some help!"

My mother was overreacting, but Mrs. Fredrickson left to get the nurse. The nurse came in with a warm paper towel and an ice pack. My nose was no longer bleeding, so it only took a moment to wipe up the blood and put a cold compress on my nose.

My mom moved Spumoni out of his seat so that I could sit down. I smiled until I saw Spumoni walk across the room and stand beside Josh. Spumoni and Frek glared at me. I held their gazes and squinted my eyes menacingly. They looked away. They probably wished someone was there to take care of them. Tony's nose had swollen, and Frek kept holding his stomach.

After the nurse left, my mother sat down in the chair beside me and put her arm around me. "Why was I called in here?" she asked.

"There was a small disturbance in the hall," Mr. Gouge began.

"*Small* disturbance," my mother said, raising her eyebrows and looking from my nose to Mr. Gouge. "Their parents better hope it doesn't scar."

Spumoni looked panicked. His mother was notorious for yelling at her son and pulling his ears when he did something wrong. Spumoni must have been imagining his ears getting pulled off. Frek turned his watery eyes to the floor.

"Mom, they didn't hit my nose," I said.

My mother pulled her arm away and looked at me. "Then who did?"

I realized my mistake too late. "No one," I lied.

"Well, *no one* should be a man and admit what he's done," she said, looking directly at Spumoni and Frek.

"Mrs. Miller, Mrs. Fredrickson was on bus duty when she heard a commotion in the hall." Mr. Gouge paused and looked at Mrs. Fredrickson.

"I saw *your* boy," said Mrs. Fredrickson, pointing at me, "throwing his fists around wildly at these boys."

"So what you're saying," my mother interrupted, "is that you didn't see *my* boy actually hit anyone."

Mrs. Fredrickson smiled. "Miranda, we have three boys who are beaten up very badly, and *your* boy was the only one throwing himself around like a wild animal."

My mother leaned forward in her seat and spoke slowly. "*My* boy had blood streaming down his face. He did not do that to himself. And I'll say it again: you didn't see *my* boy actually hit anyone."

The room was silent. Mrs. Fredrickson took a deep breath and spoke to my mother like she was trying to explain something to a small child. "Miranda, Josh was in a fit when I found him. Tony and Edward had already been party to his wrath. I wasn't going to wait around until he did more damage."

Mr. Gouge dropped his head into his hands and shook it back and forth. "You didn't see Mr. Miller hit anyone?" he asked.

"Not only did she miss the fight, but she has mistaken Jerrod for his brother." My mother sat back in her chair and smiled.

Mrs. Fredrickson was the last one to confuse Josh and me. Kelly had branded me with the combination lock. The horseshoe-shaped scar became the only physical difference between my twin and me.

Mrs. Fredrickson couldn't speak. Her eyes enlarged, and her mouth moved to explain her mistake, but she couldn't voice words in her defense. She leaned forward and narrowed her eyes at my face. Then she looked at my brother.

"You have their records. You can look up their files if you don't believe me." My mother casually glanced down at her fingernails and crossed her legs. She knew she had won the right to negotiate my punishment. "Or you could take my word for it." She looked at Mrs. Fredrickson. "Because I know *my* boy."

"The fact remains that no one wants to explain what happened, so I'm going to have to suspend all the boys," Mr. Gouge explained.

My mother jumped out of her seat again. Her pregnant belly was large enough to keep me from seeing Frek's face. "You mean where his work will get counted as zeros? No, my son may have to get stitches. His grades won't suffer, too, because of some backwoods bullies!"

"That's enough, Mrs. Miller," Mr. Gouge said, but he remained calm. "We don't judge children based on their circumstances. It makes us bullies, too."

"*We* should also know our students," my mother argued, raising her voice and pointing at Mrs. Fredrickson. "Especially if we had them for their entire second-grade year!"

Mr. Gouge held firm. "Mrs. Miller, I hope you can understand my position. I have three boys here who were obviously in a fight. They need to be punished, and they certainly need to cool off before they come back to school."

My mother lowered herself back into her chair and smiled calmly. "I agree with you, Mr. Gouge." Everyone's eyes snapped toward my mother. "I think the boys should have some time apart. However," she said and raised her index finger, "I'm probably going to have to take Jerrod to the emergency room for stitches and x-rays, and Mrs. Fredrickson didn't actually *see* him hit anyone, so I would like to make a suggestion as to his punishment."

Mr. Gouge looked tired. He leaned back in his chair and folded his hands over his stomach. "I am not an unreasonable man," he sighed.

"I feel Jerrod should be suspended." My mother must have seen the horrified look in my eyes, but I could read from her expression that she was getting to something. "But I don't think he should receive zeros for his work."

Mr. Gouge leaned forward in his chair as if to object, but my mother held up her hand and continued. "I think that Jerrod should have to do double the work, but he should be given grades for his assignments. It's only fair. No one saw him hit anyone, and it gives the boys a chance to cool off before they come back to school and deal with each other again."

Mr. Gouge rubbed his chin. "I think it's a good idea, Mrs. Miller," Mr. Gouge began, but Mrs. Fredrickson stepped forward to protest. He held up his hand to stop her before she could speak. "But I think I will add that Mr. Miller does something for the school."

"What do you have in mind?" my mother asked.

My mother would have agreed to anything Mr. Gouge added. She was so happy that my punishment wouldn't affect my grades that Mr. Gouge could have said that I had to shovel coal into the fiery furnace of the netherworld, and my mother would have bought the shovel.

Mr. Gouge motioned to Mrs. Fredrickson. "I think the scene she witnessed has agitated Mrs. Fredrickson. Maybe Mr. Miller could clean up her room at the end of the school day for a month."

My mouth dropped open. The action made my nose throb, so I quickly closed it. I stole a glance at Mrs. Fredrickson. She was smiling like she'd won a prize hen. I'd rather shovel the coal.

"Okay," my mother said. "And maybe Tony and Edward could mow my lawn and tidy up my yard for a month because the situation has *agitated* me."

Mr. Gouge chuckled. "Mrs. Miller, I think you have won your point, so there's no need to be ridiculous. Mr. Miller's grades won't suffer during his suspension, unlike Edward's and Tony's grades." His smile faded when he looked at me. "You are lucky to have such a concerned parent, young man. You will be suspended for the rest of the week, and your assignments will be doubled. You must complete all the work your teacher sends home with you, and I expect you to clean Mrs. Fredrickson's classroom after each school day for one month. After you have completed your punishment, you will receive credit for your work. Do you understand?"

"Yes, sir," I said and extended my left hand. I took it back quickly and put out my right hand. Josh and I were left-handed.

Mr. Gouge placed his hand in mine, and we shook firmly. "In that case, Mr. Miller, your family may leave. I will discuss your punishment with your teacher, and your assignments will be sent home with your brother tomorrow."

My mother and I got up from our chairs and turned to leave. Mrs. Fredrickson looked satisfied, but Tony and Frek were scowling at me.

"Mrs. Jackson," Mr. Gouge called to his receptionist as my brother opened the door, "were you able to contact Mrs. Spumoni and Mr. Rice's grandmother?"

I smiled to myself. As my brother closed the door, I saw Tony's and Frek's frightened faces. I grinned a bloody smile and waved at them.

Chapter Fourteen

My mother didn't overreact to the fight like I thought she would. We drove home, and she started dinner. I heard her make a call to the doctor's office.

Josh and I were playing chess when my mother walked into the bedroom. She had gone next door to get Sydney, and the baby was pulling her earrings.

"Of course, you are grounded until you go back to school." She waited for me to get upset. When I calmly stared back at her, she said, "I rescheduled my appointment for tomorrow. You'll have to go with me."

I continued to look into her face with what I hoped was an even stare. She threw up the hand that wasn't holding Sydney and looked at the ceiling. "Why couldn't you have gotten a teacher?"

Josh finally spoke up. "We didn't have time, Mom." That wasn't the whole truth, but my brother didn't want me to suffer for helping him. "Jerrod saved me." *Aw, it almost sounded sweet.*

My mother turned and left the room before we could see her tears. My brother had played the right card. He had exploited my mother's sensitivity to prevent me from getting into any more trouble.

"Thanks," I said.

"You're welcome," Josh said simply and took another of my pawns.

I couldn't think of another move. Josh and I silently watched the chess board until we were called down for dinner.

Our father had come home from work, and he was washing his hands in our small downstairs bathroom. "Jerrod!" he barked as I walked toward the kitchen.

I doubled back and stopped at the bathroom door. I grabbed hold of the side of the door and pushed it back and forth between my feet.

"Your mother told me about your punishment," my father said. "And Josh told me why you were fighting."

I stopped moving the door. My father's face was unreadable.

"You did the right thing, but next time, just avoid those boys." My father took the hand towel from the ring and dried his hands roughly.

I started moving the door back and forth again. I watched as it hit my left shoe, then my right shoe.

My father reached out and stopped the door. He didn't exert a lot of force, but I couldn't have moved the door if I had tried.

"Did you hear me, Jerrod?" he pressed.

"Yes, sir," I said, looking into his eyes. Working man's cologne was radiating from him. I didn't find anything wrong with the smell of wood and sweat on my father's skin.

"Okay, then," he said and relaxed his grip on the door. "I don't want to hear a word about it over dinner." I opened the door wider for him to go into the hall.

My mother sat the last plate on the table as we came in for dinner. She smiled at my father and stood on her toes to kiss him. He rubbed her belly and bent down to kiss it.

Sydney was in her highchair. She was concentrating on hitting her spoon on the tray in front of her.

"How is my little man," my father asked my mother's belly.

My mother sighed. "We won't know what the baby is until tomorrow, Johnny. I'll call you and let you know."

"You won't have to, babe." My father rose to his feet. "I'm not going to work tomorrow."

My mother beamed at him. "You got the day off!"

He stroked a piece of hair behind her ear. "I asked today when you called me about Jerrod. I want to see Elliot up close."

My mother crinkled her nose. "Elliot, like on *E.T.*? I don't like that name."

"It was never up to you," my father stated matter-of-factly, sitting down at the table. "He decided," he added, pointing to my mother's stomach.

My mother looked at her baby bump and smiled. "I'm going to laugh so hard tomorrow if the doctor tells you the baby is a girl."

My father took a roll from a bowl in front of him. "I don't think you'll be laughing tomorrow. And don't mention *E.T.* again. I don't want you to ruin the movie for him."

My mother's mouth moved like she was going to make a retort. Instead, she sat down with her family and joined the warmth at the table.

Chapter Fifteen

My mother woke us at seven the next morning. Josh jumped off the side of the bed and ran for the bathroom. I was still too sleepy to race him when there was another bathroom downstairs.

"Why do I have to get up early?" I complained. I kicked my covers wildly and pouted. My mother didn't mind. I would have to fix them before breakfast.

"Because my appointment is at nine, and we are going to go to the doctor's office after we drop your brother off at school," my mother explained impatiently.

"Why can't I stay home?" I asked, throwing my pillow across my face. "Dad's going with you."

I took the pillow off my head and looked up after I didn't hear a response. My mother was staring at me with tears in her eyes. "You should be happy that you have a chance to meet your brother," she said quietly, and she walked out of my room.

Great. I had been conscious for ninety seconds, and I had already hurt my mother's feelings. She was probably going to tell my father, and then I would feel both guilty and ashamed. When my father was proud of me, I was on top of the world, but I'd rather be grounded for a month than see his disappointed face.

I rolled out of bed and onto the floor. I was groaning, face down on the floor, when Josh walked into the room.

"You don't have to play sick. You already get a pass on school today," he said.

"I know, but I just hurt Mom's feelings because I said that I wanted to stay home."

"Wow! That was a real jerkish thing to say," Josh said, walking over to our dresser. He got out two pairs of jeans, two pairs of socks, and two shirts. He passed me one of each.

"I didn't mean it like that," I defended, putting on the socks.

"Oh, no, Mom!" Josh mimicked while he pulled on his jeans. "I don't want to share the joy of your pregnancy with you, especially after you bailed me out at school yesterday. Could I just stay home and sleep?" Josh stopped putting on his socks to mock me. "Why would that hurt our pregnant mother's feelings?"

"Whatever," I said, but I felt shame creep onto my face.

I made my ravaged bed and put on the rest of my clothes. I ran a comb through my hair and looked in the mirror. I was a pre-teen dream.

My mother was in the kitchen, and I put my arms around her waist. She stiffened for a moment before her posture softened.

"I'm sorry," I whispered. "I didn't mean that I didn't want to see Elliot. I wasn't thinking."

My mother put her arms around me. "I shouldn't have gotten upset. I knew what you meant, but pregnancy has confused my feelings."

"Get over here and eat, Son," my father said as he rose from the table. "I'm going to take the baby to the neighbor's house."

Janet Wilson watched Sydney while my parents worked, went on errands, or had date nights. She had watched Josh and me until we were ten and our parents trusted us enough to stay home alone.

Janet was in her fifties, and she was slightly disabled, so the cash from watching my sister helped her buy extra groceries and presents when her grandchildren visited. She was a sweet woman, but she never stopped talking. My parents had to make excuses to leave almost every time they dropped off Sydney or picked her up. Most times, they just had to walk out the door while Janet was still talking.

"Okay, but don't talk all morning," she said. "We need to be out of here in ten minutes."

My father lifted Sydney from her highchair and wiped her mouth with his palm. He rubbed his hands on his pants and let the food particles fall to the floor.

"Wipe her face with a diaper wipe," my mother scolded. "You never wash your hands. I don't need her to get sick and then get me sick."

My father rolled his eyes, but he did as he walked away from his wife. Josh came down for breakfast, and my father moved Sydney's hand up and down to wave at him as they left.

Josh and I ate and brushed our teeth quickly. Our mother used to wake us up earlier so that we would have ample time for breakfast, but we would just move more slowly. Josh and I still stuffed food down our throats or jerked a toothbrush in and out of our mouths while our mother impatiently tapped her foot at the front door.

My father hadn't returned by the time we got into the van. My mother backed out and stared at the neighbor's house. "I should have taken the baby over," she said, shaking her head.

My father opened the door to the neighbor's house and stepped out. He turned around to talk. My mother waited ten seconds before she rolled down her window.

"Johnny!" she shouted. My mother was an impatient person, and my father was a carefree talker who never met a stranger.

He held up his index finger without turning around. Then he put his hands in his pockets and smiled.

"Johnny!" my mother called again. "We'll all be late. I can't miss another appointment!"

My father held up his hands apologetically. He jogged to the van and opened the passenger door.

"Why do you have to stand and talk for hours?" my mother whined. "You know we're in a hurry."

"Do you want me to drive?" my father suggested. He flashed a playful smile.

My mother scrunched her eyebrows together. We all knew she drove slowly. She was a safe driver, but she was sometimes late because of her caution.

My mother waited until her husband jumped into his seat and his seat belt clicked. She pulled out and slowly rolled through the neighborhood.

"So *I'm* the one making us late," my father said, looking from the speedometer to my mother. He was really pushing it.

"Leave me alone," my mother snapped. "I just want us to get to our respective destinations in one piece. I know what time we have to leave to keep from being late. You were the one who pushed us past that time."

"Whatever," my father grumbled. He looked at his watch. "We should still be able to make your appointment in plenty of time."

My mother let Josh out at the front of the school. My father opened the door to the van. I could see a few kids walking by, not bothering to conceal their laughter at the Ta-Ta van. I mentally marked their faces.

"Have a good day, son." My father patted my brother's back and moved him along before my mother could call him back for an embarrassing kiss.

"I love you," my mother called. "And don't forget to pick up your brother's work. I'll see you at three."

"Drive away, Miranda," my father said as he shut his door. "You're embarrassing him. What ten-year-old boy wants his mama callin' after him when he goes into school? No wonder he gets beat up."

My mother opened her mouth in an o. "He does not get beat up!"

"No, you're right," my father said and gestured to me. "Josh doesn't get beat up, because J-Rod takes care of him." He turned around and winked at me. "Which is totally wrong, of course," he added sarcastically. "He should have gotten a teacher." He put air quotes around his last three words.

My mother sighed. She finished talking, but she wasn't conceding the point.

Chapter Sixteen

I saw Elliot for the first time on a Wednesday. I remembered the day of the week, not because of my suspension, but because we lived in a town that still believed that most businesses should close by noon on Wednesday. I thought it was because people went to church on Wednesday nights, but I was surprised to learn that church wasn't the only reason.

"Why do we have to go so early?" I complained, forgetting how I had hurt my mother's feelings.

"Because the doctor's office will close by noon, and I have to get a reference for my ultrasound."

"No one goes to church on Wednesday nights anymore, so why is Erwin a ghost town at noon?" I asked.

"It's hardly a ghost town," my mother said. "Only doctor's offices, the courthouse, and insurance agencies still close by lunchtime, and it's not only because of church."

I pulled at my seat belt while my mother talked. "Then why Wednesday? What's so great about the middle of the week?"

I had asked my mother, but my father answered me. He told me that agriculture had been very important in our community, and many people worked a job in town and farmed their land. The town was closed on Sunday, but it was a day of rest, so no one could tend to their gardens or run errands. The town would shut down by lunch on Wednesdays to let people catch up on their farms or small gardens. Men would go home and weed their gardens, or they would work in food stands by the main road. Housewives would manage the stands most of the week by selling any surpluses the fields had yielded, but on Wednesdays, men would relieve their wives by supervising the stands. The women could go home and catch up on housework.

"What about during the winter?" I asked. "They couldn't grow tomatoes and corn when the ground froze."

"They would take that time to run errands and chop wood for fireplaces," my father explained. "There was always work to be done, and not all farms grew fruits and vegetables. Many farms had animals."

"Well, that's ridiculous! If the town's closed, how can they run errands?" I asked.

My mother sighed. "We are fifteen minutes away from a city, Jerrod. Only agricultural communities closed their businesses. The city was open."

I let the matter rest as we pulled into the parking lot. I wouldn't have even questioned the practice if the schools would have closed at noon on Wednesdays.

My mother, my father, and I walked into Dr. Phyllis Shelton's office five minutes before my mother's appointment. Dr. Shelton was a general practice physician, but she treated my mother's pregnancy because she had known my father's family for years.

My father and I stood just inside the yellow waiting room while my mother waited for the receptionist to scan her insurance card. The fragrance of fresh-cut flowers filled the room. I reached for a magazine on a rack but stopped when my father grunted and shook his head. I studied the magazines and realized they all had babies and pregnant women on the covers. *Good save, Dad.*

My mother waddled over to where we stood and breathed a heavy sigh. She looked at my father and smiled.

"See," my father said, "I told you we'd make it."

My mother's smile went away, and she narrowed her eyes, but her husband was purposely staring in another direction. She blew a piece of hair out of her eyes, a little too loudly, and crossed her arms.

My mother saw a fellow child-bearer and started talking. My father walked away quickly before he was pulled into a conversation about swelling, back pain, and dilation.

I followed my father. He never met a stranger, so even though there were over a dozen empty chairs in the waiting room, he sat down in a seat next to an old man.

"What're ya in for?" my father asked. He always lapsed into the Appalachian dialect when he spoke to a fellow Erwinite.

"'S not me," the man answered. "'S my bride."

The older adult straightened in his seat. My father had long legs and a long waist, so the man still had to look up into my father's eyes. My father extended his left hand, then drew it back and put out his right hand. "Johnny Miller."

The aging man put his shaking hand in my father's hand and said, "Granger Cole."

Granger Cole looked at my father sideways. "You ain't Crazy Lyle Miller's boy, are ye?"

My father's smile faltered, but only for a moment. He was used to hearing "crazy" attached to his father's name. "I'm Lyle Miller's son."

Granger Cole remembered his country manners and said, "I'm sorry, son. I was doin' what my wife calls 'blartin'." He saw my father's confused expression and added, "Fartin' with my mouth. Blurtin' out things I should 'ave kept inside."

My father laughed good-naturedly and introduced me to Granger Cole. I noticed his cane had a silver fox on it. I was about to ask about the fox when my mother's balloon-like shadow fell over us.

"They're ready for me now," she said.

My father introduced her to his new friend, and my mother tried to be polite while pulling her husband away. "It was nice to meet you, Mr. Cole," she said. "I'm going to drag my husband into this room before the nurse changes her mind."

"Nice to meet cha, young people," Granger Cole called after us.

I didn't know why nurses bothered calling you into an exam room. They should have just kept you in the waiting room until the doctor was ready to see you. The nurse weighed my mother, took her blood pressure, and ushered her to a room with a large, yellow number two on it. The nurse told my mother to remove her clothes, put on a paper dress, and sit on the table. She said the doctor would be in to see her shortly.

Shortly must've meant about half an hour. My father started to pace the room after five minutes. He didn't like tight spaces.

"Do you think they do this on purpose?" he asked my mother.

She shook her head. "It seems like it, but they had to work me in today because I missed yesterday's appointment."

"I know," my father said. "But what if we're part of an experiment? What if they see how long it takes each person to get irritated before the doctor sees you?"

"Then they'd already be in here, because seeing you pace irritates me," my mother joked.

My father had been serious, but he flashed a small smile and didn't offer any more of his insight. It made me a little sad for him. I loved hearing about the way my father saw the world.

We played "I Spy," and my mother quizzed me on state capitals and multiplication tables before we heard the doctor approach the door. My family silenced and stared at the door when we heard the doctor's footsteps. I could see small movements of the shadow the doctor cast on the floor as she quickly looked over my mother's file.

After a few seconds, the doctor knocked quickly two times and entered the room. She looked at my family, and her gaze settled on me.

"Why aren't you in school?" Dr. Shelton asked. I could tell she was prepared to give a speech against truancy from school.

"He was suspended for sticking up for his brother," my mother said quickly. *So that was the story she was giving everyone.*

"Oh, that's understandable," the doctor said. She smiled at me. "I would have done the same for my younger brother, too."

I didn't tell her Josh was my twin or that he was technically older. I just smiled to myself.

Dr. Shelton turned to my mother. "Lie back on the table."

My mother complied, and the doctor adjusted the paper blanket over her from her hips to her knees. She lifted my mother's paper dress at the top and placed it at my mother's pelvic bone. She pulled a cloth measuring strip vertically across my mother's belly. "Looks like twenty-three weeks, but your last ultrasound would put you more at twenty-five weeks now," she told my mother.

"What does that mean?" my father asked.

Dr. Shelton shrugged her shoulders. "The baby is a little small but within a normal growth range. We're still going by the due date." She turned to my mother. "In a perfect pregnancy, you've got about fifteen more weeks, but I would make sure you have a suitcase ready in ten weeks. Just in case."

Little did Dr. Shelton know that my mother had packed a suitcase when she turned thirty weeks pregnant with Sydney. It waited in the downstairs hall next to the bathroom door. I had tripped over it about twice a week.

"I guess you want your ultrasound papers," Dr. Shelton said with a smile.

My mother tensed up. "We want to know the gender so we can buy baby clothes."

My mother was a terrible liar. If the baby was a girl, she would wear Sydney's old clothes, and if the baby was a boy, he would wear hand-me-downs from Josh and me.

"You missed your appointment last month, so I need to look at the fetal growth rate and anatomy anyway," Dr. Shelton returned.

My father's head whipped around, and he raised his eyebrows at my mother. She shrugged her shoulders. Maybe she had been too busy to go to the appointment.

She wrote on papers from my mother's chart and helped my mother into a sitting position. "The receptionist will have the paperwork for your ultrasound when you check out. Do you have any questions?"

Dr. Shelton looked from my mother to my father. They both shook their heads.

Chapter Seventeen

M y family enjoyed a quiet semi-rural setting at home, but we could be almost anywhere in the next city within twenty minutes. It was convenient for my mother to be that close to specialized hospitals since she seemed to be setting a track record for pregnancies.

The building where we would see Elliot was right off the main road to a local university, and it had a green, metal roof over the beige block. It was only a couple of stories high, but my father insisted that we take the elevator.

"We can't be too careful," he said, patting my mother's bulge. "You can walk for exercise, but taking the stairs is just too much."

My father smiled to himself and asked me to push the button for the second floor. My mother softly sighed and shook her head. I didn't think she minded my father's protection as much as she let on.

My mother waddled to the check-in window as my father and I found a place to sit. It was closer to lunchtime, so there were a lot of people waiting. Almost all the patients were men over the age of thirty. Blue-collar men talked to worker's compensation representatives about their injuries, and brittle old men stared straight ahead with their hands on their canes or walkers.

"Why don't the old guys read the newspaper or a magazine?" I asked my dad. "They look creepy."

"J-Rod, I think they've been alive so long that nothing surprises them," my father mused. "They've lived through wars, economic crises, news of serial killers, and crazy celebrity tales. I kind of respect that," he continued, leaning back in the chair and placing his hands behind his head. "They see the real world around them, and they don't let anyone tell them how to see it or other people."

My mother waded her way through injured and ancient men and lowered herself into a seat next to me. She patted my hand and closed her eyes. Pregnancy seemed to make women tired.

"I'm not happy about your suspension, but I'm glad you could come with me today," she said.

I remembered my early morning outburst. "I'm much happier with you than I am at school." I tried to smile reassuringly.

Crap! That wasn't exactly what I meant. I was trying to make it seem as though there was no other place in the world I'd rather be, but it sounded like I was just happy to be away from the walls of education.

My mother patted my hand again and smiled. I opened my mouth to explain, but she stopped me. "I know what you mean," she said.

A nurse opened a door, and one of the creepy old men rose from the seat by my mother. My father moved from his seat next to me to the chair beside her. He placed her head on his chest, and my mother winced as she moved her body to a more comfortable position. It only took moments for me to hear the slight snore that all women deny.

Unlike doctor's offices, ultrasound waiting rooms were real waiting rooms. My mother visited a second check-in window to update her insurance information, but when the nurse called her name, the technician was ready to see her.

My mother's ultrasound technician was a young brunette in a large, white lab coat. She made adjustments on the computer, and she turned and smiled when she finished. She had large blue eyes and deep dimples.

"Good afternoon," she said. "I'm Leslie Ingram, and I will be helping you see your baby today."

When Leslie stood up to shake hands with us, I could see why she had on a large lab coat. She was about as pregnant as my mother.

"Do you homeschool?" Leslie asked my mother. She was as suspicious of my presence as Dr. Shelton.

My father's smile faltered a little. "He got into a little trouble."

"Oh," Leslie said, giving me a knowing look. "I have three brothers."

I was almost offended. I made wonderful grades, and I didn't cause problems *all* the time. I didn't like to be seen as a troublemaker.

My mother looked down at the technician's stomach. "When are you due, Mrs. Ingram?"

"I have about two more weeks," she said. "And, please, call me Leslie."

My father tried to make conversation with Leslie as my mother settled onto the table. She adjusted the pillow until my mother was comfortable. Then she pulled up my mother's maternity shirt to her chest and tucked her stretch pants down so that my mother's blooming pregnancy showed.

"I've had this on the warmer," Leslie said, showing my mother a clear bottle of blue gel. My mother still made a face when the gel landed on her stomach. She relaxed when her body recognized its warmth.

I had been standing in front of the door. I could hear the quick, padded footsteps of the nurses in the hall. My father motioned me over to him. I took my place at my mother's head, opposite the computer monitor.

"Is this your first child?" my father asked. Leslie was busy adjusting the ultrasound equipment, but she had been carrying on an easy conversation with my parents.

"No, I have two other children. My oldest is two, and the baby will be a year old in nine days." Leslie must have been frequently asked the reason for her stair-stepped children. "I see babies all the time." She motioned to the computer screen as she placed an electronic roller on my mother's gelled stomach. A baby's profile was clear on the monitor. "How can you see the miracle of life every day and not be affected by it?" Leslie beamed.

My father chuckled. "I think my wife is in the same league as you. Our daughter was three months old when she got pregnant with Elliot."

"So you know the sex of your baby?" Leslie asked.

"No, we don't," my mother said quickly. "But he thinks it's a boy." She jerked her thumb at my father.

"I *know* he's a boy," my father said, laughing at my mother.

Leslie smiled like she saw this sort of exchange all the time. "Well, I guess the mystery will be solved for Mom in a few minutes."

My father smiled foolishly when he saw the baby on the monitor, and my mother started to cry when Leslie turned up the volume on the baby's heartbeat. It was a truly magical time for our family, and I was glad that I was there to share it with my parents, but I missed my twin. Josh was probably learning how to multiply and divide fractions while I was watching our little sibling.

For the first part of the ultrasound, Leslie took a lot of measurements. It was amazing for me to see my brother or sister, even though he or she looked like a ghostly skeleton on a black screen.

My mother tensed several times when Leslie had to push on a certain part of her stomach. "Your placenta is in an anterior position," she said. "I know it's uncomfortable, but I have to get a few more measurements of the head."

The baby's head was near my mother's hips and the baby's feet were around her ribs. I nudged my father. "When I'm upside down, all the blood rushes to my head," I whispered. "How can the baby stand it?"

Leslie had heard my question. "The baby is surrounded by fluid, so gravity doesn't affect the baby the way it does us. Like when you're upside down in a swimming pool," she explained. "You don't feel the blood rush to your head in the same way you do when you stand on your head on the floor or ground."

I thought about it for a minute. I shrugged my shoulders. I'd have to try standing on my head in a pool.

"Hmm," Leslie uttered.

Someone should have explained to Leslie that you shouldn't make sounds like that with nervous parents in the room. My mother straightened, and we all moved in to see if we could tell what she was talking about.

"What's wrong?" I asked.

Leslie glanced at me and then looked back at the screen. "Nothing's wrong," she said slowly. My mother visibly relaxed. "Do you see this?" Leslie asked, pointing to one of Elliot's hands. I could make out a thickness on Elliot's hand between the right ring finger and the pinky finger.

"Yes," my father and I said simultaneously.

"As far as I can tell, the baby has webbing between those two fingers." She pointed to the screen. "It's nothing to worry about. It's just a genetic flaw."

My father had gone pale. He moved a little closer to the screen and squinted his eyes.

"Okay," Leslie said. "Do we want to know the sex?"

My father recovered himself. He cleared his throat and smoothed the nonexistent wrinkles from his jeans.

"Yes," my mother said. My dad nodded and smiled at his wife.

"Looks like Dad is right. You're having a little boy."

My father gave my mother a shrug and smiled at her. He didn't say "I told you so," but the words were in the air.

My mother sighed and lifted her head off the pillow. "Are you sure?"

I couldn't tell if my mother had wanted another girl or if she was upset that my father had predicted the gender. Her face was unreadable.

"If you look here," Leslie said as she moved the cursor over the monitor, "you can see the penis."

I looked at the white object on which the cursor rested. Even at my age, I could tell that I was looking at my brother.

"Uhh!" my mother exclaimed as she threw her head back on the pillow. She turned to my father. "Does the name really have to be Elliot, though?"

"I told you," my father said, "It was never up to us. He picked it."

Leslie gave our father a funny look. My mother and I noticed it, but my father just kept smiling at the screen. I felt deep red embarrassment travel from my chest to my neck and face.

"Isn't that sweet?" my father said. "Elliot's waving to Jerrod."

He lifted his hand and started waving at the screen. My mother shifted uncomfortably when she caught Leslie staring at my father with concern. We were used to my father talking to his unborn children, but the technician didn't seem to understand my father's fascination with his on-screen progeny.

"Jerrod, wave back at your brother," my father demanded.

I shook my head at my father, but I raised my hand to wave at the screen. I looked at Leslie with a playful smile and shrugged. I tried to pretend that he played games like this all the time to save my family some humiliation, but I stopped when I caught the image on the screen.

It really looked like the skeletal baby was waving at me. The bony hand on the monitor rapidly moved left to right.

I watched my father bend his fingers and move them up and down. Seconds later, the image of my brother bent his skeletal fingers in a mock wave.

My mother saw it, too. The room grew silent, and Leslie must have felt like she was fanning the flames of a crazy fire, because she quickly removed the ultrasound wand from my mother's abdomen.

Leslie rapidly gathered her paperwork, handed my mother some ultrasound pictures, and gave my father a tissue to wipe the congealing gel off my mother's stomach. I was the only one who noticed the relief in Leslie's face when she ushered my parents to the door.

"Congratulations on your baby boy," she said briskly and closed the door.

Chapter Eighteen

I had always heard that something good never lasts. I disagreed. Everything could have remained wonderful in my family if only I had quit playing my stupid jokes.

I loved hiding my brother's model cars and trucks. Very little got my brother upset, but when he was ignoring me, I could always get a rise out of my twin by hiding one of his model cars. Anger would flash in his eyes, and bright red blood would embrace his features when he found out one of his precious models was missing.

Josh's favorite model was a replica of a 1934 Ford Model B truck, and he doted over it more than the other model cars that sat in his display case. He took it out once a month to dust it and polish its wheels and black, metallic paint, but he would always hold it with care, like he was holding a super virus or something.

Most people, when they were asked what they would save if a natural disaster took their home, would say that they didn't care about material possessions as long as their family was safe. My brother was not one of those people. My brother would have grabbed his model truck and then alerted the rest of his family of their impending doom as he ran his precious truck outdoors.

I had hidden every model car and truck in Josh's display case except his favorite truck. My plans for revenge on my brother succeeded any time I hid one of his models, but I never hid the truck. I told myself that I was saving it for a time when I was really mad at my brother, but I actually knew that hiding my twin's truck would seriously damage his trust in me.

I found really cool places to hide Josh's models. I wouldn't just conceal a favored possession under the bed or in a bush. I would hide it between the mattresses or in the gutter of the house.

It would sometimes take days for Josh to find his possessions, and he wasn't the only one looking. My mom once found a model 1976 Chevrolet Corvette in the sugar container, and another time Sydney handed a slightly chewed 1982 Pontiac Firebird to Josh from her playpen.

My hide-and-seek with his model cars sometimes backfired. At times, Josh wouldn't notice something was missing.

One time, I had hidden one of Josh's model cars behind my dad's tire over the weekend. My dad wouldn't take the truck out until Monday morning, and I thought Josh would find it well before our father left for work. I was severely punished when my dad walked into the kitchen that Monday morning carrying the broken pieces of a blue model 1976 Chevrolet Nova.

I sat in my theater seat, eyeing my twin's collection of model cars the Saturday after my suspension. It was a beautiful, cold day, and I had extra energy and extra homework, but I didn't want to write reports or play outside.

Josh was being a real pain. He had been trying to turn boiling water into fog with a bottle and an ice cube, and he was upset because he couldn't get it to look like the internet photos. I thought I would try to get his mind off of it by flicking rubber bands at him. He got mad and screamed something about how I wasn't going to amount to anything, then ran downstairs to complain to our mother.

I was going to race out of the room behind him to tell our mother my side of the story, but then my eyes rested on his display case. I had hidden all the cars in the case except one. I already knew how enraged my brother became when one of his models was missing but taking the model truck would send him over the edge.

I wasn't really mad at my brother. I was just irritated that he wasn't playing with me. I knew I was going to get in trouble with my mother, so I decided to make Josh feel as frustrated as I would be after my mother delivered my punishment.

I opened the case and lifted the black truck to my eyes. Its metallic surface gripped my fingers, and the spotless windshield reflected the light in the room.

I closed the display case quickly and ran downstairs with the car behind my back. I peeked into the kitchen. No one. Josh was talking to our mother outside as she threw salt on the icy walkway. She lifted the hood on her coat to look at him as he gestured wildly at the house. She dropped her hands to her sides and dusted the snow off her maternity jeans. She picked up Sydney, who looked like a bundled marshmallow, and walked up the stairs of our back deck. The back deck opened into the kitchen, where I was standing with Josh's model truck.

I had almost forgotten about the truck! I realized I was about to get caught just in time to place the evidence inside the oven.

Our mother saw the guilt on my face when she entered the house, but she thought it was because of the recent fight I had with my brother. She switched her face into disciplinarian mode.

My mother handed Sydney to Josh. "Put her in the playpen and watch TV until you calm down a little."

My brother didn't need to calm down. He smirked at me as he took Sydney from our mother. He already knew I was in trouble.

My mother peeled off her coat carefully and motioned for me to sit down at the table. She maneuvered her large belly into the space left between the chair and the table.

She rested her face in her folded hands and took a deep breath. When she looked up at me, I could see slightly raised, purple circles under her eyes.

"Are you okay, Mom?" I asked.

My mother smiled warmly at my concern. "I've just been having bad dreams about people I once knew," she said. "It must be a side effect of pregnancy hormones." She shrugged.

Even at my young age, I wondered how pregnant women could blame everything on hormones. *Bad dreams?* Hormones. *Hold up a taco stand?* Must be hormones!

"Josh is a good brother." She rubbed her hands together to bring back their warmth. "He does his experiments because they mean something to him. And frankly, Jerrod, they should mean something to you."

"I was just messin' with him because he gets so worked up over boiling water!" I explained to her.

My mother shook her head. "Have you ever loved something?"

"Sure," I said. "I love you and Dad and—"

"No," my mother said, "like your Star Wars video games or fig-urines."

"Well, yeah, but—"

"Has Josh ever said anything against your obsession with Star Wars?"

"Well, no, but—"

"Then why would you make fun of his hobbies or terrorize him while he tries to do his experiments?" my mother asked.

I hung my head. I knew my mother was still looking at the top of my head. She was waiting for me to admit that I was wrong and apologize to my brother. Even though I didn't feel like I had done anything wrong, I told my mother what she wanted to hear. "Okay, I get it. I'll leave him alone."

My mother lifted my chin. "Good. You can go back upstairs, but after some time has passed, tell your brother you're sorry."

"Okay, Mom."

My mother relieved the chair of her weight and touched my arm. Her other hand rested on the top of her swollen belly. "Jerrod, you are very important to me," she began. "Our family is important to me. We are each a piece of a whole—like Josh's model car engines. And just like Josh's engines, we all have to work together to keep our family running."

I nodded to show that I understood what she meant. My mother dropped her hand to the table and let her gaze drift to the window.

I went back upstairs and lay down on my bottom bunk. I closed my eyes and decided to take a nap.

I recognized the smells of the roast my mother was making in the cooking pot. I hoped she was making it with whole potatoes, carrots, and a pan of cornbread.

My father's work boots pounded the kitchen floor when he arrived home with his overtime pay, and I listened to Josh complain about my rubber band flicking. I decided that a few more minutes of dozing would be great before I dealt with Josh or my father.

I was drifting off to sleep when the screaming started.

Chapter Nineteen

I had been thinking a long time about the past, and the early morning light had run away the shadows. I didn't want to relive those terrible moments in time, but my mind kept pushing me back to them.

My mother's bedroom door creaked open, and her feet padded softly down the carpeted hallway. I thought she'd go downstairs, but her footsteps stopped outside of my room.

I lay frozen on my bed, looking at the door. I could hear my mother's breath, soft and sad.

The knob turned, and the door inched open slowly. My mother stood in the doorway with a laundry basket against her hip.

Oh, she was putting away laundry. No big deal.

"Hey, Mom," I said, rising from my bed. "I'll get that for you," I offered, motioning to the laundry basket.

My mother didn't move. She seemed like she was unsure about something.

She tried to get her emotions under control, but she let a tear fall. "I never blamed you," she whispered. "You never hurt anyone."

The last words seemed to be too much for my mother, and she burst into tears. I watched her with my hands up. *What was I supposed to do?*

Before I could decide on a course of action, my mother turned around and closed my door. I lowered my hands and stared at the door.

I had waited almost a year for my mother's forgiveness. Now that she had pardoned me, I still felt cold and alone. I had pictured us holding and hugging each other, but my mother had left without a show of affection.

My mother may have been trying to keep her emotions in check, like her father had taught her to do when she was young. She was probably ashamed of her tears. Besides, she was from the city, and city girls weren't supposed to cry.

I settled under my comforter and attempted to push the gnawing emptiness away. I tried to pretend my twin was on the bed above me and that he was only sleeping. I wanted to talk to him, and I knew he would understand. No matter how mad I made him, he always listened to me and tried to help.

The morning light landed on Josh's model car collection, but it was dusty and mostly forgotten. One of the models was missing because of me.

I enjoyed most of my memories of the past, but I had been avoiding one of the worst times for our family. My thoughts shifted back to the day I had hidden my brother's favorite model truck in the kitchen stove.

It was nice to hear that my mother didn't place blame on me, but her actions over the past year suggested otherwise. We both knew I had hurt a lot of people during my seventeen years, and Josh wasn't the only brother who had died because of me.

Chapter Twenty

"Johnny, get the baby!" my mother screamed.

I could hardly register what was happening. I jumped out of bed so fast that I hit my head on the bottom bunk. Dizzy stars danced across my vision.

Footsteps pounded up the stairs, and my mother's voice shouted, "Jerrod! Fire! Jerrod!"

I got to my door just as my mother flung it open. Her face was red, and her eyes were wide. Thick, black smoke wound behind her. I didn't do or say anything before she grabbed me and pulled me toward the stairs.

"Jerrod. Jerrod." My mother kept saying my name over and over again as we ran down the stairs and out the front door. At the bottom of the steps, I smelled an oily, melted smell that choked my breath. I felt like it would coat my lungs and blanket my oxygen if I continued to breathe it.

Our father had walked Josh and Sydney across the street, and Mrs. Fredrickson was trying to calm Sydney as she screamed in her brother's arms. My father was on his way back to get his wife and son out of the house. He met us on the porch.

"Are you okay?" my father asked, but my mother ran past him with me still in tow. She continued saying my name until she reached Josh and Sydney. Mrs. Fredrickson yelled to her husband to call 9-1-1.

Our neighbors trickled out into the road and walked down to see about the commotion. My father placed a hand on his wife and shook her gently. "Miranda!"

My mother's eyes darted back and forth, and she said, "We're all out, right?"

My father confirmed that we were all fine and reached to embrace his wife. His hands closed around my mother just as she fainted.

I had never seen my father cry. He was sensitive to his wife's feelings, but my father was always strong and protective whenever unfortunate events visited his family.

Josh, Sydney, and I sat silently in a family waiting room at the hospital for almost three hours. Our father smelled of antiseptic when he finally entered the room and fell into a chair with a drained look.

He nodded his head slightly when Josh asked about our mother's condition. He had been told to stay in the waiting room with his minor children and leave his wife in the hospital room. There was no one he could call. I rubbed my father's shoulders until he fell asleep.

He woke in less than an hour and rubbed his eyes with his fingers. I got the impression that my father was waiting for more news about his wife. When the doctor came into the waiting room, we all looked up with expecting eyes, but the doctor told my father to go into an adjoining room.

The doctor had brought along a plumpish woman with kind eyes and a ready smile. She wasn't dressed in scrubs or a white uniform. She had on a soft blue button-up shirt with a pair of beige slacks. One plain gold ring stood out on her left ring finger.

I could see my father through a clear glass window, and I watched the doctor place his hand on my father's shoulder. He looked directly into my father's eyes and then turned his attention to the woman. My father shook her hand and stared back at the doctor with fearful eyes.

The doctor mouthed a few words, and my father's face crumpled as he backed against the wall. The doctor turned to leave, and my father slid down the wall to the floor. He pulled his knees to his face, and his body shook as he cried. Josh and I looked at each other. *What could we do?*

The woman went into action. She spoke to my father for almost half an hour, patting his shoulder or hand from time to time. Her eyes never left him.

Thirty minutes after the doctor had spoken with him, my father dismissed the woman gently but firmly. The woman gave him a card and left the room. On her way out of the waiting room, she wordlessly smiled at us and handed Josh a card. Her card said that she was Maureen Cole, Grief Counselor.

Josh had been in charge of Sydney since the fire. She was sleeping pleasantly in his arms, and a small bubble of saliva had formed at the corner of her mouth.

I hadn't been scared during the fire as I stood and watched most of the lower part of our home burn. I didn't care about my material possessions, but I was terrified now. *Did we still have a mother?*

I turned to Josh and realized that he had been staring at me. Josh was eight minutes older, so he always considered himself the oldest. He could be trusted to be the most mature, and he was kind of a spokesperson for the children. Josh took the blame if we had done anything wrong, and he was expected to watch over Sydney and me if my parents were busy. Before Sydney was born, our mother would often tell Josh, "You are your brother's keeper."

Josh was definitely in charge now, and we both knew that Sydney was his first priority. That meant that I would have to comfort our father and find out what had happened.

I nodded to Josh that I understood what I needed to do, and I quietly raised myself off the bench we shared. As I walked toward the door that separated my father and me, my father's cell phone rang.

My father didn't even try to camouflage his tears when he answered. I was close enough to hear him say that he was John Miller. My father's expression changed from sadness to concern and then to rage. He barked his thanks to the person on the other end of the line and threw his phone at the wall.

He jumped up and flung the door open. My father's eyes met mine. I never thought I would see my father look at me with such contempt.

"I hope you're proud of yourself," he yelled. Sydney stirred in Josh's arms and cried.

I couldn't move. I stood frozen and horrified as my father closed the distance between us and put his finger an inch from my chest.

"Your little games are so funny, aren't they?" he raged.

Sydney was in a full wail.

"You don't care who gets hurt as long as Jerrod gets a good laugh out of it!" he screamed at me. I wondered if the hospital staff would run into the room to save me from my father's wrath.

Josh said what I was too afraid to voice. "What did he do, Dad? We've been together all day."

"Oh, then you must know," our father shouted sarcastically. A nurse had peeked in the door to find the source of the commotion. "I just got a call from the fire department. Someone put a model car in the stove," my father explained, looking at Josh. "And since I know you wouldn't damage one of your models, that leaves only one person." My father turned his attention back to me. "A person who thinks it's so *funny* to hide his brother's stuff."

My father poked me in the chest with his index finger to emphasize the word funny. I had been slowly processing my blame, but when my father touched me and I saw the loathing in his face, I burst into tears.

"I will pay to fix the house," I sobbed. "I am so sorry. I don't care how hard I have to work. I'll fix—"

The nurse entered the room. She seemed filled with a purpose to stop the domestic disturbance, but she stopped short when she heard my father's next words.

"Sure, you can fix the *house*, but you'll never fix my *home*," my father yelled. Grief had edged his words. "Tell me, Jerrod, how are you gonna fix our family?" My father's face changed, and his voice hardly choked out his next words. "Especially after you killed my son."

Chapter Twenty-One

I stole a glance at Josh. He was sitting with a red-faced Sydney, who was trying to wiggle free of his grasp. My father read my thoughts.

"No, Jerrod, my *youngest* son," my father spat.

I fully understood what had happened. My mother wasn't dead; she had lost the baby.

I cried harder. My father looked at me in disgust and threw his hands up.

"He didn't know Mom was going to miscarry," Josh offered. He switched Sydney in his arms, but she was still trying to get away from him.

Our father rounded on Josh. "Your mother didn't miscarry. A miscarriage happens when a baby is deformed." My father's words were not entirely true, but he was fueled by rage and grief instead of facts. The nurse moved a little closer into the room with every word my father bellowed at him. "Your brother was perfect!" he continued. "I watched his birth and his first breath." Our father's voice changed a little. There were cracks where there was once force and venom. "His little body wasn't ready to be born." He pointed at me, and the spite in his words returned. "But Jerrod didn't care! Now my little Elliot is *dead!*"

The last word hung pregnant in the air. After a moment, it seemed to echo off walls and absorb into my skin.

My brother had been born. I found out later that his condition had been stabilized, and he had been sleeping peacefully in an incubator when a complication extinguished my younger brother's life.

My father noticed the nurse in the room. She took the opportunity to say, "If you don't calm down, sir, we're gonna have to ask you to leave. And if I see you touch your son like that again, I'm calling Child Affairs."

"My *son*," my father spat on his way out of the room. "He's not my son."

Chapter Twenty-Two

J osh worked some magic on the nurse by explaining that our father was only grief-stricken. He told her that he would be fine after he calmed down and smoked a cigarette.

I had finally gotten Sydney to quit crying. She was on the waiting room floor, happily ripping pages from a magazine.

The nurse left the waiting room, satisfied that she had resolved the situation. Josh moved closer to me and whispered, "When do you think Dad will come back?"

Our father didn't smoke. He was probably taking a drive to calm down. I shook my head; I didn't know what to say.

"I'm sorry," I said to Josh.

"That's okay." He put a sympathetic arm around my shoulders. "Just out of curiosity, which one went up in flames?"

I hung my head, and fresh tears flowed. "Your favorite. The black truck."

My brother looked away. His jaw clenched and unclenched, but he turned back to me and patted my shoulder. "I really don't understand you sometimes," he said, but his words were soft. "I don't think you intentionally try to hurt people, but you need to think before you play your jokes." Josh looked at the door as if our father would step through it at any moment. "I think you've suffered enough for what you've done. And Elliot's death wasn't your fault. I think Mom was having trouble because of the position of her placenta."

Hearing our brother's name caused a fresh wave of sadness. *Elliot had waved at me!*

I felt like my heart was being kicked by the gods of pain and chaos with its every beat. I may not have been the only reason for my sibling's death, but I felt like I was the main reason for all the darkness that had touched our family.

Josh wrapped his arms around me. The best thing to happen to me that day was my brother's forgiving hug. He let me cry, and I hugged him back. Josh was the only one in the world who truly understood me.

Two hours later, when the doctor walked into the waiting room, our father had not returned.

"Where is your guardian?" the doctor asked. He was the same doctor who had delivered the news about Elliot's death.

"He stepped out to get us some food," Josh lied.

The doctor searched our eyes for a lie. "Okay. Tell him that he can see his wife now. He can take one of you older ones for ten minutes each. He'll have to make arrangements for the three of you if he wishes to spend the night with his wife."

The doctor was straightforward. I hoped he had a better bedside manner when he spoke with my mother. We nodded our agreement, and he closed the door.

"Dad may not come back, and someone needs to check on Mom," Josh said.

"One of us has to stay with Sydney, but how can we get by the nurses without a guardian?"

"That's why I have to go now," Josh explained. "The nurses are changing shifts, and I know I can sneak past them."

I didn't have to ask why I couldn't go. I had done enough to upset the family.

If Dad comes back, send him to Mom's room," Josh said. "I don't know which one it is, but I'll peek into the doors until I find it. Dad can just ask a nurse."

I nodded my head, but my stomach sank. I didn't want to face my father alone.

Josh waved as he eased open the door and disappeared from view. The door clicked as it closed.

Sydney and I were alone. She yawned. She had taken a short nap during the day, but it was close to her bedtime.

I scooped her up and we sat in a chair. I placed her on my lap easily, but soon she started to squirm. *Oh, please don't let her want a night bottle,* I thought. There was only one more bottle in the diaper bag, and I had no idea when my father would return.

Sydney placed her head on my chest and yawned again. She grabbed a handful of my shirt in her hand and squeezed it. As her eyes drooped closed, the rest of her body relaxed. I knew she was asleep when I had to adjust her heaviness across my legs.

The door clicked open, and I panicked. My Dad was back, and I was alone to face his wrath again.

I was surprised to see Josh walk into the room. He grabbed Sydney before I could protest. "Mom wants to see you," he said with a trace of bitterness. "I gotta tell you, she looks awful, but don't act like you notice."

"Is she okay?"

Josh was tired, and he didn't hide his sarcasm. "Yeah, Jerrod. She's just great! She had a baby early, and he died. Then, for added fun, I had to be rushed out of the room so she could be given a sedative, or tranquilized, or whatever."

"What? They had to do *what* to her?"

Josh took a deep breath and softened his voice. "They had to do *something*, Jerrod. She was screaming that Nana took her baby."

"But Nana's dead," I protested.

"Yes," Josh said as if he were explaining something to Sydney. "Maybe Mom is having hallucinations from losing her baby, or from too much blood loss, smoke inhalation, or stress. I don't know."

"How am I gonna get to her?" I asked.

Josh sighed heavily as he sat down with Sydney. "I don't really care, Jerrod, but she wanted to see you."

I was upset about Josh's indifference to my situation, but I was determined to see my mother, especially if she had asked for me. I found the maternity ward easily. I acted as though I had a purpose and expected no one to stop me. I got as far as the electronically sealed doors of the labor and delivery rooms. Josh must have snuck in when a nurse was leaving.

I was still deciding what I should do when I felt a hand on my back. I recognized the nurse who had been present for my father's tirade.

"Are you okay, young man?" Her touch was gentle, but her words were firm.

This woman was either my ticket inside or back to the waiting room. *What would my mother think if I didn't show up? Would she think that Josh loved her more because he had found a way into her room?*

"My dad sent me to get a soda for my mom, but I forgot the money."

At first, her features hardened, and I thought she would send me away. I noticed her relax a little, and she said, "Your brother tried the same tactic."

The nurse grabbed my hand and led me to the doors. She swiped her identification card under an electronic screen, and the doors opened. A fresh breeze from the heating unit constantly blew on us as we walked down the hallway.

We moved down a long hall and stopped at the last door on the left. She bent down to be level with my eyes. "Your mother is not up for trivial discussions," she said. "She has had a little trouble accepting her situation, so only say happy things to her. It could be worse for her if she gets upset. Give her all the love you can in ten minutes, and don't tell anyone I let you or your brother in."

I nodded that I understood. The nurse nodded back and swiftly walked back down the hall.

I stared at my mother's door. It was different than all the other occupied room doors. It didn't have a banner that said *It's a Boy* or *It's a Girl*. There was a corner piece of blue silk taped to the door. I wondered if my father had ripped down the banner when he heard my brother had died. *Had he even seen my mother since Elliot's death?*

I grabbed the knob and pulled open the door. The smell of over-dried linens and chlorine bleach filled the room. The steady beeps of the equipment attached to my mother echoed against the almost bare walls. One canvas picture of a purple flower adorned the wall. I didn't know the type of flower, but it looked too bright for my mother's mourning room.

I had decided that I was going to be cheerful like the nurse had suggested, so I skipped in with a large smile. My expression melted like wax when I saw my mother.

My mother's skin was so pale that you could almost see through it. The swell of her belly was gone, and the brightness in her eyes had died with her son.

Her gaze was fixed on the wall in front of her, but my mother knew I was in the room. I stepped over the cords around her bed and wedged my hand beneath hers.

"Jerrod," she spoke. The sound that came from my mother when she said my name was scratchy and squeaked at the finish. It was like she hadn't used her voice in a long time. "Your brother told me about your father's outburst."

She moved her body upward with the hand I wasn't holding and tried to sit straighter on the bed. I held up my hand to indicate that she should relax. "He shouldn't have blamed you," she continued, locking eyes with me, "but there is a lot you don't know about your father." She sighed. "I still have a lot to learn."

This was not going well at all. I would probably get kicked out of the hospital if my mother continued. I decided to breathe sunshine, even though I felt gray and empty.

"Everything's going to be fine, Mom," I said with a forced smile. "It just takes time. Time heals all wounds." I probably would have spit out every cliché I knew, but my mother's eyes reflected my artificial face.

I was trying too hard. My mother always said she preferred genuine people, but I decided too late that I should have been more sincere.

She gave me a small smile and dropped it quickly. She gathered the thin sheet on her bed into her fist. She let it go and turned her face away from me.

My mother clenched her jaw and took several deep breaths, like she was preparing to tell me a story, but finally, she just dropped her head. She was very good at controlling her tears.

I could hear the seconds tick by on the clock in the room. I had eight more minutes, and I wanted to leave my mother smiling. I didn't want to disappoint the kind nurse who had helped Josh and me.

She slowly lifted her head and locked eyes with me. "Don't breathe a word to anyone about what I'm about to tell you," she said quickly. "I was told in confidence by your father a month after you and Josh were born."

My mother looked around as if she suspected someone to be listening in the shadows. She had always talked to me like I was another adult. She confided in me even though some people would have told her it was inappropriate. Josh and I were smart for our age, and in a lot of ways, we were miles more mature than our peers. I tried to comfort her by squeezing her hand. My gentle pressure must have reassured her because my mother continued.

"Your father was very excited when he found out I was pregnant for the first time. He lifted me over puddles and took me to organic food marts to make sure I had the healthiest and best pregnancy. He was very sweet and supportive until we went to the doctor for the first time. I had always had irregular cycles, so I didn't think I might be pregnant until I was almost eight weeks. I went into the doctor's office full of life and love, and I came out feeling alone and almost empty."

I was trying to follow along with my mother's story, but I must have looked curious when she said she'd felt alone. My mother stared at the blanket she had wadded up in her hand. When she began again, I could hear the sorrow in her story.

"I knew your father had had a difficult childhood. His father did strange things, and he loved to chase women. Your nana kept herself busy with household tasks and society meetings so that she could seem like she didn't notice her husband's infidelities. One of the reasons I think your father wanted a large family was because he grew up alone. But he wasn't always alone."

My mother didn't turn her face to see my reaction. She looked out the window. The night was dark, but I could see the lights that marked the emergency helicopter landing pad.

"I hadn't started to show yet, but the doctor placed a Doppler on my belly. We heard a strong heartbeat, probably yours. I'll never forget the way the doctor scrunched together his eyebrows and moved the device lower. Another heartbeat echoed in the room.

"The doctor told us, 'I can't be positive, but given the location of the fetal heartbeats, I think you're having twins.'

"Your father turned white and looked at the floor while the doctor felt around my belly and congratulated us. He didn't even lift his head when the doctor shook his hand. The doctor smiled at me. He must have been thinking that your father was in shock over having more than one child at a time, but that wasn't it, and I knew it.

"I had a sinking feeling in my stomach, but I didn't ask your father about it until we got to the car. He said he was just thinking, so I left it alone. He stayed that way until after you and your brother were born. He was silent, contemplative." My mother sighed. "It was a very difficult time in our marriage."

"Your father and I still had some happy moments during the pregnancy," she conceded, "but I felt more alone than I ever have. That's why I waited so long before I had another baby. I was afraid of reliving that horrible experience of loneliness. Living alone is better than living with someone and still feeling lonely."

My mother paused and settled her gaze on me. I was past my ten-minute limit, but I didn't think my mother would ever tell me this story again. And for some reason, she thought it was important for me to know.

"One month after you and your brother were born, I was washing dishes when I heard crying. I knew the cries of my babies, so I figured your father was watching someone cry on TV. When the crying didn't stop, I went into the living room and saw your father looking into the playpen at you and your brother.

"You had fallen asleep with your heads together and your hand over your brother's. It was one of the cutest things I had ever seen, and I ran to get the camera, but I didn't get a picture.

"Your father stopped crying when he noticed me in the room, and he sat down hard on the couch. I walked over and put my arm around him. I told him that it was okay to get emotional over you guys, but he shook his head.

"'They just remind me so much of me and Ly,' he said.

"I smiled sympathetically at him. I think he knew that his mother had told me Ly's story, but I wasn't going to give anything away. He opened up to me that night about his true concerns, and we were able to have a good relationship again."

My mother was so tired that her eyes could hardly stay open. She tried to adjust her position in her bed, but sleep was overtaking her. I knew that doctors sometimes gave patients a sedative to calm them after a traumatic event. My mother wasn't talking as quickly and coherently as she usually did.

"I'm sure you're wondering what happened to your Uncle Ly, but I can't tell you. I've been through a lot today, so please forgive me."

My mother looked back out the window. She shuddered when she took her next breath.

"You already know that your Uncle Ly isn't around," she started with tears in her eyes. She quickly blinked them away. My mother took another deep breath and continued.

"I will tell you this: Elliot was a twin. The other one was lost, or *absorbed*, somehow. It happens a lot. The doctors saw twin fetuses during my first ultrasound, and then one of the twins disappeared before my next sonogram visit. I guess your father felt a special attachment to Elliot because of the missing twin."

Sneakered feet were padding down the hall. I hoped it wasn't the kind nurse who had let me into my mother's room. I didn't want her to be disappointed in me, too. I was usually very good at keeping my word, but my mother's tongue had been loosened by her grief and the sedative. I hung on her every word.

"Jerrod, your father loves you, but he's very different. He's lost people who were very close to him, and I'm afraid losing Elliot has pushed him over the edge. He bonded with Elliot in a way that he could never have bonded with you or your siblings."

I was stung, but I tried to keep my face unreadable. I hoped she hadn't told the same story to Josh since he seemed to think he had a special connection with our father.

My mother's body was giving in to the sedative. She couldn't fight it any longer, but she told me one more thing before she drifted into a medicated slumber.

"Your father told me that he felt like Elliot would be the only one who could ever understand him since Elliot's twin was lost in the womb. The reason he became so attached to his unborn son was because your father lost his twin, too."

Chapter Twenty-Three

I glanced into the waiting room. Josh was asleep with Sydney across his lap. His head was turned up sharply against the wall at an angle, and his hand was on Sydney's back to keep her from a fatal fall.

I had no trouble getting from my mother's room to the waiting room. The nurses didn't even look up as I pressed the button to open the electronic doors.

My mother had tried to explain my father's feelings to me, but I was more confused about my father than I was before visiting her. *Why hadn't we been told about my father's twin until now? Why couldn't Josh and I sympathize with our father? Josh and I couldn't live without each other!* I felt a weight growing heavier on my shoulders.

I was responsible for the death of the only person who my father thought would understand him. I probably killed Elliot's twin, too, with one of my stupid pranks.

I wanted to spring into action. I wanted to do something to make my father forgive me and to show that Josh and I were able to understand his loss just as well as Elliot.

Reality came knocking, and I had to answer the door. I had con-tributed to the stress that had ended Elliot's short life. It would be a long time before things could go back to normal, and my father would never feel the same about me again. I had seen it in his eyes.

Josh didn't move when I opened the door. I took Sydney from Josh's lap and placed her on a long row of seats. I lay down on the other side of her so she couldn't roll off. She stuck up her chin in a determined way, still dreaming, and I patted her belly. Her face relaxed, and her lips parted. Steady baby breath washed over me.

I thought I was too upset to fall asleep. I lay next to my sister and thought about all the terrible things I had done. I wished I would have left the truck in the case. Then Elliot would have been born healthy and fully developed in a couple of weeks.

I didn't feel sleep creeping up on me. I was overtaken by dreams before I could think of another pitying thought for myself.

***

Luckily, no one checked the waiting room to see if my father had attended to his children. We slept the rest of the night in the family waiting room without incident.

The morning after Elliot's death, my father came into the waiting room with the smell of alcohol coming off of him in waves. The only reason Sydney, my brother, and I left with him was because my father's eyes were clear, so I figured he had slept it off without taking a shower.

None of us moved when my father walked into the room. I could feel him standing over his sleeping children. He was calm, but there was bitterness under his surface demeanor.

My father gently shook Josh awake and picked up Sydney from my side. He spoke collectively when he said, "You need to get your stuff together. I'm taking you to a hotel so I can spend time with your mother."

We drove to our makeshift home in silence. My father's eyes kept darting from the road to my direction in the van.

The beat of my heart was stirring the sadness in my soul. I felt every condemning thought my father didn't voice. I wished he would turn on the radio so I could have a small distraction.

My father had rented a room in a local hotel while he had been absent from the hospital. It was a nice place on the outskirts of town, near a gas station. I had a little change in my pocket, so I decided I would buy my mother one of the roses that always seemed to be for sale at the counter.

I used to get excited over a stay away from home. I looked at it like a new adventure, but I could only feel dread and heartache tumbling over each other in my stomach as we pulled into the hotel's parking lot.

Our room was up two flights of stairs, and our father had packed some bags with necessities from our home, so Josh and I labored up the stairs while my father carried nothing heavier than Sydney. He stood at the room door, balancing Sydney on his side, while he found the key to the room.

Hot air burst from the room. The unit hummed, and I smelled the lemon cleaner the maids had used to sanitize our accommodations. I took in an aroma that told of my father's alcohol dreams.

We had three and a half rooms. Josh and I stood with the bags in our hands in the bedroom. There were two large beds, one dresser, and a television. We had free cable, because the television was on, and the national news was monotonously recapping domestic kidnappings and celebrity misdemeanors.

A space between the living room and the bathroom served a variety of uses. A mirror and a stand with a hairdryer were attached to a mount on the wall. A small cabinet hung beside the mirror for food and dishes. A stove was pushed under the cabinet, and a small refrigerator was placed next to it. I held a bag of perishables my father had grabbed at the service station, so I opened its small door and put them away. I placed half a jug of milk, a carton of eggs, two small bottles of orange juice, and a sixteen-ounce bottle of Coke inside. The refrigerator could hold no more.

I glanced into the bathroom and spied a stand-up shower and a basin. It looked like Sydney would have her bath in the sink.

"Go get the rest of the stuff out of the van," my father said to Josh, but his directions were meant for me, too. "You can put it all up while I'm gone."

I walked out of the emotionally frosty room and into the bright sunshine. The day was only mildly chilly, but that didn't cheer me up.

Josh came out behind me and started down the steps. I couldn't see him when I bounded down the last flight of stairs, but I heard my father's car keys jingle as Josh found the button on the fob to unlock the van.

I grabbed all the smoke-soaked bags that I could carry, and Josh got the rest. I had to go back and help Josh pick up oatmeal packets that had spilled from one of his bags, but we managed to carry everything else without any other problems.

My father had changed Sydney's diaper and was feeding her a bottle of formula when Josh and I reentered the room. She was falling asleep in his arms, so he motioned for Josh to take her and sit on the bed.

"With any luck, she'll go to sleep, and the two of you can get some rest," he said, smiling at Josh. He meant Josh and Sydney, not Josh and me.

My father kissed the top of Sydney's head and hugged Josh. "I love you, son. I don't have to tell you that you're in charge. You are your brother's keeper."

I was hurt, but I quickly found a bag to unload to try to mask my feelings. A trace of cigarette smoke lingered on the boxes as I put them in the cabinet. My father didn't smoke regularly, but he smoked when he drank, and he certainly had been drinking the previous night.

He walked with his back to the door and opened it. He kept his eyes on me the whole time as he addressed the room.

"I'll be back with your mother when she gets her release papers," my father said. "Make sure she doesn't come in to see to a mess or a crying baby, and don't even *think* about trying anything."

He opened the door again and disappeared into a sunny day. I could hear him thumping down the steps, and I imagined that I heard the van start and pull out of the parking lot.

What did my father mean when he told me not to try anything? Did he think I would run away? He had been watching me in the car and in the room like I would attack him. *Did he think I would grab the keys to the van and go join the town delinquents?*

I had all the stuff my father had packed from the house put away in less than half an hour. I discovered a newspaper that reported on the fire at my home on top of the bathroom counter. *That was fast!* It must have just made the paper's deadline.

It stated that a toy had caught fire as a woman heated the stove. *She was probably making cornbread for the roast,* I thought miserably. The firemen that the reporter had interviewed called it "an unfortunate household accident."

Unfortunate! My little brother had died because of that fire! I slung the newspaper on the floor next to the toilet.

Josh and Sydney had fallen asleep in each other's arms. I sat on the bed and watched them.

After a few minutes, I picked up the television remote from the small nightstand that separated the beds. I found some cartoons and lay back on the bed. I wished for a video game that would take my mind off my situation, but I had to settle for reruns of animated figures my parents had probably watched when they were my age.

Now that my father's resentment wasn't in the air and I was still, I could feel my lack of sleep inching over me. I closed my eyes and tried to forget that I still had more consequences to face.

I dreamed that Elliot was chasing me. He was a bloody mess, and his umbilical cord dragged behind him as he ran. He was Sydney's size, so his newborn body didn't prevent him from chasing me like a rabid dog. His hand held tightly to a black model truck. I knew that if he threw it at me, I would burst into flames.

My mother, my father, Josh, and Sydney were lined up as if they were watching a marathon race. I ran in slow motion and screamed for my family to save me, but no one came to my rescue.

My father yelled to Elliot, "Get him, Son! Get him before he kills us all!"

My mother was holding Sydney. They were both waving and smiling obliviously. My mother said, "You should respect Elliot's dreams. We all have to make sacrifices for the family to stay intact."

Josh was standing away from our parents and Sydney at the end of the line. As I passed him, he advised, "This is getting you nowhere. You can go on blaming yourself, but you can't change the past."

Josh was always the voice of reason. Most of the people in my dreams seemed to be like people in the movies. They were cast in various roles and given a subconscious script. Josh and Ella were the only ones who could enter and exit my dreams with their own true thoughts and feelings.

We never talked about it, but my twin and I had shared our nighttime fears since I could remember. Whenever I saw Josh, I knew that I was dreaming, and I was safe.

I willed myself awake and reached for consciousness. It was like I was flexing all my muscles at one time. After a couple of seconds that dragged on forever, I felt the dream lose its hold on me.

Elliot's bloody blue eyes reflected my father's anger. He smiled maniacally, an image that was imprinted on my mind when I woke up.

"I'm sorry," I whispered to my fading baby brother. My apology didn't move Elliot. I watched in horror as he aimed and threw the black truck at the remains of my family.

Chapter Twenty-Four

That night, my father helped my mother into the hotel room. He wanted to pick her up and place her on the bed, but she insisted on taking a shower first.

It had been a long day. Josh and I had spent all our time caring for Sydney and cleaning our space. I lay on the bed and pretended to be asleep. Besides, if I became active, Sydney would probably wake up, and that might make it harder for my mother. Josh must have thought the same thing. I could see his open eyes stare back at me in the light from the open bathroom door.

My father prepared my mother's shower and left the bathroom after she told him she did not need his assistance. He walked into the bedroom and sat on the edge of my bed.

"Get up," he spoke at me without a touch of affection. "Your mother and I will sleep on this bed. You can sleep with Josh or out in the van. I don't care."

Josh held my gaze for a moment before I moved to a chair and put on my shoes. He used his eyes to tell me to climb into the bed next to him, but I wasn't sleepy. I picked up the keys to the van and walked out the door.

The sun had set, taking any warmth with it. I was so angry that I didn't feel the chill of the night air.

The van was cool, but I was still hot from my father's words, so I didn't notice the temperature for over half an hour. I was thinking up elaborate scenes where my father would regret his harsh words to me. I particularly liked the story where I got a rare form of cancer, and he apologized through his tears as he nursed me into remission.

My family kept a blanket in the van beside Sydney's car seat. It was folded there because my mother couldn't stand the cold temperatures that screamed out of the air vents in the summer. My father was a tall, muscular man, and he overheated easily, so everyone wrapped themselves in coats and blankets when he had control of the van's thermostat. I folded the blanket around me and stared out the back window.

Movement in the parking lot caught my eye. I almost froze in fear when I realized that the figure was headed straight for the van, but I was able to make out my brother's form.

I climbed out of the van before Josh could make his way to me. His eyes were wide, a strong sweaty smell coming off his body.

"What's wrong?"

"Dad told me to come get you, but he's mad," Josh started. "Mom was crying and defending you, so he yelled, and the baby woke up, and Mom was crying, and...and..."

"It's okay," I said, patting my brother's arm. Large tears rolled through his hands, and sobs shook his body.

"I can't get upset," Josh said, suddenly straightening up. "I gotta help Mom and Sydney."

"What do you mean?" I asked with growing horror.

"Dad is threatening to leave."

"Let him leave," I said a little more loudly than I intended. A distant dog barked its disapproval.

"No, Jerrod." Josh looked up from his tears. "He's gonna *leave* us!"

I opened my mouth to tell my brother something, but I forgot what I was going to say. My mouth stayed open as I let Josh's words register.

"Okay," I finally said. "I'll go help you take care of Mom."

I wasn't upset anymore about my father's frustration and grief. He was acting like a selfish child. We were the children, and *he* was supposed to be strong and take care of *us*. Besides, if my father didn't want to be in the family anymore, then *I* would take care of my mother and siblings. I could be more of a man than my father, and I was prepared to tell him so.

I didn't get the chance to tell my father I was a better man, because when Josh opened the door, I saw my mother crying into my father's chest. My parents sat on the bed, my father holding Sydney in one arm and stroking my mother's hair with the other.

"You know I could never leave you, Miranda," he told her. "You are my first and only love."

My mother continued to cry, and Sydney looked up and smiled at Josh and me like nothing was wrong. I felt out of place, having never felt so isolated around my parents.

Josh shut the door, and the sound announced our presence. My mother's face was a shade of red only brick layers are used to seeing, and her eyes were swollen with despair. Her eyes darted from Josh to me, and she tried to get up off the bed.

I rushed to her side without thinking of my father's anger and helped her, feeling my father tense. My mother looked down at him, and he fixed his gaze on the floor.

My mother's embrace was more calming than a warm bath. She gently turned my face, and I noticed that we were almost equal in height, and I could feel the post-pregnancy skin through her nightshirt.

"Your father wants to tell you something," she said deliberately. It was hard for her to stand, but she wanted to make her point.

I stared at my father and waited. I felt like saying, *"Hey! It's your turn!"* or *"You're on!"* but I let my father choose his words. He finally looked up and handed Sydney to my mother.

I was sure my mother had begged my father through her tears to resolve our situation. He had always complied with my mother's wishes when she turned on her tears, and he would say, "Who can ignore a woman when she's upset?"

My father didn't meet my eyes. He only conceded, "I know Elliot's death wasn't your fault. You are my son, and I love you." He practically spit out the words.

I wish he had been sincere. I wanted to hug my father and tell him that I was sorry, but I saw he was unmoved, and it hardened me.

I put my hand on his shoulder. My father reached up to pat my hand, but I withdrew it before he could touch me.

"Thank you, Dad," I said tonelessly. I hugged my mother and went into the bathroom.

I spent a long time in the bathroom that night crying silently and reflecting on the last two days. Before I left the bathroom, I decided one thing. I would be his son, and I would play along with the idea of a happy family, but I would never let myself get close to my father again.

Chapter Twenty-Five

Other than the usual pleasantries, I only spoke to my father two more times before he left. We saw each other daily, but we tried to ignore one another or treat the other person with polite indifference.

I didn't believe my father's lame apology, and he never truly forgave me. I think he was content because he stayed away from me. I was comfortable living with a man I no longer respected and calling him my father. Our alternating periods of resentment and apathy worked well until the spring.

Our estrangement put a strain on the rest of our family. We still had good times, like Christmas and the announcement of my mother's pregnancy, but my father still treated me coldly. My mother and Josh could see it in his actions, and Sydney could feel my exclusion, but I was indifferent to my father's resentment.

A mild aroma of alcohol followed my father for several months after Elliot's death. Occasionally, I'd hear him yell at my mother about someone watching him or trying to kill him. I think I heard my mother tell my father once that I would never hurt him.

How could I hurt him? My father was eighteen years older than me and almost two feet taller.

I had not heard my father yell at my mother until after Elliot's death. He quit drinking as much, and the yelling stopped after he found out that she was pregnant again.

My mother tried not to approach my father about his bitterness toward me after that night in the hotel room, and Josh took the blame for anything I did after Elliot's death before I knew I had been caught. I didn't know Josh had taken punishments on my behalf until my father was gone.

My mother tried only once to interfere. She was convinced she could reunite her husband and her son. She almost succeeded.

I never forgot that day, but it was because of a story my mother told me. The story caused me to go looking for him on a cold December night. It also led to my brother's death.

* * *

I entered the kitchen on a bright day in early spring with the intention of helping my mother with dinner. We all treated her like glass once we learned that she was pregnant again, afraid that she might break from daily routines.

"What can I do?" I asked brightly. My mother turned from the stove. There was already a significant bulge pushing against her shirt.

She looked contemplative. "I don't need anything, but I think your father could use some help in the garage."

My smile dropped. "That's more Josh's thing. I'll just do my homework."

I thought my homework would provide the perfect excuse, but my mother put her hand on her hip and narrowed her eyes. "*It would mean so much to me if you helped your father."* She put emphasis on every word.

I took in some air to sigh heavily, but my mother held up her hand. She continued to smile warmly as she opened the door to the deck. She gave a wave with her hand that elaborately indicated the direction she wanted me to go.

I gave in and walked out the door. The garage was behind the house, and my family rarely used it. My father's truck would have barely passed into the garage, and the van was almost as tall as the building.

The structure was painted the same color as our house, but it had not been repainted after the fire. The paint had been scarred slightly from smoke damage, but priority had been given to repairing the kitchen when my parents had fixed the destruction I had caused.

The garage door was up, and my father was working on his motorcycle. I heard the clank of heavy tools moving in his toolbox. I could smell the grease and the dankness of the old, musty dirt floor before I stepped inside. It felt ten degrees cooler inside its walls, and I wished I had put on my jacket.

It was a wonder that my father had a motorcycle. My mother saw how carelessly he drove, so she adamantly refused to allow a motorcycle. My father was very sneaky, though, and he told her that he would fix it up and sell it. He just didn't say *when* he'd sell it.

My mother was an intelligent woman, and she could read people well. She must have known my father and I were in more than just agreeable moods, so she suggested that we work together in hopes that a sincere reconciliation could be reached.

My father had the radio on, and he was singing. He would have listened to music from the time he woke up until he went to sleep at night, but my mother liked periods of quiet. "Feels like the first time..." he sang and then whistled the parts he didn't know.

"I guess we're supposed to work together," I said loudly into the garage.

My father jumped so high that I thought he was preparing to hit me. I cringed.

"You scared me," he said, out of breath. "What did you say?"

"Mom sent me out here," I told him. I straightened my posture and tried to look indifferent. "I think we're supposed to bond or something."

My father smiled at me for the first time since Elliot's death. "Women know more than we think they do." He chuckled. The sound was better to me than a Christmas symphony.

My father met my eyes and winked. "Believe me, J-Rod, our women know us better than we know ourselves."

My father hadn't called me by his special nickname for me since Elliot's death. He used it when he thought he was being confidential with adult information. He must have thought it made me feel more like his friend than his son.

He gazed out of the garage, toward the kitchen window of the house. "I thought *I* could sense things, but women are emotional creatures, so they can see a problem or a solution where men sometimes can't."

My father sat on the garage floor. It looked uncomfortable for a man of his size to sit with his legs crossed, but his face didn't betray a trace of displeasure.

"I love you J-Rod," my father began, "but I don't trust you with these tools. You can stay and talk to me, though."

I was puzzled by my father's words, but I didn't show it. *Why didn't he trust me with his tools?* We had worked with those same tools on projects when Josh and I were in Cub Scouts. I was older now. *Shouldn't my father trust me more?*

I decided not to analyze my father's remark anymore. I sat down on the floor next to him and drew circles in the dirt. I really didn't have anything to say to my father, so we spent the first ten minutes in quiet company. Finally, the silence became too loud for me, and I didn't mean the lack of conversation. I was tired of the emotional distance.

"Are you still mad at me, Dad?" I asked. After I spoke, all my muscles tightened at once, and blood pounded a marching rhythm in my ears.

My father stopped working. The strained look on his face dropped into the unhappy expression I had gotten used to seeing. I would have been afraid to ask him if he had still been drinking, but there were no more bottles hidden in the house. He got up and turned off the radio.

"I was never really mad at you, Jerrod," he said. The pet name was gone. Oh well. I needed to know where I stood with my father. "I'm supposed to protect my family, and when something happens to any of you, I feel like it's my fault."

He rubbed his temples and paced the length of the garage as he spoke. "I couldn't help your mother, I couldn't help Elliot, and I couldn't help Ly!"

Was my father finally going to tell me about his brother, or was it the name he used to reference his father since they no longer spoke to each other?

"What use am I as a protector?" he continued and pointed at himself as if to clarify his point. "I'm worthless! I could have saved all of them, probably even my mother, but the cards are always stacked against me!"

My father scrubbed his face with his large hands. He looked at me and said, "Tell your mother I'll be back. I'm goin' for a ride."

My father didn't wait for my reply. I hurried to my feet so that I would be clear of the motorcycle when my father started it. He hopped onto the bike and kicked up the stand. My father didn't thrust the motor to life until he had backed it into the driveway.

I watched him turn out onto the road. I felt tired and upset all over again. *Why had I even tried to talk to a man who didn't care about his son as much as he had cared about a baby who he only had known for a few minutes?*

Chapter Twenty-Six

I stood in the garage until my mother walked out onto the back deck. She was smiling but worry lined her features when she noticed her husband and his bike were missing.

"Did your father leave?" she asked. There was a strain in her voice, but I was too miserable to investigate its origins. "I had hoped I was hearing things."

I nodded my head and walked toward the house. I felt ashamed. My father and I could have had a great conversation about the weather or his motorcycle, but I had to bring up bad feelings.

I thought I'd see disappointment when I looked into my mother's eyes, but concern and pity were trained on me when I reached the top of the stairs. She had a dishtowel in one hand, and she put the other hand on my shoulder.

"Let's go in the house and finish dinner," she said with an encouraging smile. I nodded and followed her through the door and into the kitchen.

The layout of the kitchen was the same, but the new countertops, flooring, and appliances made me feel like I was visiting another house. It was nice to have an updated kitchen when there were so many little things that needed to be fixed throughout the house.

My mother handed me an apron, and, even though I kind of knew, I asked, "Who is Ly?" My mother stopped and sucked in a breath.

"Did your father mention him?"

I squinted at my mother suspiciously. "You said his name when you were in the hospital. But Dad just told me he couldn't save you, Elliot, or Ly."

My mother gave me a puzzled look. "I guess I could have said anything while I was under the influence of the drugs they kept pumping into me at the hospital." She sighed. "At any rate, I wondered when it would come out." She went back to chopping vegetables. "It's no wonder that he would mention Elliot in connection with Ly. Your nana had to tell me the story, and I understood your father much better after that."

My mother stopped chopping vegetables and turned to face me fully. Her posture was tight and rigid. "Are you sure you want to know?"

"Yes," I said before I had another thought.

She turned down the stove, crossed the kitchen, and took down two mugs. She spooned the chocolate we shared for long talks into our mugs.

After my mother ran hot water into our mugs, we sat down at the kitchen table. She stirred the hot liquid with the tip of her finger.

"First of all, Elliot was a twin," she started, sucking the chocolate off her finger. "The ultrasound you went to was not my first. Your father was thrilled when he heard we were going to have another set of twins. He had originally wanted to name one of them Lyle."

"After his father?" I asked. My father didn't seem to like his father. In fact, I always thought he hated him.

Crazy Lyle Miller had always been a fountain of disappointment to his family. He had finally been diagnosed with schizophrenia soon after the fire that killed his wife. He was admitted into a mental institution because it was possible that he had set the fire, and everyone wanted him out of their sight. We never visited him.

"No, after his brother."

I gave my mother a puzzled look even though she had already told me part of the story. She was expecting my bewilderment, but she placed her hand on my arm to let me know that she would tell me in time.

"Your father and I almost didn't last," my mother said. She looked into her cup as if using the liquid as a medium into the past. "Your nana stopped me from giving up on him, though.

"Your father and I had been living together, but I brought his clothes to your nana one Monday after he left for work. We had fought all weekend, and I was convinced that your father and I weren't right for each other. I was going to end our relationship without another argument.

"I drove out to your grandparent's house. Your grandfather was on one of his famous drinking binges, so he wasn't there.

"Everyone knew your grandfather only worked odd jobs for money for groceries or electricity. He'd bum money for liquor."

My mother spoke plainly to me. She never treated me as if I couldn't understand the duplicitous adult world. I respected her for that.

"I knocked, and your nana called for me to come in. I felt like a traitor, but I opened the door and picked up the two trash bags I had filled with her son's personal items. I carried the bags to the kitchen, where she sat reading the paper with a cup of coffee.

"Your nana looked over her reading glasses at me, but when she saw the bags, she knew I was planning to break up with her son. I'll never forget the way she calmly put down her paper and placed her open reading glasses on it. I loved her, and I was unprepared for the tears I saw in her eyes when she looked up at me.

"She asked me, 'What has he pushed you to do?'

"If she had asked me anything else, I would have been defensive. I realized that my reasons for dumping your father's stuff off were all really lame. I think I was really going to let your nana clean up my mess for me. I was a gutless coward, and I thought that if I dropped off your father's things with your nana, then she would be forced to call him at work. Then I could avoid a confrontation because I could have the locks changed and be anywhere else before he came home. I had even fantasized that your father would bypass returning to our apartment ever again.

"Thank God your nana didn't make it easy for me. I think I muttered something about your father getting too jealous. Your nana relaxed a little, but she didn't speak. She slid her chair back and crossed the room. I was still holding the bags, but when she didn't take them from me, I was forced to turn sideways so that she could move past me.

"I followed her to her bedroom. I thought it was a real intrusion of her privacy since I was still planning to leave her son.

"I stood in your nana's bedroom with two garbage bags in my hands while she pulled out an old photograph album. She blew a fine coat of dust off the cover and stared at the golden title: The Miller Family.

"'If you're not in a hurry,' she told me without looking up, 'can I tell you some of the reasons for his strange ways?'

"I told you that I loved your nana," my mother explained. "It was my love and respect for her that made me drop the bags and sit on the bed beside her. I let her narrate the album.

"The first picture showed two boys asleep on the floor. Their heads were together, and they were smiling. I was surprised that they both looked like your father. I thought it might have been a reflection picture until I read the caption: Little Lyle and Kyle.

"The next picture showed twin toddlers in a kiddie pool, waving at the person taking the picture. The only difference between the boys was a web on the right hand of one of them that stretched from the boy's ring finger to his pinky.

"I had a lot of questions after looking at that picture, but I stayed silent. Before I left, your nana told me Ly's story, or maybe it's your father's story, but I understood your father much better after I heard it.

"I listened to your nana talk for almost an hour. It was easy to follow her southern dialect because I had been living in Erwin for several years.

"I can relate the story to you because your nana was so descriptive that afternoon. She had probably had a lot of time to relive and think about the moments before she told them to me that day.

"Most of the time, my eyes followed her mouth, but I would look at a wall or the little album when her story brought tears to my eyes. Sometimes she would point to a picture or wipe her eyes with the back of her hand, but no matter the weight on her heart, your nana told the story to its end.

"She knew something was wrong with Lyle Miller before she married him. He threw stones at her window and sang love songs, and then he would yell at the trees for watching them talk.

"Lyle was jealous, too! He broke the arm of the school's quarterback just because he smiled at your nana and asked about her family."

"Why did Nana marry him when he was so violent?" I asked. My nana had been a thin, frail woman, and I knew jealous men could be mean to their wives.

"Well, Jerrod, it was because her father had acted the same way with her mother," my mother answered. "She thought that was how men were supposed to behave.

"I know you know better," she interjected. "Your father chose to end that cycle of violence."

I pressed my lips into a thin smile. My father may not have survived long enough to have had children if he had chosen to physically assault his wife. My parents argued, but my mother's fiery spirit was too much for my father's temper. Thankfully, their love canceled out their most heated emotions.

My mother returned to her story. "Besides, Lyle made her laugh, and that is very powerful magic in the dating world." She nodded as if she was sharing a special secret with me.

I never planned to use the knowledge. The girls I knew were annoying.

"Anyway, she thought she loved him, and she became pregnant quickly," my mother resumed.

"They weren't married!" I blurted out. My mother must have been more accustomed to that type of situation because she only shook her head.

"They were married very quickly," she continued. "Of course, everyone knew she was pregnant. They could already see her belly poking out of her mother's old wedding dress, but no one spread rumors about their family.

"She had witnessed abuse between her mother and father, so she thought it was normal when Lyle started hitting her. He would kick her legs or punch her back so bruises wouldn't catch the attention of the doctor. She never fought back until the day his fists missed her back and hit her growing belly.

"She had already felt the baby moving, and she enjoyed the little hand or foot she felt in her ribs or pushing on her bladder. Those little pokes and pushes made your nana smile when there was nothing else to smile about."

My mother had been raised in the city, but I could hear parts of the dialect she had absorbed when she spoke. She was telling my nana's story, so my mother explained situations, and she used phrases that she normally would have spoken in a different way. It made me feel like I was hearing the story from my nana even though she was no longer alive.

"She knew Lyle didn't hit her stomach on purpose," my mother said, "but she saw red when it happened. She smacked him full across the face, and Lyle jumped like he was going to hit her again, but he saw his mistake.

"That was the first time he left for what the town called his 'drinkin' binges'. Your nana knew he was seeing other women, even her best friend, Judy, but it got her through the day to ignore his dalliances. Besides, he always came back.

"Lyle liked to hunt when he could see past the end of a rifle. Sometimes he'd go into the woods for days and hunt. She was happier when he hunted because she knew he hadn't been out running around on her if he brought a squirrel, rabbit, or deer home.

"He always thought the trees were watching him—"

"Wouldn't that make it hard to hunt if you thought a tree was sneaking up on you?" I asked sarcastically. I rolled my eyes and shook my head in disbelief, but my mother wasn't amused.

"I thought you were mature enough for this story," she said. "Everyone knew Lyle had a mental condition, but no one troubled themselves to help your nana or him. Lyle did a lot of terrible things, but he was still a person, and he may have been able to better control his condition if he had received the proper treatment."

My face reddened in shame. My mother was right. I should not have been so unfair, but I still didn't like Lyle. He had been physically violent with my nana, and I doubted that it was all related to his *condition*.

My mother clenched and unclenched her jaw before she began again. "Lyle thought the trees watched him," she said. "Sometimes he liked that they watched him, but certain trees would send him into fits. He went into the woods for days, and when your nana asked him about it, he'd say the trees made him stay. Lyle would have scratches that would almost make you believe that he had to fight the trees to get back home."

I would have made another sarcastic remark, but I was still wounded by my mother's reaction to my last comment. *At least the trees took up for my little nana*, I thought.

It's possible that she sensed my sarcastic thought because she took a drink of her cocoa, staring at me over the rim of the cup. "He called the two maple trees in their front yard *good trees*. Lyle said they watched the house and protected your nana and him. But he also said those trees told him that she was cheating on him."

During the story, my mother referred to my father's father as *Lyle* or by a pronoun. She never called him my grandfather. It didn't bother me. I didn't know him, and the story hadn't given me a favorable opinion of him.

"Lyle got mad at her one day because dinner wasn't ready on time, and he stormed out the door," she said carefully. He had probably acted violently before he left, but I didn't ask about it. His hostility was implied in every scene of the sad tale. "She was only a little worried that she would go into labor before he came back. The doctor said it would be at least another week even though your nana was much bigger than the usual measurements.

"She started having contractions the next day, and they wouldn't go away. She decided she was in labor, and she started the long walk to the hospital. Your nana had never learned to drive, so she passed Lyle's old black truck parked in the yard and headed to the road with a suitcase in her hand.

"She had been walking twenty minutes before her father saw her and pulled his car over to pick her up. They went straight to the hospital.

"She gave birth to a baby boy about half an hour later. Maybe the walk helped it along. I don't know, but your nana said that the Lord didn't 'visit horrible child-birthin' pains' on her. She said she hurt a little and was 'terrible uncomfortable,' but her baby came into the world while she was still waiting for her father to bring her mother to the hospital.

"She was holding a beautiful baby boy, but she still felt uncomfortable. She asked a nurse how long it would last, and the nurse peeked beneath her gown. The nurse's face turned pale, and she said, 'I see another head!'"

My mother chuckled. "At the time, there weren't a lot of multiple births in this small town, so I'm sure there was quite a commotion. Your nana must have thought that some alien had gotten into her body when the nurse said she could see another head!"

I smiled, but I was too curious about the outcome of the story to appreciate the hilarity my mother tried to convey. I wasn't even bothered by the details of childbirth. Josh and I had been in the delivery room with my mother and father when Sydney was born.

"Your nana gave birth to another baby that was identical to the one she had held in her arms," my mother said. "She was trying to figure out how she was going to nurse two babies at the same time when her mother finally got there to help her.

"In this area, you couldn't have people in the delivery room with you back then," my mother explained. "Your nana's mother filled her in on the things she needed to know after she and the babies were cleaned. There were no baby classes in our town back then, so a woman's mother, grandmother, or aunts told her the way to care for her babies.

"Your nana had delivered the twins easily, but something had gone wrong in the hospital. She didn't really explain it, but the doctor told her that she couldn't have any more babies.

"Three days later, they let her go home. A nurse asked what she had named her boys. She had thought a long time about it. She named the first baby Kyle John and the other one Lyle John. The names rhymed. One child was named after his father, and both children were named after her older brother, John, who died in the war."

I was glad my parents didn't give Josh and me rhyming names. Having the same first letter in our names was enough.

"Your nana said her father had a fit," my mother recounted. "He shouted, 'Your husband was in bed with another woman while you birthed his sons! He doesn't deserve his name to carry on. You know he's already got another girl down on the river in the family way?'"

I thought about the prospect of a half-uncle or half-aunt somewhere in the town, but I quickly dismissed it. Surely, my father would have known about a half-brother or half-sister by now.

"Your nana's mother gave her father one of her *mean stares*," my mother emphasized. "Your nana's mother was not like her. She would fight back when your nana's father hit her. Her father didn't challenge your nana's mother when she was really mad, and her mother didn't think she should be upset so soon after giving birth.

"Her mother held her hand to let your nana know that she was not alone. Your nana's father had not always been faithful.

"Her mother stayed with her for a week after the babies came home. Lyle came stumbling home drunk when the twins were a week and a half old.

"Your nana's mother took one look at Lyle and got up to grab her bag. She kissed both the babies and your nana before she walked to her house. She didn't speak to Lyle. She walked past him and out the door.

"Lyle watched her leave. 'That's no way to treat a man in his own home. Where's her manners?' He laughed at a joke that was only funny to him.

"Your nana tried to go about her business and ignore him, but he kept stumbling through the house, so she was afraid he would wake up the twins. She finally caught his eye and told him to quieten down.

"Lyle looked at her through his booze and said, 'Where's your belly?'

"Your nana had prepared herself for that question. 'I can't stay pregnant forever,' she told him. 'I had the babies while you were gone.'

"Lyle's eyes widened. 'Doctor said the baby ain't comin' for another week. Whose baby'd you have?'

"'You were gone almost two weeks, Lyle,' she said to him. 'I had the babies last week. My father drove me.'

"'You women lie about babies,' he slurred. 'You think the trees didn't tell me about that man visitin' while I was gone? You can't trick me, woman. I don't have any babies.'

"Your nana walked up to him and spit in his face," my mother recounted with pride. "Lyle raised his hand to strike her, but she didn't back down. She gave him what she hoped was one of her mother's furious looks. She had never raised her voice much more above a whisper, so Lyle was shocked enough to hear what she said.

"'You are not gonna accuse me of birthin' someone else's babies!' she yelled at him. 'Those babies in there are ours, and you know it. They have your last name, as dishonorable as it is, and you *will* call them yours!'

"The babies had started to cry while she was screaming, so she left him to tend to himself. The next morning, he was kind to her and the twins, but she knew he was waiting to put her in her place."

This type of family dynamic was a bit of a culture shock to me. I knew about the detestable situations on television, but it was hard for me to process that my sweet nana had endured such abuse.

"Your nana's babies grew into boys and then into young men," my mother said, carefully avoiding calling them Lyle's children. "At twelve, they could read any book and figure large numbers in their heads. The teachers talked about college, but she knew they were too poor to send them.

"Lyle hated Ky and Ly. He would never come out and say so, but he was jealous of their intelligence and that your nana gave more attention to them than she did to him. Lyle would pat them on the back or teach them to shoot a gun, but it was an unspoken understanding that the boys were her children. She only stood up to Lyle when it came to them, so Lyle left them alone, and she let Lyle do whatever he wanted without causing trouble.

"The twins were peculiar to everyone but your nana. She was around them all the time, so she was used to the things they did. Ly could read a book, and Ky would know what happened in it without reading it himself. They could always find each other whether they were in the house or out in the woods, and Ky would tell her about Ly's dreams before Ly stumbled into the kitchen for breakfast."

I nodded my understanding. It wasn't so different from the things Josh and I could do.

"There was this section of the woods, near the river," my mother continued, "where Ky and Ly always played. Your nana was scared of the woods, but they were boys, and they played near the house, so she tried not to worry. Besides, Ky was very protective of his brother.

Ky took the idea of being the older brother seriously, even if he was only minutes older.

"There were drops into holes and caves all over those woods, and she always worried that the boys would fall in one. She worried about ticks and snakes. She worried about bears and mountain lions. Most of all, though, she just worried about losing her sons. They were her only children, and she felt like they were all the family she had after her mother and father died.

"She wasn't concerned enough to speak her mind about it until the day she heard a shot in the woods. She had been stringing beans on the front porch, and the boys were playing in the woods. Around mid-afternoon, she heard the crack of a gun echo off the mountains.

"She jumped up, no longer caring about the beans in her lap, and called for Ky and Ly. They didn't yell back at her, so she hastily concluded that they had been shot by mistake by some hunter in the woods.

"She thought about trying to find her husband, and then she decided against it. Lyle was off on one of his binges, so it would have taken too long to find him. She called for the twins from the porch a couple of times, and then she put on her shoes and headed to the woods.

"She walked around the edge of the woods, yelling their names for almost half an hour. Then she steeled herself and walked into the trees.

"It was a little darker and colder because the sun couldn't get through the trees, and that didn't help her nerves. I saw your nana shiver a little when she told me, like she could still feel herself in the forest. She was so spooked that she just kept moving and calling for the boys.

"She was lost before she realized she couldn't see the edge of the forest. Your nana wandered around until almost dark calling and crying for Ky and Ly. She had talked herself into believing that her children were dead.

"Ky found her a few minutes after the sun set. She ran to him with tears running down both sides of her face. Ly joined them while she was hugging Ky. She was so scared about the woods and for their safety that she thought they were angels rescuing her.

"I like to think of them in that moment," my mother said softly. "I could feel so much love radiating from your nana when she told me that part of the story.

"Ky told her that he and his brother heard the gunshot and realized there was a hunter in the woods, so they went home. They looked for their mother in the woods when they saw the bowl of beans scattered on the porch.

"Your nana finally told Ky and Ly about her fear of the woods, and they seemed to understand. Ky promised to be more careful, and your nana believed her sons would play more safely."

My mother took a sip of her cocoa and grimaced. It must have gotten cold.

"She confided in me that she always told Ky that he was his brother's keeper, and she depended on him to take care of Ly," she said. "Ky and Ly were the best of friends, so she never had to discipline them. Lyle was more of a disciplinarian.

"Ky woke their father up early one morning, and your nana thought Lyle was going to kill him. Lyle had a temper anyway, but he had been drinking late, and he probably had a hangover."

My father had periods of time when he would drink. I knew about hangovers. My mother would give my father headache medicine and lots of water on those days.

"When Lyle was home, your nana wasn't allowed to move out of the bed until he told her that she could start his coffee," my mother said. "It always woke him when her weight lifted off the mattress.

"She was lying with her eyes open, thinking about the things she had to do during the day, when she heard the boys stir. It was almost the middle of the day, so they were hungry. She knew they were sneaking around the kitchen, trying to be quiet, but her body went cold when she heard a bowl drop and break into pieces.

"Lyle was up like a shot and charged into the kitchen with his fists clenched. Your nana ran after him and hoped she could get Lyle to take his anger out on her instead of her boys.

"Ky tried to explain that he had dropped a bowl getting it down for Ly to have some cereal. Lyle wouldn't hear it. He jerked Ky up by his arm and started hitting his back, shoulders, and behind over and over.

"She tried to get in between them, but Lyle shoved her away every time she got close to them. All she could do in the end was cry and scream for Lyle to stop. She tried to think of any way she could make Lyle stop hurting Ky. Her eyes found Lyle's hunting gun by the door, and she started to inch her way over to it.

"Lyle may have stopped beating Ky sooner if he had cried. If Ky had started crying or screaming from the first, Lyle probably would have stopped after a couple of swats, but Ky wouldn't break.

"Ly and your nana were the ones screaming and crying for Lyle to stop, and they were hoarse before the beating was over. Lyle finally worked through his rage and dropped Ky on the ground.

"Ky got up and looked his father in the eyes. He was shaky and bruised from the older man's beating, but he stood straight in front of Lyle and held his gaze. He spit in Lyle's face.

"Your nana had finally made it over to Lyle's hunting gun. She checked that it was loaded and then she did something that was both brave and stupid. She put the gun in Lyle's back.

"'If you touch him again, Lyle, I'll kill you!' she screamed.

"'Woman, you don't know the first thing about a weapon like that,' he told her, but he had his hands up, and his voice cracked.

"'Do you wanna bet your life on that?' she asked and pushed the gun harder into his back.

"Lyle turned his face to the side so that she could see him smile cruelly at Ky. 'I'll make sure you know real pain, boy,' he promised. 'In the end, I'll break you.'

"Lyle kept his hands up as he got dressed and walked out the door to town. Your nana kept the gun by her side until she couldn't see him on the road anymore.

"Ly fixed up Ky's wounds and put him in bed while she waited for Lyle to leave. She went into Ky's room to check on him, and she was surprised to see him awake. She could see mean, purple knots forming on his neck and arms.

"Ky was facing the wall, but he asked, 'Why do you stay with him, Mama?'

"She had to think about that question for a minute, but she used her religious background to answer him. 'It's sinful to get a divorce.'

"Ky turned over to face her. She could see the red marks on his cheeks and the bruises on his shoulders. 'So God thinks it's okay to beat your wife and children?' he asked her.

"'It's not our place to judge,' was all she could think to say. Ky didn't like her answer, and he rolled over and faced the wall again.

"Your nana felt so drained and powerless. She told me that her boys were the most important thing to her. She couldn't stand to see them disappointed in her. She kissed the top of Ky's head and got up to pack.

"She spent the better part of the day taking care of Ky and filling two suitcases with her boys' clothes and the few toys they had. She hoped they would be long gone before Lyle stumbled back home. She thought she could sleep at the church for a couple of days and make a more solid plan for their future. She was almost ready to walk to town when she heard the front door open.

"She ran to the door to make sure that the wind hadn't knocked it open, and she came face to face with Lyle. She almost ran into him. Lyle's unsteady gait and red face told her what he had been doing.

"She was shocked that Lyle was back so soon. Her thoughts immediately rested on the suitcases in the hall. *Would Lyle hurt them if he knew they were leaving?*

"'Well, if it isn't my lovely bride!' Lyle beamed.

"Your nana didn't know how to act. She wondered if he was tricking her into believing he wouldn't hurt her.

"Ly stood outside his brother's room like a sentinel. Everyone was on the defensive, but Lyle just acted like he was a normal father returning from a trip into town.

"Lyle braced himself against the wall. 'I've got something for ya,' Lyle said with a wink. 'Actually, I got somethin' for all of ya.'

"All your nana could think was that he had bought a new gun in town to shoot them with. She wondered how long it would take before their bodies were found.

"She noticed the bag in his hand for the first time. A red rose was peeking out of the top.

"'A rose for a rose,' he said, handing her the flower. She took it carefully and stared at the rose like it was a rock from outer space.

"'You still like flowers, don't cha?' he barked at her. She nodded her head. 'Good,' he said and surprised her with a brief kiss.

"Lyle gave Ly a box of peppermint candy and patted the boy's head. She saw Lyle's jaw twitch when Ly cowered before his touch, but Lyle managed to keep a crocodile smile on his face.

"Lyle pulled another box of peppermint candy from his bag. 'I guess Ky's still under the weather,' he said. 'I'll take his treat to him.' No one mentioned that the beating Lyle had given him was the reason Ky was feeling "under the weather."

"She took advantage of Lyle's absence to move the suitcases out of the hall. Ly helped her throw clothes back into drawers and toys into their bins. They finished and were standing casually in the living room when Lyle left Ky's room. Ky had accepted his father's gift, and there had been no more fighting.

"Lyle pulled her to him. She stood there with her arms at her sides, smelling the sweat and alcohol that was the only scent he wore.

"'Things are gonna be different now,' Lyle promised. 'I've acted stupid, and I'm gonna be a better dad and husband. I promise.' He looked into her eyes when he made his pledge, like she would believe him more.

"Your nana knew that the truce wouldn't last, but she wanted to believe Lyle so badly that she gave in to his lies. She was too scared to be alone with two sons and no home. Back then, women in her position didn't have a lot of options.

"She threw her arms around Lyle and cried. He walked her to the couch and sat. He soothed her until he passed out.

"She thought that Lyle would be back to his old ways the next day, but he woke up with a great disposition. He placed a kiss on her cheek when he got out of bed, read the comics to Ly at breakfast, and carried Ky's food to him in his bedroom.

"The biggest surprise was when Lyle *stayed* nice. He taught the boys to play football and took them fishing. He came home almost every night and didn't go on drinking binges very often. He was really winning your nana over, and she was glad. She finally felt like they were a family.

"One day that summer, she was shucking corn when Ky came running into the kitchen. 'Ly's hurt!' he yelled at her.

"It took a second for her to understand what he was saying. She was scared, and she followed Ky out the door without thinking. She didn't even stop to put on a pair of shoes.

"Ly was in the woods. She could hear him screaming a long time before she saw him. As a mother, it must have been agonizing for your nana to hear the cries of her child before she could reach him. She ran the rest of the way to him with rocks and twigs tearing at the bottoms of her feet.

"She finally found her son. Ky was trying not to cry, but she suspected that he could feel his brother's pain and fear.

"Ly was under a large maple tree. His foot was caught in a bear trap. Blood was streaming onto the ground, and Ly was pale with shock. He kept picking at the teeth of the trap but without a lot of energy. She knelt down next to him and tried to think of a way to loosen the trap. The catch to release it was welded into the trap.

"'Mama, please help me!' Ly cried. 'I'm sorry.'

"I guess that tells you a lot about Ly's character," my mother said. "He was terribly hurt, but he apologized for being in that situation." My mother squeezed her fist with her other hand, like she was holding back anger, and continued.

"Ky tried to explain how it happened, but your nana barely heard him. She understood that they were playing in their usual place in the woods and that Ly had walked into the trap when he ran to climb into his favorite tree.

"She saw a wooden sign on the tree that said *Ky and Ly's Hangout*. It was clear that children played there.

"She knew that she could not help Ly on her own. Ky was frantically talking about no one ever setting traps in that part of the woods because kids played there, but she shook him and said, 'Go get help! Whoever you see on the road, stop them and bring them here!'

"At that moment, Ly's screams stopped, and your nana swore to me that Ky and Ly seemed to speak to each other without words. She thought she knew what they had said. Ky had wordlessly told Ly he'd be back, and Ly sent that he would wait for him."

My mother met my eyes. "I didn't fully understand it when your nana told me the story," she admitted, "but I've seen this type of communication between you and Josh."

I gave her a small smile, but I said nothing. Secrets between twins were sacred.

"Your nana tried to get the trap's teeth out of Ly's ankle," she resumed, "but it wouldn't move. She thought she had started to release it a couple of times. She could hear the metal pulling out of the skin, but she would lose her grip, and the trap would spring back into Ly's ankle.

"Ly reached a point where he didn't cry or scream, but he almost passed out. Ly was in shock. He grabbed her arm, and his fingernails made scars that I could see on the day your nana told me this sad story. Fresh blood flowed from his leg every time she moved the trap. It stained the summer grass a darker red than wine.

"She knew Ly was losing too much blood, and he would have to go to the hospital in the city to receive a blood transfusion, but she couldn't free him from the trap to get him there. She tried to pull the trap at the other end, but it had been securely nailed to a tree.

"She tried to make Ly as comfortable as possible. She sang to him and tried to talk to him about his place in the woods. Ly started to pass out, but she slapped his arm and told him to look at her eyes. Your nana never struck her children, but she was scared, and she couldn't keep Ly awake. Ly smiled at her through his pain.

"After some time, there was movement and voices in the woods. Ky had found Sheriff John Moore to help him rescue his brother.

"Sheriff Moore had been in office for almost a decade, and all the families in Erwin trusted him. He was a portly man, and your nana hoped his weight could help him free Ly.

"Sheriff Moore looked at Ly like his death was certain. Ly was concrete pale and easing in and out of the world, but your nana was convinced her son just needed a blood transfusion.

"Sheriff Moore swept into action. He had brought a metal tool from his cruiser, and he used it to loosen the nails that held the trap to the tree. He and Ky pulled until the trap was freed. The sheriff picked up Ly and ran. Ky and your nana followed him and tried to match his pace.

"Sheriff Moore laid Ly along the back seat of his cruiser, and Ky sat in the floorboard beside his brother. Your nana jumped into the front seat and turned around to hold her son's hand.

"'Keep him awake,' Sheriff Moore bellowed at them over the cruiser's motor and his adrenaline.

"They sang every religious song they knew, as if God would hear their pleas more readily if they lifted their voices in reverence to Him. They asked Ly to tell them stories about things he remembered from his childhood. Ly whispered a memory about making apple pie for the Apple Festival, and your nana and Ky vowed to make a hundred pies with him after he came home.

"Poor little Ly kept asking if *they* were okay. They tried not to get too emotional. They just smiled at his snow-white face and prayed with all their hearts that it would be the Lord's will to save him.

"Your nana kept looking at the growing pool of blood in Sheriff Moore's back seat. The good sheriff had taken off his shirt, and Ky was trying to put pressure on the worst of Ly's punctures, but the blood flowed out steadily around the material, and the trap maintained its hold.

"I don't think your nana realized she was losing her son on the ride to the hospital, but Ky seemed to understand that death was taking his brother. She said Ky would look Ly in the eyes and talk with his 'non-speak words', and Ly seemed like he was responding to his brother as he nodded in and out. Inevitably, Ky started shaking his brother and shouting, 'I can't hear him anymore!'

"Sheriff Moore had been standing on the gas pedal, and he tried to make the cruiser go faster, but the car was protesting the 100 miles per hour it was traveling. They were lucky to be in a police cruiser. Traffic parted for them when they saw flashing blue lights.

"Sheriff Moore pulled right up to the doors of the hospital. Your nana jumped out and flung open the back door of the cruiser.

"She had a vivid memory of a nurse wheeling out a new mother and her baby," my mother said, but it took her almost a full minute to gather enough composure to continue. "She didn't realize she was witnessing the irony of life and death, but I recognized the cruel joke.

"The nurse saw the police cruiser, handed over the young mother to her husband, and ran back inside for help. Ky had barely gotten out of the car before the nurse rushed back outside and shouted for an explanation of the accident.

"Sheriff Moore recounted the parts he knew while the nurse checked Ly's wrist for a pulse. Two nurses jogged out a stretcher, and they easily lifted Ly onto it.

"They raced inside the double doors of the hospital. Ly's face had turned grayish-white, and his body seemed silent. There was no resistance from his muscles as they moved him into one of the emergency rooms.

"The doctor breezed into the room and analyzed the hospital machines the nurses had hooked to Ly. His face was grim as he watched a nurse giving CPR in an attempt to revive Ly. Five minutes stood still in time as Ky, the sheriff, and your nana watched her efforts and prayed. The line on the machine stayed flat, so the doctor placed his hand on the nurse's arm to let her know to stop. The nurse looked completely defeated, and the doctor recorded the time of death at five-eleven.

"Your nana knew that her little Ly had been dead before they arrived at the hospital. He had died just as his consciousness went beyond Ky's reach. The loss of blood had been too great.

"Ky and your nana had the opportunity to be alone with Ly's body after the nurses unhooked the machines. They stood and cried miserably over the boy they couldn't save. She signed a certificate of death and thought about the day when she signed his birth certificate. The time in between had been too short.

"Sheriff Moore drove your nana and Ky back home. They walked into an empty house without turning on a light.

"She lay down on Ly's bed and stared at the wall. A few minutes later, Ky lay down beside her. They held each other, and she draped her arm loosely around his chest so that she could feel his breath going in and out of his body as he slept.

"She woke up the next morning and called her relatives and friends. Her friend Judy drove Ky and your nana to the funeral home to make arrangements. Several of the community churches donated money to help pay for the cost of the funeral and burial. The funeral home overlooked the remaining balance.

"Of course, Lyle had been away on one of his binges, so he didn't even know his son had died until two days later. He was too drunk to understand it, and he was gone again before he could touch reality.

"Ky and your nana held one another during the viewing and the funeral. She didn't cry until they closed the casket over her son. She didn't remember Ky shedding tears for his brother.

"She didn't see Lyle at the funeral. Someone told her that he had tried to go, but he was drunk, so Sheriff Moore had beaten him until he passed out."

My mother's jaw clenched. "Sheriff Moore was a good man," she said to herself.

"Ky didn't want anything to do with Lyle after Ly passed," my mother said. "Lyle stopped trying to talk to him, and he stayed gone most of the time until Ky moved out.

"Ky started to tell people his name was John because it was the name he and Ly had shared that was not a part of their father. John wanted to adopt his mother's maiden name, but she wouldn't allow it. She told him to bring honor back to the Miller name.

"Your nana told me that his brother's death was the main reason he was so protective over me," my mother explained. She had a small smile that reflected her pride over my father's commitment to her. "Johnny had lost so much," she went on, "and I was the first woman he let get close to him."

My mother looked at me squarely. "I'll say to you the same thing your nana said to me when I thought about leaving your father: Please think of his sad story before you give up on him."

"I wasn't mad at your father anymore," my mother said as she concluded my nana's story. "I could hardly remember why I had been angry in the first place. I had made up my mind to forgive your father long before the conclusion of your nana's pitiful recounting of her life with Lyle Miller.

"Your nana put her hand on my leg. I looked down at her hand and then up into her face. She was moving her mouth, but sounds wouldn't come out. Finally, words spilled from her lips as tears poured onto her cheeks.

"'People are hopelessly flawed,' she said. 'Our experiences make up who we are, and we're lucky if we don't let the world beat us down. Please don't pass judgment on me for my poor choices. I have told you my story, but Lyle has his reasons and his own story. I just wanted to help you understand John a little more so that you could love him for who he was, who he is, and the man he wants to become.'

"I kissed your nana's cheek and got up to leave the room. I picked up the bags with your father's stuff in them on the way out.

"When I got home, I put away everything in the bags before your father's shift ended. I fixed a nice dinner and waited for him to open the door.

"I didn't have to wait very long. I heard his footsteps on the stairs, and I felt a moment of apprehension as his key slid into the lock. *What if he was still mad at me?*

"Your father opened the door and called my name. I'll never forget his worried eyes or the way his mouth trembled when he told me that he thought I had left him. He relaxed when I hugged him, but he wasn't convinced that everything was okay. He didn't know that my heart had been softened by his mother.

"He asked me to promise everything was okay. I promised him, but he wasn't satisfied.

"He said, 'Pinky swear.'"

My mother modeled her hand with an extended curved pinky. I didn't need a demonstration. I had seen my parents pinky swear a hundred times.

"I had a feeling your father was showing me a glimpse into something confidential he shared with Ly," she admitted, "It was almost like a secret handshake. I took his pinky in my own, and I made my first pinky swear. I never regretted it."

Chapter Twenty-Seven

I didn't know how to respond to my mother's story. I wanted to smile because it had ended happily, but something told me to keep my face sober. I reached out and patted her hand, "I'm glad you didn't give up on Dad."

My mother blinked the tears out of her eyes. Her gaze had mostly rested on her cocoa mug throughout the story, but now she looked at me with a determined stare. "I still haven't given up on him," she insisted, "and I won't let you write him out of your life."

I pretended to be shocked. I even opened my mouth a little like I was going to object, but I was too stunned by her accusation.

"Don't look so surprised," my mother said. "Everyone in the house can see the way you've distanced yourself from your father."

"My father hasn't exactly been all warm and gooey to me!" I defended.

My mother straightened in her chair and raised her eyebrows. "Jerrod, I told you that story for several reasons. One, so that you could understand your father a little better. Two, so you could see why he has been more upset over Elliot than he would have been if he had not already lost a close family member in childhood. And three, so that you could get a real idea about Lyle Miller."

My mother waited to let me absorb her points before she continued. When she spoke again, the edge was out of her voice.

"There were a lot of clues in your nana's story that I didn't think about until later," she confessed. "I realized that a monster was just beneath Lyle's skin when I had time to reflect on your nana's words. I know one day you will connect all the dots, but I can't go into that story now. Right now, I want to talk about how you're going to make peace with your father."

I looked at her indignantly. "Why do *I* need to make up with *him*?" I shouted. "I walked out there to help him work on his stupid bike, and he rode it away from me. I'm just a child! What more do you want from me?"

My mother controlled her breathing and her anger by looking at the table as she spoke. I felt momentarily ashamed of yelling at my pregnant mother, but only momentarily.

"You may only be eleven, Jerrod, but I think we both know that you're intelligent for your age," she said. Once she had uttered that sentence, my mother visibly relaxed. She locked eyes with me. "But we need to get back to the main reason I shared the story with you." My mother slowed her speech and placed extra emphasis on every word. "Your father wanted to protect Elliot, especially after the unexplained disappearance of the twin, because he thought of Elliot like a second chance. He felt like Elliot was his way to make up for not being able to save Ly."

"What about Josh and me?" I asked. "Why didn't he think of us as a second chance?"

"I don't know," my mother conceded. She moved in her seat. Her pregnancy made the hard wood of the chair even more uncomfortable.

"You know how your father *talks* to his unborn children?" my mother asked. She put air quotes around the word she emphasized.

Sure I did. I was only embarrassed that he might do it in public, like he did at the ultrasound.

I nodded. "I have to be honest, Mom. I think he actually can communicate with us before we're born."

"Me, too," my mother said, still holding my gaze. "And that's why I believed him when he told me part of Ly's spirit was resting in Elliot." Tears fell from my mother's eyes. "So I understand his grief. He lost his son and a second chance to save his brother."

"Mom, you know I don't believe in recycled spirits."

My mother shook her head. "I know, but your father does. He especially believed that his brother's spirit was residing in Elliot when he saw that little bit of webbing between Elliot's fingers."

I remembered my father's shocked face when the ultrasound technician pointed out Elliot's genetic flaw. I had dismissed it as something in the Miller DNA.

"What do I do?" I asked my mother. I knew that was all she wanted me to say.

"I honestly don't know, Jerrod," she returned, "But you're smart. I know you'll figure it out."

I nodded at my mother's words, but I thought she had too much faith in me. Maybe I could find a way to make up with my father, but even after hearing his sad story, I didn't feel sorry for him. My father blamed his son when things went wrong, and it sounded like it ran in the family.

Chapter Twenty-Eight

It had been hard to transition back to a normal routine after my talk with my mother, but I thought I heard Sydney cry out, so I walked to the steps to call for Josh to bring her to our mother. I stopped abruptly at the foot of the stairs.

Josh was standing three steps up, holding a sleeping Sydney. He put his finger to his lips and silently climbed up the steps. I followed him to our room and closed the door. My mother rattled dishes as she set the table.

No one could have heard our full conversation. We had been sending words to one another for so long that it felt perfectly natural.

I looked at Josh. *You heard.*

He nodded. He rubbed a hand over Sydney's head. *The baby was crying, and I was bringing her to Mom when I heard her telling the story.*

Did you know?

No.

"How can I fix this?" I whispered.

"I think you just have to try a little harder to be nice to Dad," Josh said. "I don't think he will ever forget it. I don't think he can forget it."

Josh rubbed Sydney's fine hair into a smooth wave across her head. "I could put myself in Dad's place. I would never forgive myself if I let something happen to you."

I waved Josh's words away irritably. *You're just a few minutes older, and nothing's going to happen to me.*

"You never know," he said. "Now I see why Dad doesn't want us to be apart and why he would never let us play in the woods."

I signaled that we should go downstairs for dinner. Josh understood and followed me downstairs.

My mother looked up nervously from her pot of green beans. "I wondered what was taking so long."

She suspected that I was sharing my father's story, but I moved to show Sydney sleeping in Josh's arms, and she relaxed. "I wish you wouldn't have gotten her out of bed. I would have let her sleep."

Josh turned to get a bottle from the refrigerator, and my mother looked at me pointedly. I understood that she hadn't told me to keep my father's story a secret, but I wasn't supposed to share it with my brother. She probably imagined that she would share it with him some other time.

My mother waited a few more minutes for my father to get home. She would have denied waiting on him, but she took a long time pouring our drinks and placing the food in bowls on the table.

Sydney woke up when my mother tried to ease her out of Josh's arms. The baby started to cry, but Josh was ready with a bottle. My mother put the bottle in Sydney's hands, and Sydney brought it hungrily to her mouth.

Sydney was the only one who enjoyed her dinner. Josh ate a few of his green beans and pushed the rest of his food around to make it look like he ate more. I consumed half my plate of food without tasting it, and my mother didn't even pretend to eat. She kept looking at the clock and out the kitchen window.

My mother always made us finish everything on our plates. We have had to consume mounds of food in order to get away from the table. We didn't even have a dog to sneak our food to, so we sometimes left the table so stuffed that we couldn't eat school lunch the next day.

"Okay, guys," my mother said, picking up her full plate and taking it to the sink, "it's time to finish your homework"

Josh and I crept toward the kitchen sink. We were sure we would be told to sit down and finish our meal, but our mother didn't even look at the dishes we put by the sink.

"I love you, Mom," Josh said, placing his arms around our mother.

Not one to be outdone, I echoed, "I love you, Mom," and hugged her, dodging Sydney's hair-pulling fingers.

Josh and I stampeded up the stairs to our room. Josh shut the door. "Do you still have homework?"

"Of course not," I lied. Even though I was labeled a troublemaker, I still breezed through my assignments. I could finish my math later.

"I'm worried about Dad," Josh said. He sat down on the floor and picked at the carpet.

I dropped down beside my brother and crossed my legs. "He's just upset because he couldn't protect Elliot or Ly," I said.

Josh gave me a rare condescending look. "I think it's more than that."

"Oh, so you think he blames himself for Elliot's, Ly's, and his mother's deaths. Why doesn't he blame himself for Kennedy's assassination, too?" I rolled my eyes. "He's just depressed. It'll work out. It always does."

Josh looked thoughtful. He didn't even snap at me for my exaggeration about President Kennedy. "I never thought about Nana's death. Dad probably *does* feel responsible."

I threw up my hands. "Why in the world would he feel responsible for an electrical fire?"

"Because I think everyone," Josh said, pausing for emphasis on his next words, "*but you,* knows that Crazy Lyle Miller started that fire."

"Then why isn't he in jail?" I asked, shaking my head in my hands. "With all the family secrets we have, we don't need a closet for our skeletons. We need a whole town!"

"This town is full of secrets," Josh said soberly.

I stared at him with my mouth open. "Josh, step out of the world of the melodramatic and back to reality. We're talking about our family and Crazy Lyle Miller."

"Okay, we'll review the facts. It's common sense." Josh shrugged. He placed a hand on my shoulder and smiled sadly. "Mental sickness runs in the family. Crazy Lyle Miller has schizophrenia. It caused him to be paranoid, so he told the police that he thought his wife was a terrorist. He acted like he was a hero. They put him in a mental institution before Dad was told about Nana's death."

I don't know what emotion showed on my face. Josh continued gently, "You know that Dad has been prone to depression, but do you remember his fits of rage?"

"No," I lied. I remembered two incidents very well. One of those occasions had been after Elliot's death.

Josh knew that I was trying to deny the problems in our family. "You remember his last outburst at the hospital, but do you remember Dad's friend Jason?"

I couldn't camouflage my thoughts from my brother. I nodded. Josh could see the visions in my mind.

"He was so mad that Jason had tried to kiss Mom that he almost killed him," Josh recalled.

I could still envision the blood all over Jason's white Mustang. If we hadn't lived in the country, my father would have been arrested for attempted murder. I don't know if Jason would have pressed charges, though, after he saw my father's reaction to his unreciprocated advances on my mother.

Josh made his point. "I think the police knew that they had to get Crazy Lyle Miller out of the reach of his son before they told Dad about Nana's death," he said. "Why do you think we never visited Dad's father in the institution?"

I looked strangely at my brother. "I don't know. Maybe because he's in a *mental* institution!"

Josh chuckled. "We still could have visited him, or we could have written him letters, but Dad doesn't want anything else to do with his father."

I was becoming familiar with that feeling. I didn't really care if my father ever found his way home, but I knew my mother needed him.

"I don't think Dad and his father had the best relationship from the beginning," I said. *Hadn't my brother listened in on the same story my mother had told me?*

Josh wasn't listening. "I guess I always knew that there was something wrong about the fire."

"Crazy Lyle Miller must have really lost it." My brother sighed. "He burned down the whole place. He even poured gasoline on those two maple trees and set them on fire. I guess they stopped being *good* trees."

My thoughts were on my father. I didn't want to consider my grandparents. I wanted to concentrate on fixing my family. I wanted to find an explanation for my father's behavior even though I was still angry with him because I wanted us all to be happy again.

"Could Dad have schizophrenia?" I asked. My voice was steady but worry lined my face.

Josh shrugged. "I researched it last year," he admitted. "Dad's behavior is similar to a person with schizophrenia, but he drinks too much for me to really tell. Besides, schizophrenia usually skips a generation. It would hit you, Sydney, or me, probably in our early thirties."

I had gotten worried when Josh mentioned that I was more susceptible to schizophrenia than my father, but I relaxed when he said it wouldn't hit until I was thirty. I'd be old by then and it wouldn't matter.

Josh and I had an uncomfortable moment where we overlapped images of paranoid fits. I wondered if Josh and I would share the disease like we did everything else.

I was brought out of my thoughts by Sydney's cries. She was just hungry or needed attention. I could tell from the sound she made that she wasn't hurt.

"Well, this is not getting my work done," I said and pretended that I wasn't worried about our conversation. I forgot that I had lied to my brother about having finished my homework.

Josh watched me get out my math book and papers. I didn't betray my real feelings, but my twin could pick them up from the unseen mental connection we shared.

I finished my homework and played a zombie video game. Eating people's flesh was not as fun as I hoped it would be, so I turned off the game and went to bed early.

It didn't take long for Josh to abandon his project of the week and climb onto the top bunk. I heard him snoring before I drifted into hazy, indefinable dreams.

I didn't hear my father come back, but I thought I heard someone crying by my door after I'd slept for some time. I must have been dreaming.

Chapter Twenty-Nine

The day my father left was brilliantly sunny. It hurt to open my eyes in the radiant light. It was early, but the rays pushed their way through my dark curtains and into my room.

I sat up in bed and blinked my eyes. Josh's familiar form wasn't outlined in the mattress above me, so he was probably getting ready for school. I went through my routine quickly and hopped down the stairs to breakfast.

I stopped on the landing with a full view of the living room. All the blood drained out of my face, and the color washed away from the day.

The lamp next to the couch had been overturned, and pieces of beige ceramic were scattered on the living room floor. The television was pushed to the edge of the entertainment center, like someone had bumped into it very hard, and all the magazines and mints had been knocked off the coffee table. The air had the odor of sweat, alcohol, and sadness.

My mother never told me exactly what happened. She seemed ashamed and embarrassed every time someone mentioned the day my father left. I was present for the end of the fight, and I didn't trust most of my memories.

My father was in the corner of the living room, next to the television. I had a crazy thought. *Don't let the TV fall on him!*

My mother was pulling herself across the floor toward my father on her hands and the side of her right leg. Shards of debris from the broken lamp cut her and left kisses of crimson carnations of blood when she lifted her bare leg to inch closer to my father.

My father's eyes were possessed, and he kept shaking his head in his hands. His large flannel shirt was torn, and dirt caked the knees of his jeans and the socks on his feet.

My father muttered, "No one I love will ever get hurt again." He repeated it every ten seconds.

I was not proud of my thoughts as I looked at my father. I had considered him a strong protector, and I respected him. My father always stood with his back straight and his eyes clear. Now, he was emotionally broken in the corner of the room with liquor roaring off of him.

I was ashamed and disappointed in the mess that used to be a man I had held in the highest esteem. I felt like screaming, *Get it together! She shouldn't be comforting you! You're supposed to be strong for all of us!*

I stood at the base of the steps, and I didn't move. I always thought people were exaggerating when they described someone as frozen stiff, but I couldn't move at all. I wasn't even aware of my motionlessness at the time.

My mother reached out timidly and touched my father's arm. He jumped as if her touch was electric, and he shouted, "Get away from me!"

My mother turned her face sharply, like she had been slapped. I couldn't see her wounded expression, but I could feel the hurt radiating off her in waves, like the ripples you see when you throw a stone into still water.

When the waves of despair reached me, my paralysis was broken. I felt heat race from my belly to my neck and face. I screamed at my father without thinking about my words. "Look at what you've done! You are selfish and *crazy*, and I think we *all* know where you get that! It seems like the Miller men are good at one thing, though," I yelled without realizing that what I said included my brother and me, "and that's ruining families! *You* ruined our family, and now you've hurt the only person who still believes in you, your *pregnant* wife!"

My mother noticed me when I started screaming and shook her head violently. When I finished, she said, "Your father's not himself, Jerrod. He thinks he's done something terrible."

"He did do something terrible," I said to her while still glaring at my father. "He acted like a sniveling, selfish, *crazy* idiot, and he shouted at *my* pregnant mother!"

My father had stopped muttering to himself when I yelled. He turned his face to me, and I looked into his vacant eyes. "You're right, Jerrod," he said flatly. "I *am* ruining my family." My mother shook her head again and offered something in his defense, but my father held up a finger without looking at her. "I'm sorry that I let you down, son. I saw so much of myself in you sometimes, but I didn't want to nurture that part of you, because I didn't want you to be like me."

"No chance of that!" I spat. "I will never be like you! There's nothing of you in me!"

My father's eyes reflected nothing but the floor as he looked down and said, "Like father, like son."

My father stood and grabbed his keys off an overturned couch cushion. He bent down on his knees before my mother. I started to protest, but my father's tender motions stopped me. I heard pieces of the lamp crunch beneath him. He took her hand and gently kissed her.

"I'm sorry, babe," he said. Tears rolled down my mother's face. "I've made sure no one will ever hurt you again. Even me."

My mother tried to grab ahold of his hand. "Please, Johnny," she begged. "I love you so much. I can't do this without you!"

My father didn't embrace my mother like he had in the past when she was emotional. He told her, "You don't need me like you think you do." His voice broke. "You've always been stronger than me."

He didn't even look at me as he walked out the front door and closed it softly behind him. The sounds of the Ta-Ta van echoed through the deadly silent living room as he backed out of the driveway.

My mother cried softly into her hands. I knew I had to do something, and I wasn't sure if she blamed me for her husband's hasty exit, so I didn't try to comfort her. I decided to clean up the mess.

I had righted the television and gotten most of the broken lamp off the floor when I heard a creak at the top of the steps. I moved over to find Josh holding a wide-eyed Sydney on his hip. I didn't know if she had heard the commotion or if she'd felt the emotional temperature of the house, but she looked scared. *So that's where Josh had been.* He was taking care of our sister.

"What did he do?" my mother spoke softly from the floor. I nodded toward Josh. *Take Sydney back upstairs.*

Josh turned and headed down the hall. When I couldn't see him anymore, I faced my mother.

Her eyes were red and swollen with tears. No amount of makeup would cover the puffy patches. Her hands and legs were bloody from the broken shards of the lamp. Little drops of blood from her hands had traced lines on her face.

Then it hit me. I was the man of the house. Josh might have been older, but I had the power to handle hard situations and get things done. *I* wasn't going to cry in the corner.

I didn't move from the landing. "You need a quick shower," I commanded harshly. "You can wear sunglasses and keep the windows rolled up when you take us to school. Josh can run Sydney over to the neighbor's house and tell her I've been giving you trouble, so you're staying home with me. That will explain the yelling and why you're home from work. Call in and tell your boss the same story. You need to get some rest."

I didn't know if it was the authority in my words or the logic in my directions, but my mother rose off the floor and headed up the stairs. She patted my arm as she passed me, denial clouding her vision. I looked at the blood on my shirt from my mother's palms. "He's a good man, and you'll find that you can forgive him and love him," she whispered.

My father was not a man—especially not a good one. A *man* does not hurt the people who love him and run away. *I* was cleaning up his mess and staying strong. *I* was the man of the house.

Chapter Thirty

I could look back on those memories like familiar reruns of television shows. The characters seemed to evolve, but the end was still the same. Unlike the sitcoms I watched with Josh, no one seemed to learn from their mistakes, and a happy ending was beyond our reach.

I wanted to think my story was building on my current life, but everything that had led me to that horrible day last December was a mix of my past and my actions at that time. My tale wasn't over, but a big part of it had been told.

After I cleaned up the mess my father had left behind, Josh and I spent an anxious day at school and ran from the bus to our front door. Josh hugged our mother, who had bandages all over her hands and arms, and walked next door to get Sydney.

We practiced the same daily routines. Josh and I did our homework, our mother fixed dinner, and Sydney toddled into trouble whenever no one was looking. None of us mentioned our missing family member.

My mother seldom spoke. She stayed in her bedroom most of the time. I heard her crying and arguing with someone on the phone a couple of times, but I knew it wasn't my father. She talked to my father with love in her voice, even when she was angry, but she spoke to the person on the phone with a resentment that she seemed to have nurtured over time.

My mother had night terrors that grew more intense the closer she got to Ella's delivery date. She screamed my nana's name once, but all her other nighttime mumblings were too low to hear.

My brother and I took care of Sydney and my mother, and we hardly ever fought. Josh and I tried to seal our family back together.

I assumed my father had run into another town to hide from whatever he thought he had done. He was probably cowering in the corner of a bug-infested hotel room, muttering to himself. The mental image didn't bring me joy.

As upset as I was with him, I thought about the good times we had experienced with my father. I remembered his jokes and the way he looked into my mother's eyes when everything seemed right with the family. He seemed like a good man. Maybe he was. *Had I been too hard on him? Had I scared him away?*

It's easy not to focus on someone's bad qualities when they are gone. Their terrible behaviors, while unacceptable when they are happening, tend to get pushed into the back of your mind when you can no longer hear their voice.

I dealt with my guilt daily until Ella was born. I was in the delivery room with my mother, and I was the one who cut the screaming baby's umbilical cord.

I threw myself into taking care of Ella, and Josh spent most of his time with Sydney. We helped our mother, who had a mild case of post-partum depression, but my brother and I didn't talk to her very much. She spent several weeks after her pregnancy staring at the walls in her bedroom. Sometimes I'd run to her at night after she woke up screaming, but I could only comfort her occasionally. I had nightmares of my own.

There were times when I wondered why we hadn't heard from my father, and there were days I didn't care. My mother refused to move anything he owned. His toothbrush and razor stayed on his side of the double vanity, and my father's clothes hung neatly in the closet.

I tried not to hear the news or read the paper after my father's disappearance. I didn't want to know what had happened. Unfortunately, news about our family still had a way of reaching me.

Around the time Ella took her first unsteady steps from Josh to me, Josh and I gained two pieces of information about our family. It was the most I had discovered about my father in almost a year, and it came from a short bus ride and an unlikely source.

Tony Spumoni hadn't said a word directly to me since our elementary school fight, but he would sometimes talk very loudly about "The Brown Noser," which I assumed was Josh, and a pink Barbie van. Tony was speaking to Johnson in the seat in front of Josh and me when he suddenly stopped, looked back at us, and laughed. I was going to let it go, but Spumoni turned toward Johnson and said, "It's been nice havin' one less Miller in the world." Then they laughed.

I assumed they were talking about my father, so I threw my arm over the seat and around Spumoni's neck. "What did you say?" I yelled. We were in the back of the bus, and the kids were loud, so no one at the front of the bus heard me or saw Spumoni kick his legs and claw at my arms. I was going to choke him until he passed out, but Josh grabbed my arm and pleaded, "He's talking about Crazy Lyle Miller, Jerrod! Please let him go!"

I released Spumoni, but only because I saw something out of the corner of my eye. I shrugged off Josh's arm, jumped over my brother, and craned my neck to look out of a back window at the passing road. A used car lot raced by, and I could just make out a neon pink van in the cars lined against the road.

I wasn't surprised when I heard that Crazy Lyle Miller was dead, but I was shocked to see an electric pink van for sale at Erwin's used car lot. I didn't even search the internet or newspaper for Crazy Lyle Miller's obituary, but I made a plan to visit the owner of the car lot where I saw the van.

I walked home from school the next day. My brother faced the unpredictable moods of the bus kids. I let him lie to our mother and say that I had to serve afterschool detention. I wasn't scared about being punished. She hardly knew I was alive.

It was windy, and the balloons on the cars were waving fiercely as I stepped onto the lot. I hesitantly approached the pink van. The shoe polish on the windshield claimed that the van was in good shape with great mileage. I took a deep breath to release the sharp pain in my heart.

There was no doubt that it was our van. It still had the chip in the door that my father had made the first time he put in Sydney's car seat.

I stood very still when the door to a small trailer creaked open and a man stepped out. I pasted a smile on my face and walked over to him with my left hand extended. The owner of the car lot greeted me and shook my hand without making me change to my right hand.

"So you're from the school paper?" he asked.

"Yes." I continued my lie from the conversation the previous night. "I was just doing a kind of economics piece about where you get your cars."

"Well, I get my cars from auctions mostly," the owner began. He had told me his name was Big Joe Harris over the phone, and the name fit him. He wore a cowboy hat over a permanently sunburned face. His jeans were worn, and a nice button-up shirt covered Big Joe's ample torso.

"Do you get your cars from any other places or from individuals?"

Big Joe stroked his red chin. "I try not to trade, but I have gotten cars from people in the town." Big Joe turned on the car salesman's smile. "I try to help out the local town folk when I can."

"Like that van," I said, pointing to my family's former vehicle. "Did you get it from someone in the town?" I tried my own misleading smile.

"As a matter of fact, I bought it from a police officer," Big Joe admitted. "Nice guy, but I think he's a transplant. Talked like a Yankee. Hey, shouldn't you be writin' this down? I don't want to be misquoted, even if it's only in a school newspaper."

"I'm good at memorizing," I said, waving my hand at him. "I've got the story. Thanks for your time."

I started to walk away while Big Joe called out something about remembering him when my parents were in the market for a car. I was too busy in my own thoughts to answer.

I walked home quickly because I already had to lie about detention, and I didn't want to explain why I was home so late. I shouldn't have been worried. My mother wasn't home yet.

Josh was sitting on the couch with Sydney, bouncing her, but she seemed to be deeply asleep. Her head hung off Josh's arm, and drool ran down her cheek in a fine, transparent string. Ella was wide-eyed and silent in her playpen.

Josh was jerked out of his thoughts when I opened the door. He stopped bouncing Sydney and asked in a rush, "What did he say? Is it the van? Did Dad sell it to him?"

"Not much, yes, and no," I answered in one breath. "He bought the van from a police officer. The policeman could have gotten it from anywhere." I threw up my hands.

"It's okay, Jerrod," he said. "You did the best you could." I watched his eyes dim.

We didn't get to talk about it anymore, because my mother's keys rattled in the doorknob. She walked in with a rare smile on her face, and all her children soaked in her happiness until we went to bed.

That night, after my mother's radiance had been covered with sleep, I lay in bed thinking of all the horrible things that my father could have done. I even worried that Crazy Lyle Miller's ghost might haunt his son's house.

I tried to bring one happy memory to my mind so that I could fall asleep peacefully. But nighttime was when the darkness came.

Chapter Thirty-One

At eight months old, Ella was very intelligent. A lot of parents bragged about their progenies, even if their children were only of normal aptitude, but I thought Ella was really a genius.

Her motor skills advanced at a reasonable rate, but her eyes followed everything. I had Sydney's development as an infant as a comparison, so I thought I knew the way to distinguish between a normal achievement and an extraordinary accomplishment.

Ella talked in words mixed with baby sounds. I could have sworn Ella spoke my name, but Josh dismissed it as a baby's nonsensical utterings. I knew that he could hear her and understand her, though.

Josh and I liked to go outside in the spring. The weather wasn't too hot or too cold during the day, so we could pass a football or play tag while barely breaking a sweat.

Some days, we would just sit on the front lawn and watch Sydney climb up and slide down her toddler slide. Ella would try crawling on a blanket, or she'd pick up colored blocks and arrange them by color or size.

One day, Josh and I were watching our sisters, lost in our own thoughts, when we heard Ella say, "Go away."

We looked directly at Ella and then at each other. *Did she really say that? Did we really just hear an eight-month-old speak a sentence?*

Ella seemed slightly upset, but when she noticed us looking at her, she smiled. "No play today," she said and shrugged.

"Okay," Josh and I said simultaneously. We took Sydney and Ella back inside and put them on the floor in front of our mother. My brother and I were so serious about our brotherly responsibilities that our mother didn't protest.

I followed Josh outside and sat on our front steps. Josh paced back and forth in front of me.

"I have to clear up a couple of things," he said. I shrugged my shoulders.

Did you hear Ella speak? he sent. We were hesitant to say it out loud.

I nodded. I repeated the words I heard as Josh stood with his mouth open.

"We didn't hear her in our head like we do each other?" Josh asked.

"No," I confirmed. "I know when you talk to me or to my mind. It's a different kind of hearing."

Josh had nodded through my explanation. "Then I only have one more question. She wasn't talking to us, and Sydney was on the other side of the yard, so who was Ella talking to?"

I didn't have an answer.

Several months later, Ella was sitting up on the floor, watching me do my homework. I was working on advanced math, and she was searching the paper with her eyes.

The sounds of Josh and Sydney bouncing a ball echoed through the house. Our mother wasn't home from work, but Josh had started a spaghetti dinner and had put garlic bread in the oven.

Ella had an array of colored toys in front of her, but she was more interested in watching me. I didn't mind the audience.

Suddenly, she pointed to a spot on my paper. It took her a moment to fix her finger on the page, but when I lifted her hand, I noticed a mistake. I corrected the problem and continued working. A couple of problems later, I saw Ella moving her hand toward my paper again. She placed her whole hand over my last problem.

I felt like I had been dipped in ice water. *Was she correcting me?*

I gently removed her hand from my homework and reviewed the problem. It seemed correct. I shook my head. I felt silly for believing that Ella had sensed an incorrect answer.

I returned to my homework, but Ella placed her hand over the same problem. I removed her chubby digits and realized my mistake. I had copied the problem incorrectly from the book. She had covered the problem with her whole hand. It was *all* wrong.

"Thank you, Ella."

Ella smiled at me. Her baby head seemed to wobble on her neck as she beamed at me.

I decided I was crazy. There was no way that a toddler was helping me with my homework. I couldn't shake the idea that it was not a coincidence, so I did the only thing I could do to prove her ability to myself.

I wrote down a problem. It was a simple multiplication fact, but Ella looked at me questioningly. I tried to tell myself that her look didn't mean *What are you doing? That's not part of the assignment.*

I had written two times three equals five on my paper. I thought I saw my sister shake her head in frustration as she placed a finger on the number five. I erased the answer and wrote the number six.

Ella smiled at me and seemed to be waiting for my praise. I couldn't speak.

I wrote another problem. I solved that one correctly, and Ella didn't move. I played the game for almost an hour trying to convince myself that my sister could not solve math problems. Finally, I admitted, "Okay, I get it. You're a genius!"

Ella looked back at me with a face that seemed to say *Wow! You're just realizing that?*

The really remarkable part of the situation was not the problems she solved but the next word Ella said. Ella pointed an unsteady finger at the couch and said, "Nana."

I wanted to believe it was just my overactive imagination, but she repeated the word. I stared in the direction of the couch, and I could see a small distortion in the pattern on the couch. A spot on the couch resembled the wavy air you see radiating from the sidewalk on a really hot day. I tried to focus on the aberration, but then it was gone.

Ella said, "Nana gone." She looked at my paper and patted it. She was finished with our game.

There was something extraordinary about Ella. She had demonstrated her gift by accident on the lawn for Josh and me, and now I could confirm my suspicion. I knew beyond a shadow of a doubt that Ella was a prodigy, but she also possessed a unique ability. She could communicate with the dead.

I told Josh about my experience with Ella, and to my surprise, he didn't laugh at me. He sat calmly at his desk and moved a pencil across the tops of his fingers.

"I've seen her do something like that, too." He put the pencil in his science book to mark his place.

"You've seen her talk to dead people?"

"Well, I thought it was like the way that Sydney used to coo and laugh when no one was around her, but Ella was definitely looking at something. I could almost catch a shimmer, but then it was gone."

"That sounds like what I saw," I said. "I saw a shimmer on the couch, but when I tried to focus on it, it disappeared."

There was a knock at our door. "Come in," we voiced together.

My mother peeked her head into the room. She had a sunny smile that was usually covered by a dark cloud of heartbreak. "Well," she said, tracing the side of the door with her fingers, "I was just starting to get hungry, and I realized I could possibly die of starvation before I finished fixing dinner."

"So what you're saying is that you need to find some way to eat quickly," I said, playing along.

"Yes!" my mother responded happily.

I was excited to see her in a good mood. She had worn the garb of depression too long.

"What do you suggest?" Josh asked.

"Well, if you're not buried under a pile of homework, maybe we could go grab a pizza," my mother suggested.

Josh and I jumped up and ran out our bedroom door. We didn't finish our conversation, and our sister's unique abilities were forgotten. In fact, we didn't discuss Ella's gift again until the day she was punished for something she didn't do.

Chapter Thirty-Two

My mother put her best face forward and didn't talk about her husband or his disappearance. I would sometimes hear her crying into the night, but it was easy to ignore because I didn't want to talk about him, either.

Sydney continued to grow into a stylish young girl. Sydney giggled with Ella at night through the wall that separated our rooms. She and Josh were always close, but he didn't understand her obsession with fashion or other feminine concerns, so I was glad my sisters had a chance to bond.

Sydney was smart, but I didn't think she wanted everyone to know it. When Sydney was four, she announced to the family that Ben Franklin was her favorite president.

Instead of being amazed that Sydney knew about Ben Franklin, we all laughed at her and called it 'Pulling a Sydney' if someone made a mistake. I should have been more supportive of my sister, since most of the silly things she said were because she didn't take time to think about something before she spoke about it.

Josh and I grew closer and happier. The only time I was sad was when I was filling out college applications and he was still preoccupied with auto mechanics. I thought it was such a waste to watch him solve quadratic equations in seconds and then talk about his future in auto mechanics.

I shouldn't have been so hard on my brother about his chosen profession. He was going to have a respectable business, but I wanted him to have plans like mine so we wouldn't grow apart.

I didn't want to be separated from my brother, but I felt a pull to go to the west. I applied to colleges in New Mexico and Arizona, but I didn't tell my brother. The acceptance letters gave me numerous options, but I wasn't happy. I wanted to be with my brother and go to the out-of-state colleges, but Josh had a business plan for his own mechanic shop, and it did not involve moving out of Erwin.

I could sometimes tell that my brother missed our father, but he covered those thoughts well, and I didn't want to share them with him. Josh told Ella a couple of stories about our father before he joined the rest of the family in the denial of our father's disappearance.

I thought every member of my family was good-looking, but Ella was exceptionally beautiful. She had my father's crystal blue eyes and long, curly blonde locks of hair. By the age of two, no one could walk by Ella without paying a compliment directly to her or to my mother about her.

Ella's intelligence was amazing. Her IQ scores were beyond her years, and she was very sensitive to everyone's feelings.

Ella horrified my mother by approaching random people and whispering things to them. Usually, these individuals would receive this angelic young girl with a smile, but once Ella had spoken to them, they would pale. Most of Ella's subjects would walk away in a daze, probably in deep thought, and Ella would skip back to us as if nothing had happened.

Ella tried to tell everyone in the house about the things she saw or heard, but we tuned her out. I think we were scared of her. I had been a little worried about her when she helped me with my math as an infant, but I was too frightened to deal with her after her insistence that her imaginary friend was real. Believe me, that is a story for another day.

Our family dealt with Ella's gifts the same way we did with everything that upset us. We ignored it, or we joked about it. If Ella spoke to a stranger and he walked away with a stunned expression, either Josh or I would nudge her and say something like, "What a life-altering talk, but you couldn't tell him his fly was open?"

Sydney may have been a little jealous of Ella, but she tried not to show it. The only time I saw Sydney's feelings truly hurt was one morning when Josh told Ella she looked beautiful and didn't acknowledge Sydney. That was the same day Sydney drove a wedge into her relationship with Ella.

It was stormy on the day Sydney felt Ella steal attention away from her favorite brother. We all had to stay indoors.

Josh and I were in our room all day, and my sisters were playing their own version of hide-and-seek. My mother was making lunch when I heard a crash.

Josh and I were the first ones to go see the source of the noise. Sydney and Ella were standing over a picture frame that had fallen off the wall. I knew without looking at the picture that it held our last family photo with our father.

Our mother reached the top of the stairs. There were no screams from children, insisting that their minor scrape was hemorrhaging, so she prepared to calmly handle the situation. She encouraged us to act like children, so she expected things to get broken from time to time.

Our mother usually handled accidents well. She would patch up the broken object or throw it away. We were never blamed for the damage we caused when we played as long as we didn't lie about who caused it.

She stopped when she saw the broken picture, and I could almost feel something inside her break. It was like a dam that had held the water back for too long and finally burst open.

She picked up the frame, and pieces of glass fell from it. Our mother probably would have sobbed a great deal in her bathroom and not punished anyone, but Ella chose that moment to declare, "Nana wanted our attention."

"What did you say?" my mother asked, rounding on Ella.

My sister wasn't quite three, but she had a strong command of the English language. Ella looked puzzled, like she was wondering if her mother didn't understand her words. "Nana wants to tell you something, so she knocked the picture down," she repeated slowly and clearly.

"Ella Louise!" she shouted. "Don't you dare lie to me! I can handle an accident, but I won't stand here and be lied to!" My mother was shaking with anger, but I think she was scared, too.

"Mommy, I told you the truth." Ella looked desperate, but then she seemed to realize something. "Sydney saw her, too!"

Sydney was surprised when our mother turned sharply in her direction and shouted, "Tell me what happened before I lose my mind!"

Maybe Sydney was frightened by our mother's reaction to Ella's words. Maybe Sydney really didn't see what happened. Or maybe Sydney was still mad at Ella for taking Josh's attention. Whatever the reason for her response, Sydney quickly said, "Ella knocked it down when we were playing. She's just too scared to tell the truth."

Ella's eyes seemed to plead with us as she looked at each one of us in turn, but she saw disappointment where she should have seen love and support. The most upsetting part was watching the bond between my sisters break. Ella glared at Sydney, "You are a liar, and I hate you!"

Sydney wasn't stung by Ella's accusation. She seemed completely indifferent to her sister's anger.

After a moment, Ella stopped trying to defend herself and threw up her hands. She brushed past Sydney with true hurt in her eyes. She stormed into the room she shared with her and slammed the door. The noise jerked the rest of the family out of our own thoughts.

My mother cleaned up the broken glass, and Josh and I went back to our room. Sydney stayed away from her room until it was time to go to bed.

We always had a low dose of sibling rivalry until the day the picture fell. After that day, Ella was always competing with Sydney. She purposely outperformed Sydney in everything she tried, from gymnastics to piano. Ella was also the ringleader when it came to making fun of her sister. Sydney tried to help Ella with something as simple as getting a bowl for her cereal, and Ella rewarded Sydney by saying, "I don't need help from a person whose favorite president is *Benjamin Franklin*."

It was hard for me to watch their feud because I knew that nothing I said would help. The worst part was never hearing the muffled laughter coming from their room in the night.

Every family can work together in small and large ways to form unbreakable bonds, but there were words and events that caused permanent damage to the relationships in my home. I had felt close to my family, but I never realized just how far we had drifted apart since my father had abandoned us. I was scared of Ella's abilities, intentionally apathetic toward my mother, mostly ignored Sydney, and was in denial about my upcoming separation from Josh when

I left for college. When tragedy hit our family again, it scattered us like ants in the rain.

Chapter Thirty-Three

"Stop talking to me!" Sydney yelled. "You're crazy! You're crazy like Dad and his father!"

I jerked out of my reverie and back to my present situation. I had been locked into the past for so long that it was almost like I had relived the last eight years.

Sydney's screams echoed in my mind. She was clearly upset, and her screams were directed at Ella.

I rushed downstairs and into the kitchen. Ella was sobbing in a chair, and Sydney was still screeching over her. "Don't you get it?" Sydney continued. "No one wants to hear it! We don't see what you see, and if we could, we wouldn't want to. You're a freak, and you're not my sister!"

"Hey!" I intervened.

Ella looked up, and Sydney stalked off. I called to her, but I saw no need to encourage another outburst, so I decided to let her stomp to her room.

I sat down next to Ella and put my hand over hers. I let her cry for a few minutes. I was gathering my courage to talk about what had happened. It addressed so many things I liked to avoid.

Ella sat up straight in her chair and wiped her eyes. Sweat covered her face, and her eyes and cheeks were red. "Maybe I am crazy," she whispered pitifully. She had to put pauses between her words to keep from crying again.

I pulled her close to me. "No, you're not." Ella resisted my comfort at first, but then she relaxed in my embrace. "You're just very special, and that makes some people uncomfortable."

"It makes you uncomfortable, too." Her words sounded muffled in my sweatshirt.

Ella was right. I had no response to her observation, but I wanted to make her feel better. "You're the coolest weirdo I know."

She laughed. Ella turned her burning face up to me and smiled, but that smile slowly melted. "I have to tell you something."

I wasn't prepared for Ella's words, but they had been sent to her by the only person I trusted unconditionally. I braced myself for anything, and I resolved to do whatever Ella asked. I leaned into her perfect features as she whispered, "Josh says to go through with the plan tonight."

I went to bed as early as Sydney and Ella that night. I wanted to have some extra time to follow through with the plan.

Once I was in my bedroom, I flew into action. I grabbed my backpack. It had been cleared of my books and packed with a rope, a screwdriver, and a hammer.

I climbed out my window and along the awning over the front porch. There were creaks from my weighted steps, but my mother wouldn't check to see the cause of the noise. She'd blame it on the nonexistent wind or nocturnal animals so she wouldn't have to face her fear of dark things in the night.

At the end of the awning, I balanced and jumped onto the paved driveway. The asphalt stung my feet. I straightened myself and paused, but I heard no movement inside.

"She's still reading," a voice spoke.

I startled and put a hand over my mouth to stifle a scream. I hadn't realized just how nervous I had been.

Ella stepped off the porch. She was dressed in a black coat and pants. Her blond hair was pulled up and covered with a dark cap.

"How did you get out here?" I asked, trying to control my anxious breathing.

"I can't let you go alone." She looked out into the cold night and watched her breath create a puffy cloud in front of her. "And besides, you need me."

"How did you get out here?" I asked again.

"I walked out the front door," Ella said simply. She crossed the landscaping and held my hand. "Mom hardly notices the things that happen right in front of her."

I herded her toward the door. "It's too dangerous for you to go with me. Go to bed, and I'll be home soon."

Ella's mouth formed a sad smile. "Jerrod, I'm going with you, and you can't stop me. The best thing for you to do is let me walk beside you, because something could happen to me if I have to try to keep up with you in the dark."

Great. She had decided to use my protective instincts against me. Ella was going to follow me, even if I tried to make her stay home.

She took my silence as acceptance. "Now, let's go before we get caught in our own yard."

My sister and I cut through the woods to the school. We had taken a little dirt path behind newly developed fast-food restaurants, and it still took us an hour to make it to the trail that led up the mountain to our school. We approached the academy from the road.

Pale Woods Academy was lighted by its own streetlights that were placed in the parking lot and at the flagpole. Ella and I ran along the tree line beside the school in hopes that any surveillance equipment wouldn't detect us.

"Now remember," I cautioned, "we'll have about ten minutes to get in and out before the police get here."

Ella nodded solemnly.

I walked slowly and softly to the first window. It was dark on that side of the building, so it provided an easy way to stay covered if the police got there before we could get out of the school. It was also a convenient way to get to the stairs.

"Remember to stay close to me," I told Ella. "In and out."

Ella rummaged through the tools in my backpack. She seemed suddenly struck by an idea. "Let me break the window!"

"Fine," I agreed. "I'll hoist you in first, and then you need to start climbing the steps while I get in."

Ella got the hammer out of the backpack. She closed her eyes and moved her lips. I didn't want to know her prayer. Ella broke the glass before I could have another thought. She was in the school too quickly for me to offer her help. I noticed blood on a jagged piece of glass as I made my way inside, and I had a moment of worry.

Had Ella been hurt?

We had broken into one of the kindergarten classrooms. I could see the large rugs with multicolored numbers and letters. The smell of bleach assaulted my nose. Ella's feet padded across one of the brightly colored carpets.

The alarm was silent, but I could see a flashing red light next to the window, and the school's emergency lights flashed on. The police had been alerted, but it helped that I didn't have to concentrate while the alarm resounded off the walls.

I ran up the steps and passed Ella as she reached the top. I took the passageway to the left and stared at the door.

Ella was by my side in seconds, a screwdriver in her hand. "When did you get that?" I asked.

"When I got the hammer," she said condescendingly.

"Great," I said sarcastically. Mom would be thrilled to know her daughter was running with a screwdriver. She would be even happier to learn Ella was out after dark and breaking and entering.

Ella unscrewed the screws on the doorknob. She finished quickly and moved to the screws in the deadbolt.

"You think you're so smart?" said a voice behind us.

Ella screamed, and I almost let water run down my leg. I steeled myself before I looked weak.

"What are you doing here?" I screamed at Sydney. My voice bounced off the concrete walls.

"You're not the only smart one," she said, glaring at Ella. "What made you think it'd work this time when it didn't work last time?"

Sydney reached into her pocket and took out a key. The moonlight reflected off its metallic shape. Ella snatched it out of her hand before I could process its possible usefulness.

"The deadbolt wouldn't have slid out of the door when you unscrewed it," Sydney said mockingly. "At least I had the foresight to bring the janitor's key to that room."

Why hadn't I thought of that? Sydney was the pod monitor, so she had the janitor's keys!

"You are not that smart," Ella shot back. "How did you know it would be useful anyway?"

Sydney looked puzzled. "I just had a feeling, and I took it without thinking about it."

"Well, that sounds more like you," Ella said mockingly.

I glimpsed the hurt Sydney must have felt every time her family made fun of her. We thought it was good-natured ribbing, but it had broken her in a way we hadn't seen. I resolved that I would not be part of the sadness that clouded Sydney's features.

Ella put the key in the deadbolt and opened the door. I figured we had three to five minutes before the police arrived.

"I was going to tell you something but forget it!" Sydney pouted.

Ella turned. "What could you possibly say to make up for what you said to me tonight?" The moisture in Ella's eyes reflected the moonlight like tiny pools in a forgotten garden.

Sydney self-consciously looked to the floor. She moved her right foot in an arch in front of her.

I felt the seconds fly away, but I was helpless. This was between my sisters.

"I only wanted to say that I really do believe you," Sydney admitted.

"Wow! That makes all the years of lies and cruel remarks just fade away," Ella barked. Tears flowed down her cheeks. I tried to comfort her, but she waved me away. I had always seen Ella as a strong girl. I had rarely seen her cry, and it was always for a good reason. Ella was a child, though, so I gave her a minute to collect herself. But only a minute.

Sydney crossed the distance to her sister and embraced her. She put her face in Ella's hair and said the one thing she knew could stop Ella's tears. "I believed you, but I was scared." Her voice was muffled by Ella's blond curls. "I was scared because I can see them, too."

Chapter Thirty-Four

My sisters' reconciliation reminded me of the bond I had shared with Josh. I hadn't allowed myself to think about the events that had led up to my brother's death, but they washed over me in a flood. It only lasted a few seconds, but everything I had known, or thought I had known, changed. I reached for the memories, and my mind floated away. It went back to a year before, when my family still loved me, and my brother was alive. It was like I was in a dream or a vivid memory.

It had been snowing outside. Big wet flakes pelted the windows. It sounded like Old Man Winter wanted to come in and warm himself.

Josh was at his desk, and I was playing a video game. My mind flew into the room and rested where it belonged. Inside my body.

"I think I've got it," I said.

"You beat another level?"

"No." I shook my head, pausing my game. "About Dad."

"Oh," Josh responded. "I don't understand how your plan will make Mom happy, and I don't like the small part you've explained to me."

"Did you get a thicker skull than me, or did part of your brain get damaged at birth?" I asked.

I meant it to be funny, but Josh's temper rose quickly. He shot up out of his chair and pointed at me. "You're one to talk about dense skulls," he accused. "Aren't you the one who never learns from your mistakes? I'm just trying to tell you that breaking into the school is a bad idea."

"Then what would you propose, Golden Boy?" I jumped up from my seat and rushed him. Josh's jaw tensed, but he didn't move. I was whispering, but the words would have had the same effect if I'd yelled them.

"I'd *propose* leaving things alone," Josh spat.

"Okay, then Mom can go on crying, and Ella can just *imagine* she sees her father. She'll never meet him!"

"*He* left *us*!" Josh yelled a little too loudly. He realized his mistake and lowered his tone. "Did you ever stop to think that maybe he doesn't *want* to see us?"

I shook my head. "Dad was stressed out when he left. He probably doesn't know how to come back. He probably thinks Mom is still upset with him."

Josh sighed. "Then he should call her! Our phone number hasn't changed." Josh waited a long moment before he added, "I'm not going to help you break into the school." I opened my mouth to protest, and he held up a hand. "But I won't tell anyone what you plan to do. I'll cover for you when you leave, and I'll help you climb in the window when you get back."

Josh paused, and then he added, "I still think it would be easier to ask Grandpa for his copy of the file. He seemed like he would be willing enough to show it to you."

Josh had made up his mind. He wouldn't let me share his thoughts, so he meant every word he said.

"I don't want anyone to know what I'm doing," I explained. "Grandpa may tell me what Dad's *doing*, but he might not let me know *where* he is. I need to know *all* the information in the file so that I have a better chance of finding Dad."

I stalked back over to my chair and sat down. I put my head in my hands. "I'm going to break into the first window to the left of the school's main entrance," I revealed. "A big tree covers the line of sight from the road to the window, so I won't be seen if the police get there before—"

Josh covered my mouth. I hadn't even felt him behind me. He let go of my mouth and moved in front of me. Josh stared down at me and said, "That's enough. I don't want to know about your plan, in case you get caught." Josh looked thoughtful. "I don't even know if I'll be able to block your schemes from my mind, but I'm going to try."

I could feel my present self in the body of my past. My past self relaxed in the chair and resumed playing video games. My present self was mortified. *Why am I reliving the past with no hope of affecting the future?* I thought.

My present self panicked. I tried to scream. I pounded on the walls of my mind, but nothing changed. No one could hear me scream. *Josh! It's all wrong! Don't let me go through with it! Please don't make me watch you die again.*

Chapter Thirty-Five

I zoomed forward in time to the night after my conversation with Josh. I relaxed in the mind of my past and started to relive the unfolding events, almost like watching a horror movie I'd seen many times. No matter how much I yelled at the television screen, the main character was still going to step outside the safety of the house and get stabbed. No matter how much I protested in my mind, I was still going to break into the school.

All I could think about was the file. My mother had told her father that she had given it to the school, and there was only one place non-academic files were kept in the school: The room at the top of the stairs.

I had once overheard a teacher tell an assistant about the use of the room when I was waiting for the principal to render one of my many punishments. The teacher had told the aide that the non-academic files were placed in that room so that the office wouldn't be overcrowded with copies of divorced parents' parenting plans or the medical histories of students with special health concerns. The school had to have a copy of court papers or medical files, but a student's personal information could be accessed by any employee of the school whenever that employee entered a student's name into the school intranet.

I went over my plan in my head. I was going to break into the school, run up the stairs, and use the screwdriver to open the door. I'd grab the file and be out of the school before the police pulled up to the building.

Josh had helped me figure out how long it would take for the police to get to the school once the alarm was tripped. He had reluctantly made some calculations based on some information he gleaned from an online site. My brother said I should have no more than ten minutes after I broke the window to get in and out of the school.

I was going to grab the file and be home before anyone noticed I was gone. I decided to wait to read the file with Josh when I got home. He deserved it for helping me, whether he wanted to see it or not.

My mother was taking a bath as night fell. Josh eased down the steps with me as I began the first phase. I had snuck out of the house by climbing out of our upstairs window many times, but my brother insisted that my plan was dangerous enough without balancing across the awning. Josh opened the door and pushed me outside. He closed the door quickly. I heard the faint echo of my mother's voice.

Josh's muffled voice replied, "It's just me, Mom. I had to bring in one of my science projects."

Phase one of the plan was complete. I made my way behind the house and ran down the streets of Erwin. I was exposed for five minutes while I ran down the road to the railroad tracks. No trains rumbled the floors and dishes of the nearby houses. They had been mostly silenced by progression.

I couldn't hide behind bushes or trees, and I wasn't exactly dressed for a nighttime stroll if a policeman spotted me. My feet barely touched the pavement as I hopped across two sets of train tracks.

I was lucky no one was out on a late, snowy night in December. The chain restaurants were closed, and the police were dealing out justice in other parts of town.

I passed another set of railroad tracks, and I flew into the cover of trees and buildings to conceal my movements. I arrived at the woods near the academy less than twenty minutes after leaving my house. I gulped air that stung my lungs like icicles, and my legs burned.

I hesitated and reconsidered my plan. The woods were the shortest way to the school, but I felt nervous about moving through them in the dark. There was a trail I had taken hundreds of times, but I had always done it in the daylight. I took a deep breath and entered the woods.

I tried to make out any alien noises, but the sounds of the woods were sleeping. I could almost hear the deep, steady breaths of the trees. Moving quickly down the path, I relied mostly on my memory, but I had to use my eyes as they adjusted to the dark. The trees seemed to flex their roots in their sleep.

The trail shortened the time it took to get to the school considerably, but every moment stretched on for an eternity. I had decided to reserve most of my energy for my escape from the school, but fear made my legs run until the muscles were shaky and strained.

I could see the security lights of the school when I first heard a sound behind me. When you hear a sound in the movies, it will stop and build suspense, but when I stopped and listened, the sound grew clearer. It was the sound of running feet.

I slid off the path and moved behind a tree. I quickly moved my backpack from my back to my chest and quietly took out the hammer. I returned the backpack to my back and prepared myself. The steps of my follower had slowed, and a shadow felt around in the dark. I raised the hammer above my head.

I didn't know if the person was planning to kidnap me or if it was a Person of the Woods, hungry for human flesh. I aimed the hammer at the figure's head.

"Jerrod," a voice whispered.

I recognized the voice one instant before I released a fatal blow. I couldn't believe that the shape of my brother had been unrecognizable in the moonlight. I hadn't even felt him in my mind.

"What are you doing here?" I yelled at him. The forest seemed to stir. I heard a few leaves whisper, or maybe it was the animals in the trees. "I thought you were a Person of the Woods."

I could feel Josh roll his eyes. "You play too many video games."

"I thought you didn't want to be part of my plan," I said mockingly. I moved onto the trail with him.

"I changed my mind," Josh whispered. "Mom went to bed, and I found a way to sneak out without being noticed. Besides, you need someone who thinks about what he's doing before he does it."

I laughed and put an arm around my twin. "We won't have time to think if what you told me about the police is right. Ten minutes seems like a long time, but we have to break into the room, get the file, and get out."

"I still think it will be easier for two of us to do it," Josh said.

"I'll definitely need your help once we're in the room," I admitted. "It will be faster for two people to find a file."

Josh stared up at the school. I could see the apprehension in his eyes. This was the most dangerous thing he had ever done, but he was more concerned with the effects it would have on his permanent record. If we were caught, I could handle the heat, but everyone would be harder on Josh.

"Well, we're not getting any younger," I joked as I led my brother to his doom.

Chapter Thirty-Six

Josh looked left and right as I prepared to break the window. His eyes were wild and panicky.

I stopped the hammer just short of connecting with the window and said, "Are you sure you want to be a part of this? I can wait until I know you've made your way home to break in."

Josh looked straight at me. "No, I'm good. I'll be fine," he said unconvincingly. His hands were stuffed in his pockets, and his eyes darted from the road to the window.

"Okay." I hit the window with the hammer without looking at it. I held my eyes on Josh's face, and when Josh heard the alarm, he jumped. I quickly climbed into the window. I felt one of the jagged edges of glass cut my stomach as I climbed into the building. I held up my hand for Josh to wait, and I knocked the bloody piece of glass to the ground. I made a mental note to pick up the glass with my blood on it on the way out. I doubted the Erwin Police Department would be able to test my blood for simple vandalism, especially since I wasn't taking anything of value from the school, but I couldn't be certain.

I helped Josh into the school and raced for the stairs. I had a head start, but Josh was up the stairs and at the file room door before me.

"Hand me the screwdriver," he yelled over the alarm. "You're too slow."

I was going to argue, but Josh whipped me around and unzipped my backpack. He was busy unscrewing the screws in the doorknob before I realized what had happened.

It was so loud! The unforgiving alarm blared its disapproval in short repetitive bursts of sound. It reminded me of my alarm clock, only louder and more annoying.

I felt useless as Josh finished unscrewing the doorknob and took apart the deadbolt. I would have brought two screwdrivers if I had known my brother was coming along.

"No!" my brother screamed. I looked down at the door and saw that the deadbolt's screws were gone, but the bolt held fast to the door.

I pushed Josh up and away from the door. He stood there with the screwdriver in his hand, trying to tell me something, but I couldn't hear him over the alarm. I dropped my backpack to the floor and took out the hammer.

I beat on the door and the lock. *I had to get in that room!*

Josh kept pulling at my shirt, but I was too enraged to stop. I didn't quit throwing the hammer until I heard a shaky voice over the alarm.

"Police! Put down your weapons!"

Maybe things would have gone differently if the officer who first arrived had been on the force for longer than a month. It possibly would have helped if my brother and I weren't over six feet tall, taller than most other boys in our school. Not to mention how beneficial it would have been to drop the tools we were holding instead of keeping them in our hands as we slowly extended our arms upward.

The officer was clearly nervous and had probably never fired his weapon at the scene of a crime. The worst he may have seen were drunk driving arrests and fatalities from car crashes.

The policeman most likely saw two grown men in front of the file room. Then he registered that they were holding weapons as their arms raised. He certainly didn't see two scared kids whose worst thoughts were of the disappointment they'd see in the eyes of their family and friends. He didn't see how heartbroken I was about my failed attempt to find my father.

My eyes didn't register the bullet that entered my brother, but I saw his form buckle as he dropped the screwdriver and grabbed his chest. Of course, I felt the pain, too. I had shared everything with my brother, and the physical pain from a bullet was no different. In the moment I reached for him, though, I felt a bullet meant for me pierce my shoulder. I lost control of my left arm and dropped the hammer. The officer had been trained to shoot weapons out of the hands of criminals. He had succeeded with me, but his shot was off with Josh, and it had pierced his lung.

"Stop!" I yelled as loudly as I could. My voice came out like a loud squeak. "We're just children." The officer seemed surprised that he'd fired his gun. He looked from Josh and me to the hand that held his gun. He squinted in the dark, and then the officer holstered his gun and ran down the steps, yelling into a handheld radio.

Josh collapsed on the ground. He convulsed and spat up blood. He held his chest, and his eyes focused on a bare place on the wall.

"Josh!" I shouted. "Stop it! Get up and come home with me! We've got to go to a hospital!"

My brother's eyes found my face and focused on me. Blood was pouring from my shoulder, and I couldn't think clearly. My injury could be fixed, but Josh's wound could be fatal.

"Go!" Josh said. It sounded like a gurgle, but I could hear the word echo in my mind.

Josh tried to focus on my eyes. Pain gripped him, but he was able to refocus. *Go get help. I love you.*

I won't leave you, I sent back.

Got to if you want to live. He looked down at my shirt. I had blood at my belly. When I looked at the blood on my shirt, my stomach started to sting. *When had I been shot in the chest? Or had I thought that the pain I felt was only Josh's and missed the bullet entering the flesh of my own chest?*

I was confused and scared, and I had lost a lot of blood. I had been shot, and my brother was dying in front of me. I bent down and held him close. I hugged him more tightly than I intended, and he let out a gasp. I set him gently on the floor and got up. I moved my backpack under his head and called over the alarm, "Help!"

The stupid alarm was too loud! I could hear it ringing in my ears in between its loud bursts of sound.

Josh's eyes were rolling up, and there was a small smear of blood below his lips. He focused on me. He shouted *Go* in my mind, but it was weak.

I nodded and ran for the steps, but all I could manage were stumbled steps of agony. Blue lights reflected off the walls of the hall. I ran outside into a cold night that took my breath.

"There he is!" a voice shouted. "He's the perp, and he's got a weapon."

The voice shook the cold from me. I looked around for its source and found the same officer who had shot my brother and me standing by two police cars. He was gesturing at me and shouting at two other officers.

One officer pulled something from his belt, and the other threw up his hands. "Wait!" he yelled.

I needed to get help for my brother, but I didn't want to die in the process. I ran away from the policemen and into the darkness. I circled around the school and stopped. Pairs of feet crunched in the snow behind me. I ran onto the playground and around the swings. I didn't even hesitate as I entered the woods.

Later, I remembered hearing someone call my name. I was too scared to wonder how they knew it was me.

I continued to run until my adrenaline couldn't support my injured body. I wanted to put as much distance as I could between the officers and me.

I finally had to stop. I was panting, and blood was pouring down my arm.

It was in the middle of Pale Woods that I started to wonder how I was going to get out. My brother needed my help, and I couldn't get him to the hospital if I was lost in a maze of trees.

Josh! I yelled in my mind. I was stumbling in wild circles, and sweat was dripping into my eyes.

Where are you?

The thought came in clearly, but I could feel a loss in my brother's strength. I didn't want to think about what that meant.

I'm lost in Pale Woods, I sent back.

The school?

No, the woods.

I'll tell Ella. Find an area that you can describe and stay there.

How was he going to tell Ella? Was she there with Mom? The rest of my family must have been in an ambulance riding with Josh to a hospital. The thought made me feel a little better. At least Josh was getting help.

I looked around. I saw darkness and gnarled tree roots. My eyes had adjusted to the night, but I was in shock. I couldn't really concentrate on my surroundings.

Then I saw it. A large hole in a tree. I wasn't sure if the hole had been made by nature or by something else, but it was definitely a good place marker. I sent the tree and its description to Josh.

Okay, they're on their way, he sent back. *I love you, Jerrod. Stay put and don't blame yourself for any of this.*

Who was he kidding? All of this was my fault. I had hatched a plan to get into the school and endangered my brother's life. All of that planning and deception for a man who probably didn't care for us anyway.

I was lost in my thoughts and definitely in shock, so I didn't notice a break in the snow before I plunged into the ground. It actually felt like the earth had opened up and swallowed me. I could see the hole in the tree moving upward as a rush of air sucked my body down.

My mind didn't even process my fall. I landed on my back, and the wind was knocked out of me. I thought I was going to die from lack of oxygen. I could see a little light as I stared into the opening. My vision was going in and out, but I focused on the light. Finally, I felt a breath jump into my lungs. When the air circulated through my body, so did the pain. All my pain. I felt my injuries from the fall, and my side hurt terribly. I guessed that I had cracked or broken ribs.

I also felt the pain from my disastrous burglary. My shoulder was a swollen, throbbing mess. Every time my heart beat, I could feel another squirt of blood pulsate out of my wound. My stomach stung, but my shoulder hurt more. I inched my shirt upward in tiny movements and ran my right hand over my stomach. Instead of a hole in my belly, I found a long gash. I hadn't been shot. It was the cut from the broken glass that reached from my stomach to my chest. I should have been relieved that I hadn't been shot in the midsection, but I was still bleeding to death in a hole.

"Help!" I screamed. Well, I tried to scream. It sounded like a croak.

My voice echoed in my head. My brain and skull hurt in a far-off way.

I tried to sit up, and I felt sick. My stomach relieved itself of my dinner before I was aware that I had thrown up.

I smelled blood, sweat, dirt, and vomit. My stomach didn't relax, but it settled into acceptance.

I attempted to look around me. I stretched my neck until my shoulder sent razors of pain through my upper torso. I was surrounded by dirt and rock.

I wanted to try to climb out of the hole, but I didn't think I could raise my body. I had a feeling that if I tried to get up I would regret it. My body would take that opportunity to process all its damage at once, and I almost certainly wouldn't be able to scale the depth of my earthly prison.

I was overwhelmed by the seriousness of my situation. I held back a sob a little too sharply, and something in me snapped. I felt a pain worse than a broken bone. It was like my soul had been ripped out of me and stabbed. I took in air, but I couldn't get enough oxygen into my body. I was broken and alone.

In my despair, I thought about my nana and the way she applied life's sufferings to *The Bible*. Nana used to say that God never gives you more than you can handle, so that must have been why my mind closed down and let the darkness fall over me.

The burning woke me. My body felt like it was on fire. The cold and lack of movement during my period of unconsciousness had made my form feel more swollen and achier. I tried to lift up, but I couldn't move.

The cold morning light did little to illuminate the hole. It was a hole or an old cave entrance. From my place on the ground, I could see rocks, dirt, and roots. I figured that I might have dropped about fifteen or twenty feet.

The hole seemed to be natural, and I didn't see evidence that it had been dug by human hands. Rocks jutted out in some places, and roots, twisted and broken, thrust their way out of the earth, obscuring some of my view of the forest above me. I thanked God that I hadn't hit my head on hard tree roots or deadly rocks on the way down. From my vantage point, I could see half of the hole and most of the mouth of the opening.

I had fallen on my side, and my arm was pinned beneath me. Fortunately, the pressure on my arm may have slowed the bleeding from the gunshot.

I processed all my thoughts in seconds and through a cloud of unimaginable hopelessness. *How could I have gotten myself, and my brother, into this mess?*

I reached a horrible conclusion through my pain and distress. I willed my energy to come back, and it seemed as though my head cleared a little.

"Josh!" I screamed into the cave. *Josh!*

I knew he wouldn't answer. I had felt our connection break moments before I had lost consciousness, but I had never tried to send Josh long-distance thoughts. Maybe we had to be near each other to connect our minds, and Josh was at least ten miles away at the hospital.

The despair in my mind grew until it filled the earthly indention I was trapped inside. Loneliness like I had never felt kept picking at my heart and peeling my soul away. I was making excuses for my lost connection to my twin, but I knew the truth.

Tears sprang into my eyes, but I couldn't cry. I knew Josh was dead, but part of my mind wouldn't accept it. I just stared at the cruel, gray sky.

Moments inched into hours. I lay looking into the freezing, winter day. The wind mocked me as it stirred through the trees and out of the woods. I trembled in the cold.

My body was hot, but I shivered. My throat felt like it had been scraped with a wire rake, and fever seared my eyes every time I blinked.

I dozed in and out. I just wanted to stop the pain. My wounds hurt worse when I awakened from a doze, but my emotions were paused when I was unconscious.

I saw Josh in a dream just as the afternoon light was giving up to the night. He appeared in front of me and knelt down beside me. I didn't remember falling asleep, but I could hardly remember being awake.

I stared into his face. His eyes were sad, and I could still see the blood below his lips.

I had lost the ability to move or talk long before Josh's visit. I had wet myself, but I didn't notice the smell over the stench of blood and sweat.

I'm sorry about your truck, was all I could think to send. There was something more important to say, but I couldn't think of it. I would tell him when we got home.

Josh's eyes measured the depth of the hole and looked back at me. *You worry about the wrong things*, he sent back.

I'll work on that.

I could already feel our connection getting weak. I had to blink. It was a long blink because when I opened my eyes, Josh was gone and darkness had wrapped around me.

I tried to move. I could climb out of my earthy prison if I could grab the roots and use the rocks for support.

Trying to lift my own body was like trying to lift a distant object. It was like I was paralyzed.

I dozed off and on through the night. I thought I heard people calling my name, but I forced myself deeper into sleep. I didn't want to wake up, because Josh wasn't dead in my dreams. In my pain-induced slumber, I still passed a football with my brother and saw him push Sydney on her swing set.

My wounds hurt less. My arm had fallen asleep that morning, and I couldn't feel the left side of my body.

I thought I dreamed of Josh trying to shake me awake. His eyes were fearful, and he kept screaming at me. I couldn't make out his words. It was only a nighttime hallucination, though, because my brother was dead.

Chapter Thirty-Seven

My mind returned to the present as if I had never left. My sisters were continuing to argue, and time was ticking away.

Ella pushed Sydney and spat at her, "You do not! Don't mock me, because I can't take it!"

"Ella, I'm sorry I lied to everyone for so long," Sydney pleaded. "I know why you're here, and I'm ready to tell everyone the truth. No one will doubt you again."

Ella's face was a contortion of skepticism. "Pinky swear?" Ella extended her right hand to Sydney, her pinky in a curve.

I hadn't seen anyone in my family ask for that kind of confirmation in years. We used it jokingly before my dad left, but we never said it with as much meaning as Ella had expressed to her sister. Anyone who watched Ella's face as she stood gravely with her pinky out would have known that she was serious.

Sydney locked eyes with Ella and joined her pinky with her sister's finger. "Pinky swear," she repeated.

"Why am I here, then?" Ella challenged, unhooking her pinky.

"Because of him," she said, pointing at me. Ella seemed unconvinced.

Sydney continued, "Jerrod never got to see the file." She looked at me with sympathy. "Would you like to know what it said?"

Ella stared at me like I hadn't been in the same hallway with them for the past five minutes. I felt warm excitement bubble up from my back and fill the empty cavity of my chest. It was the first time Sydney had addressed me directly in a year.

"You have it?" I said with wonder. I couldn't help but feel some happiness. She had come to help. *Had Sydney finally forgiven me?*

"I have it," she said softly, pulling an orange packet from under her sweater. "I took it from Grandpa's filing cabinet the last time I asked him to pick me up from school."

I remembered the day my grandfather had dropped off Sydney after school. She had been so mysterious. *Was that the day she took our father's file? Had it been in the house all this time?*

Sydney pulled out the file's contents and looked up at me. "This is the complete file. The file in that room"—my sister pointed to the academy's file room—"wouldn't have shown you the picture."

Sydney held up the picture for me to study. The photograph showed the Ta-Ta van surrounded by woods. An old wooden sign hung by one end of a large maple tree. I could barely make out the words on the sign: Ky and Ly's Hangout.

The piece of paper was a death certificate. I read the name on the certificate, and I almost lost my breath. The name Kyle John Miller stood out from the paper like a neon sign.

I wanted to deny it, but I kept reading. Ella's and Sydney's faces contorted and grimaced in reaction to the changes in my expressions.

The cause of death was a self-inflicted gunshot wound to the left temple. My eyes hung on that line for a long time, trying to absorb the words. I thought I was finished reading, and then I noticed the signature at the bottom of the page. My mother had signed it, and she had signed it years ago. Josh and I had just turned twelve. Ella had barely been born.

Ella measured my reaction. "They found him a couple of months after he left," she explained. "He had gone out to the woods, where he and Uncle Ly had played, and committed suicide."

I stared at Ella, with her angelic curls and beautiful blue eyes. *How could she talk so casually about her father's death?*

"Mom and Grandpa kept it hushed because they didn't want to bring any more shame to the family," Ella continued. "Mother didn't accept Father's death, just like she didn't accept his sickness. Father showed signs of mental instability for a long time." Ella paused and looked at the paper in my hand. "Mother still hasn't gotten over him, and she would probably deny his death to the face of his ghost. She wouldn't even have a funeral for him, and Grandpa helped her keep our father's death away from the public." She saw my unbelieving expression and added, "Jerrod, Father was sick. He had untreated mental problems, and he was too proud to get help. Mother thought if she ignored Father's fits and episodes of paranoia, then he would get better."

I was disgusted and angry. I could feel the heat come up from my stomach and spread across my neck and face. I was livid with my grandfather and my mother for hiding my father's death. I was frustrated with my father for not getting the help he was intelligent enough to know to get, and I was mad at Ella for stating the facts about his death so coldly.

"How long have you known?" I asked both of them.

Sydney shrugged, and Ella continued to stare at me. They offered no response to my question.

"Don't get upset, Jerrod," Sydney said. She cried so hard that sobs rocked her body. She held out her hand, but I just glared at her.

"Why would I be mad?" I spat. "I only killed my brother and ruined everyone's lives for nothing!"

"You didn't kill Josh," Ella said. She was still the cold angel.

"I may not have fired the gun," I yelled, "but I led him to his death just the same." My words echoed down the hall.

Ella rolled her eyes. The police would be responding to the alarm soon. I didn't care. Let them find me and take me to jail. I wanted to be away from my family of liars.

"We're getting off track," Ella said. She had a determination that no seven-year-old should show. She flipped her hair away from her face and sighed. It was almost like she was exasperated at having to explain something everyone else could clearly understand. Ella's condescending attitude unfroze the remaining cool I possessed.

"News flash, Princess!" I shouted. "We don't have to break into the room anymore! I get it! Dad's dead, Mom's eternally depressed, and I'll never get to see my brother again!"

"That's not exactly true."

The voice was as clear and level as it had been in life. I didn't have to turn and see my brother to know it was him.

I stared in disbelief at the form of my once-living twin. Josh appeared as more than a shimmer of heat but less than a corporeal being. He was wearing the same brown jacket I had covered him with before I left him to die. The smear of blood had never left its place below his lips. He seemed to be a shade of his living figure.

I ran to my brother and hugged him. I thought I must have been imagining the warmth of his embrace.

When I pulled away, I noticed that Josh was looking at Ella. Sydney had pulled herself into the fetal position on the floor. She held her knees and rocked, but she never took her eyes off Josh's shimmering presence.

"Why didn't you tell me you could see him?" I asked, drawing from her earlier admission to Ella.

Sydney's eyes cleared a little, and she looked confused. "I can see all of you," she said.

"I know," I began, "but you told Ella that you could see Josh."

"Of course I can see Josh," she said, still puzzled, "but I was talking about you."

"I know. I can see him, too," I said to her. Sydney must have been in shock because she wasn't making any sense.

"Jerrod," Ella's innocent voice rang. I turned to her. The cold determination was gone, and her eyes were kind. I couldn't help but feel like she was patronizing me. "I just want you to answer one question."

"Well, what is it?" I asked hatefully.

Ella stood in front of Josh. I could see his shimmer behind her tangible form. Ella's words were soft as she pulled the world out from under me. "How did you get out of the hole?"

Chapter Thirty-Eight

My brain fumbled for the answer. "Well, I—" I started. I finally settled on, "They found me."

"Who, Jerrod?" Ella asked. "Who found you in that hole?"

"I don't remember, but how would you know about the hole if I didn't get out?" I lifted my head a little higher. I had started to get scared, but now things were making more sense.

"You know how I would know, Jerrod," Ella replied evenly. "I can see things that no one else…" She paused and looked at Sydney. "That most people cannot see."

My voice rose as I recounted part of the previous year's disaster to Ella. "Josh told you where to find me on the way to the hospital. I always thought you saved my life." My heart was breaking. I wanted to cry, but I refused.

All my siblings looked surprised. Josh was the first to recover. "I don't remember going to the hospital."

"Jerrod, Josh died before the ambulance arrived," Ella said. "He died almost where he is standing." Ella looked like she was concerned about something.

"How did you know where I was?" I asked. I could hear panic in my voice, and I was really tired of playing games. "Someone tell me what's going on!"

"I can tell you," Sydney said. Her small voice was shaky, but her face was firm. She got up and smoothed the wrinkles from her clothes. Ella and Josh were staring at her. We were all shocked that she'd spoken.

"I had been asleep in our room," Sydney began, gesturing to Ella, "when I heard her get out of bed. She told me to go back to sleep, but I listened in. You see, I could hear your voices in Ella's thoughts."

"Are you trying to say you can read my mind?" Ella asked. "How can you do that without me noticing?" It was a rare moment when Ella was genuinely shocked about something Sydney could do.

Sydney stared at her feet. "You concentrate pretty hard when you get messages. I just listen in while you're preoccupied."

There were a couple of beats of uncomfortable silence. Ella tried to move her lips around another question, but the ability to produce a sound escaped her.

My curiosity and the need to conserve time overtook me. "What did you hear, Sydney?" I prompted.

"I heard Josh talking to Ella," Sydney said. She looked at Josh and started to cry before she could finish her next sentence. "He said he was dying, but there was still time to save you."

It only took a couple of seconds for Sydney to recover. She brushed the tears away like bothersome flies and continued her story. "He told her about a tree with a hole in it in Pale Woods. Ella jumped out of bed and ran to Mom's room. I pretended I was still asleep. I could hear Ella telling Mom about Josh, and I heard Mom's screams. I thought it would be safe to get up and pretend I didn't know what was going on. We were in the car in less than two minutes.

Mom tried to call Grandpa on the way to the academy, but his phone went straight to voicemail."

I realized that one of the officers outside the school had been my grandfather. No wonder I had heard my name shouted after I entered the woods.

"I heard when you fell into the hole, and I heard—Sydney took a deep breath—when Josh died." She looked at Ella. "I still *felt* him, though. I think it's because *you* could feel him."

Ella nodded. "I could hear him better after he died," she said. "His thoughts weren't confused by pain or sadness." Ella sighed and held up her hand. "This is all true and enlightening, but we are still off track. I want to know how you got out of the hole, Jerrod."

I started really searching my brain for the answer. I remembered drifting in and out. I felt the pain of my injuries and the frustration of my position. I couldn't remember leaving the hole.

The story was too much for me. I backed away from my siblings and ran for the stairs. I ignored their screams of protest as I bounded down the stairs and skipped out the window. I wasn't sure I knew what I was doing until I reached the edge of the woods.

I retraced my steps without thinking. Trees waved in the wind like old friends.

I was on autopilot until I came to the tree with the familiar hole in it. I already knew what I would see if I looked down. The decomposed body of a boy who died looking at the only way out. I thought I saw a glimmer of metal in the moonlight.

I didn't know Josh was beside me until I ran into him. *Why didn't I know I was dead?* I shot at him angrily.

You never accepted it, he explained. *Remember, we always thought that ghosts were spirits that had unfinished business in their lives? You had unfinished business. Or you thought you did.*

I thought about my time in the hole. *Why didn't anyone find me?*

They searched for you for five days. They combed every inch of these woods. Finally, Grandpa called off the search. Mom wouldn't accept it, but she agreed to a memorial service. That was when you followed Ella home.

I was puzzled. *I thought I died.*

You did. Josh changed his tone. *You really don't remember, do you?*

I wanted to deny it all, but I was starting to get flashes of memory. I had recollections shot at me like bullets when I had arrived at the hole where I had died.

I could feel my last moments clearly for the first time since they'd happened. I saw the waning light of the day brushing my eyes. I knew I was dying, but I didn't care. I wanted death to take an express train with my soul. I would have shaken hands with the Grim Reaper if he would have made the pain stop. Every shallow breath was agony, and I couldn't even think about my brother.

My brother had visited me more than once in my hole. His first visit was to comfort me, the second visit had been to try to save me, but the third visit was to collect my soul.

You were there, I said to my twin, and then I corrected myself. *Your spirit was there. You tried to save me, but after I died, you came back to get my spirit out of the hole.*

Josh nodded. He looked into the hole briefly and then back at me. *I thought I could ease your transition, but I lost you.*

What do you mean, you lost me? I sent, but I already knew. I had followed Josh to the opening of the hole, but once my spirit left, I thought I was free. My thoughts became mixed, but I finally settled on the last task I was trying to accomplish. The next thing I remembered was holding hands with Ella in the back of a black limousine. She was dressed in black, so I had assumed that we were returning from Josh's funeral.

Ella wasn't surprised to see me, I recollected, *but she must not have known what to do when she realized I thought I was alive.*

She sent for me. He crossed the open space between us and took my left hand. *I thought I could help, but you couldn't see me for the longest time. You must have been in serious denial.*

We laughed. The wind rose, and the trees joined our mirth.

My laughter ended quickly. *I am so sorry about what I did to you.*

Josh's face was unreadable. *You certainly had a way of getting people to go along with your crazy antics.*

Apparently, I still do. I chuckled, but there was no happiness behind it. *I left Ella and Sydney at the school!* I exclaimed. *How are they going to get home?*

Josh placed his hand on my arm. *They will be fine*, he assured me. *The police were responding to the alarm when I left to find you. They'll call Grandpa.*

I relaxed a little and stared back at what I could see of my remains in the unmarked grave. *Will they ever find my body and bury me?*

I don't know, Josh sent. *None of us can see the future.*

I want to be buried next to you. I really am sorry that you died because of me.

Josh paused thoughtfully. His hand closed more tightly around mine, and I noticed that we shimmered in the same way. I could see the ground and trees around Josh, but there was interference in the air. I wondered just how much my spirit had affected the physical world.

In the end, though, Josh conceded, *it was my decision to break into the school with you. I was curious about the file, and I wanted to make sure you would be okay.*

We looked at our shimmering spirits and laughed again. *Maybe you should have stayed at home.* We chuckled around my grave until I was startled by the reality of the situation.

So, what happens now?

Josh hesitated before he answered. He may have thought the answer was obvious. I felt like I still had limitless possibilities. After all, my spirit had been living like it was human for a year. Well, that wasn't quite right. I thought everyone had ignored me because I had caused my brother's death, but I finally realized that they couldn't see me. My mind wandered to the homeless boy in the lunchroom before I decided that it didn't matter anymore.

Don't you feel it? Josh's eyes narrowed. *Don't you feel the pull?*

Of course I had felt a pull, or physical suggestion, like I should be somewhere else. It tugged like when you get really upset, and you know that the only way to feel better is to resolve the situation immediately. I thought it was because of the guilt I felt over Josh's death. I had a little relief when I came back to the place of my death. Josh was right, though. I could feel a strange, strong tugging at my inner being.

I think we have to let go. I let go a little, but Ella called me back before I reached wherever I was going.

You came back for me, even though I was the reason you died. I squeezed his hand.

Josh shifted his gaze to the ground and gave a sideways grin. *I told you. I came back because Ella summoned me, and who can ignore a woman when she's upset?*

I smiled good-naturedly. *I won't get to see her again, will I? Or Mom? Or Sydney?*

Josh looked at the sky as if trying to decide if it would snow. *I don't think so. You realize the truth now, so there's no reason for you to go back.*

Josh was right, but I still felt a longing for my family. I wanted to tell Ella and Sydney that I was sorry for all I had done. I still needed my family's forgiveness.

I had fleeting regrets. I never really had a girlfriend. I would never go to college. I couldn't watch out for Ella and Sydney as they grew older.

Guilt overcame me when I realized Josh would never fulfill his dreams, either. He had always had hopes and goals, but he wouldn't live to see them happen. Sadness frosted my heart.

I'm okay, Jerrod. He had been following my thoughts. *I have had a little longer to accept my death, and I'm okay with it. I had a good life with a great family. Besides, I think no matter how long you live, you will always wish you had more time.*

Do you think Nana was right? I pulled my arms around myself even though I was past needing warmth from the elements.

About her religion? He moved his head slowly up and down as he thought. Soon he began nodding vigorously. *I think she was on to something,* he finished with a grin.

There's only one way to find out. I took his other hand.

I let go of everything that was tethering me to the physical world. Wind, memories, and voices spun around my brother and me as our souls lifted. Josh never took his eyes from mine. I smiled at him.

My brother and I left the world the same way we had entered it. Together.

Epilogue

Ella ran down the steps and out the door of the school. Blue lights were casting strange shadows on the snowy trees. She could feel Sydney behind her when she opened the door into the blustery night air. Snowflakes kissed her face and melted.

"Hold your fire!" yelled a familiar voice.

Mother ran to the steps and embraced Ella and Sydney. She didn't need to worry about potential shots. The policemen's weapons were safely in their holsters. The entire police department had undergone additional training sessions after Josh and Jerrod had been shot, and they weren't going to take a chance with another incident at the school.

"What in the world are you two doing here!" she screamed hysterically. Ella was reminded of the losses her mother had suffered during her life. Her daughters and her semi-estranged father were all she had left.

Ella gathered up all her courage to appear normal. She didn't need the police to suspect that she was Crazy Johnny Miller's daughter.

Ella whispered, "Jerrod's with Josh at the place he died. I think they will finally be able to be at peace." She locked eyes with her mother, and her mother's expression hardened. Her mother's eyes darted to the left and right to determine if anyone had been close enough to hear Ella's declaration. Her jaw clenched and un-clenched, but she didn't yell at Ella about her gift in front of the police. She took one of Ella's and Sydney's hands in each of her own and walked to the cruisers with determination.

Grandfather was standing by the open door of a cruiser, his face lined with age and worry. She liked him, but she didn't feel sympathy for him. He was surrounded by angry souls and old secrets. The whole town had secrets. One of those secrets had not stayed buried, even after several generations.

As she had grown, Ella had watched Grandfather's secrets surround him like shadows. They tried to touch her with their dark breath, but they only came as close as a whisper. Nana kept most of them away.

"Are they okay?" Grandfather asked Mother, inclining his head at his granddaughters.

Mother nodded and told him something that Ella didn't care to hear. She was busy staring at the edge of the woods.

She sensed Josh and Jerrod let go of the world and move on. Ella felt a little sad that she had not told Jerrod goodbye, but she had gotten more time with him than most people who had lost their loved ones.

Ella glanced briefly at her sister. Sydney seemed to be ignoring her surroundings again. That was fine. Sydney could go back to being self-consumed. It would only make their family seem more typical.

Mother had finished talking to Grandfather, and he was shouting orders at the other officers. Her mother looked at her and smiled like she had contained the situation. Ignorance must be blissful.

Mother would sweep everything under the rug and expect Ella and Sydney to pretend nothing had happened. Sydney would oblige, but Ella wouldn't let them believe they were a normal family.

Mother hadn't seen Josh and Jerrod after they had died, but she had felt their presence. She wouldn't admit that she had spoken aloud to Jerrod at the kitchen table and in his room early one morning, but Ella had heard her. Sydney had sensed Mother's conversations with her dead son, too, but she busied herself with selfish concerns and ignored them.

Sydney walked to the car with her nose up and slid into the backseat of Mother's car. Ella climbed into the other side of the backseat and gazed out the window. There was a small space between Sydney and her, but Ella could feel their emotional space growing again.

Sydney had been scared. Ella thought the pinky swear would have meant more to Sydney, but it was a manipulation.

Ella sighed and stretched her legs. Her toes could almost touch the back of the seat where Jerrod's spirit had sat during car rides for almost a year. She reached her hand to the side of the passenger seat, but his spectral fingers didn't find her own. Ella decided that she couldn't trust anyone, living or dead, with her secrets now.

Mother might have thought that all the excitement was over, but Ella knew it would just continue. Her nana had tried to warn her as a baby, but Ella thought she had control. Back then she believed almost everyone could see the sad and angry spirits moving around them.

She thought about stretching her mind to tell Miles about Josh and Jerrod. Miles had kept an eye on Jerrod at school for her in case he realized he had died. Miles could see the dead, but he struggled with the spirits that haunted him. Ella decided to let Miles's mind rest. It was very seldom people like them had a reprieve, even in sleep.

Ella shivered despite her resolve to seem strong. The being at the edge of the woods smiled sinisterly and waved.

Ella knew that there would be more problems and death if she didn't help the spirit. Not all spirits were good or confused like her brothers. Some were evil, and they wanted to affect the physical world in wicked ways. This being was evil, and he wouldn't let Ella go until she did what he asked of her.

Ella closed her eyes and waited. She hoped the spirit would be gone when she opened them. But when she looked again, he was still smiling at her, reminding Ella that she had to help him, or he wouldn't go away. And he would hurt everyone around her until she complied.

As Ella watched, the spirit pointed his pale finger at Sydney. Ella didn't respond, but the spirit could sense her fear. He smiled ominously and disappeared into the woods. Ella was left alone with her own thoughts and guilt.

THE END

About the Author

Courtnee Turner Hoyle is a writer and an author of the books in the Pale Woods Mystery Series and It's About Time Series, in addition to several short stories that have been anthologized. The culture and views of her Tennessee home have forced her to find her own perspective. While she may embrace the traditions of her area, she has set non-negotiable boundaries, especially against sweet tea, chocolate, and unannounced visitors. Courtnee graduated from East Tennessee State University with multiple undergraduate degrees and a master's degree and developed unique ways of dividing the personalities of the people in her life to create quirky, relatable characters. She's a travel agent who hopes you'll allow her to plan your next adventure, and she volunteers with several local organizations. She encourages you to write splendid reviews of her books on any platform. Good reviews from her readers make her jump up and down in her kitchen and spin her children around happily. Courtnee lives with her husband and numerous children, braving the adventures of homeschooling and tree climbing, and believes there is a story in every experience.

Learn more about Courtnee, her hometown adventures, and her books by visiting www.courtneeturnerhoyle.com, plucking the leaves of her Link Tree (linktr.ee/Courtnee_), and on Instagram @pale_woods_mysteries, Facebook, and other accounts.

Acknowledgements

I owe my love of reading to my mama, who led me to a converted bank vault where children's books were plentiful. She read the first draft of this book, and she loved it, even though it wasn't her favorite genre. Since the first publication of the book, my mama has passed. Unfortunately, our conversation wasn't over...

My eldest daughter, Tosha, has always been my core support, and the rest of my children are huge fans of my work, even if some of them can't read it yet. My eldest son, Stereling, was the inspiration for Jerrod, long before he went through his detached phase.

In a way, Connor Murphy's character was a tribute to my late father. Chief Murphy had all my father's good qualities, and it was nice to bring them back to life, even if it was only in the written world.

I appreciate Sweet 15 Designs for reimagining the cover and making it reflect the story more. I feel like Jerrod is a real person now, and maybe he is one.

This was my debut novel, and I feel like it's one of my children. Thank you, God, for allowing me to write the type of book I would want to read.

I appreciate my readers, who have encouraged me to keep writing. Thank you for supporting my journey as an author!

Can You Help?

If you enjoyed the book, will you please leave a review on a reader's platform? It will help me gain more readers, and I love to read positive comments!

A book review can be as short as a couple of sentences, like, "It was a great book! I'm so glad that I read it!"

Thank you for your help!

Miranda and Jerrod's Hot Cocoa Recipe

Prep time: 10 minutes

Ingredients

- 3 cups of milk powder

- 1 1/2 cups powdered sugar

- 1/8 teaspoon table salt

- 1 1/2 cups of cocoa powder

- Dash of cinnamon (optional)

- 1 cup of water or milk* (per serving)

Milk may make the cocoa more flavorful.

Procedure

1. Whisk the dry ingredients into a mixing bowl. Store the mixture in an air-tight container for up to eight weeks. Canning

jars with metal lids may be used.

2. When you are ready to make the cocoa, spoon one-third of a cup of the mixture into a mug or cup.

3. Add one cup of hot water or milk to the mixture and stir.

4. Finish with marshmallows.

5. Allow to cool to taste but enjoy warm!

Pinky Swear

After a heartbreaking loss, thirteen-year-old Sydney Miller develops a toxic friendship with her classmate, Lydia Sneed. When the relationship comes to an end, and a spirit influences an almost fatal accident, Sydney strengthens her bond with her grandfather and decides to live with him. Sydney finally finds the love and support she needs in her grandfather's home, but Lydia begs her for help, and together they must solve a murder that will change their lives forever.

Pinky Swear
Pale Woods Mysteries, Book 2
Available now!

Finding Emma

What if the only anchor to your identity was a tattoo with a name?

David Winsome answers the door for a beautiful woman who can't remember how she ended up on the hill near his family's home. The woman assumes the name on her tattoo, Emma, and blends into the community while questions about her past plague her.

Why is the town familiar, even though no one seems to know her? And why does she feel an intimate attraction to David, even though she just met him?

As Emma accepts her new life and begins a loving relationship with David, a person who claims to know her enters her life. Does this person hold the key to Emma's past, or is there a mystery much deeper than Emma's identity?

Someone has manipulated the events in his favor, and he has a much larger plan in mind.

Finding Emma
It's About Time Series, Book One
Available now!

www.ingramcontent.com/pod-product-compliance
Lightning Source LLC
Chambersburg PA
CBHW061236310726
48971CB00007B/2088